MATRIMONIAL CONSPIRACY

"Randolph, no young man who knew and loved Janey could refuse. . . . You'll forgive me for saying that my fancy-free girl could learn to care for you—under favorable circumstances."

"What are they?" asked Randolph.

"I'll swear I don't believe Janey has ever met a real man. My plan is simply to give her a terrible jar—and then nature will do the rest."

"Believe me, it will have to be a *terrific* jar."

"Believe me, it will be. At an opportune time you throw her on a horse and pack her off to one of your ruins in the desert. Kidnap her! Keep her out there a little while—scare her half to death—let her know what it's like to be uncomfortable, hungry, helpless. Then fetch her back. She'll have to marry you. I would insist on it!"

Books by Zane Grey

Published by POCKET BOOKS

Most Pocket Books are available at special quantity discounts for bulk purchases for sales promotions, premiums or fund raising. Special books or book excerpts can also be created to fit specific needs.

For details write the office of the Vice President of Special Markets, Pocket Books, 1230 Avenue of the Americas, New York, New York 10020.

ZANE GREY

LOST PUEBLO

POCKET BOOKS

New York London Toronto Sydney Tokyo

POCKET BOOKS, a division of Simon & Schuster Inc.
1230 Avenue of the Americas, New York, NY 10020

Copyright 1954 by Zane Grey, Inc.
Cover art by Murray Tinkleman

Published by arrangement with Harper & Row, Publishers, Inc.

ISBN: 0-671-50141-0

First Pocket Books printing July 1965

15   14   13   12   11

POCKET and colophon are trademarks of
Simon & Schuster Inc.

Printed in the U.S.A.

1

JANEY ENDICOTT did not see anything of Arizona until morning. The train had crossed the state line after dark. New Mexico, however, with its bleak plains and rugged black ranges, its lonely reaches, had stirred in her quite new sensations. Her father had just knocked upon her door, awakening her at an unusual hour. She had leaped at her father's casual proposal to take a little trip West with him, but it had begun to have a rather interesting significance to her. And Janey was not so sure how she was going to take it.

They had arrived at Flagerstown late in the night, and Janey had gone to bed tired out. Upon awakening this morning, she was surprised at an absence of her usual languor. She appeared wide awake in a moment. The sun streamed in at the window, very bright and golden; and the air that blew in with it was sharp and cold.

"Gee! I thought someone said it was springtime," said Janey, as she quickly got into slippers and dressing gown. Then she looked out of her window. Evidently the little hotel was situated on the outskirts of town. She saw a few scattered houses on each side, among the pine trees. There were rugged gray rocks, covered with vines and brush. The pines grew thicker and merged into a dark green forest. In the distance showed white peaks against the deep blue of sky. Janey had an inkling that she was going to like this adventure.

She did not care to admit it, but, although she was only twenty years old, she had found a good deal to pall on her at home in the East. Serious thought appeared to be something she generally shunned; yet to her, now and then, it came involuntarily.

1

While she dressed she pondered upon the situation. She had never been West before. After college there had been European travel, and then the usual round of golf, motoring, dancing, with all that went with them. She was well aware of her father's dissatisfaction with her generation. Despite his attitude he had seldom interfered with her ways of being happy. This trip had a peculiar slant, now that she scrutinized it closely. They were to meet a young archaeologist here in Flagerstown, and probably arrange to have him take them to the canyon and other scenic places. Janey had become acquainted with him in New York, where he had been lecturing on the prehistoric ruins of the Southwest. Phillip Randolph had struck Janey as being different from the young men she played about with, but insofar as her charms were concerned he was as susceptible as the rest. Randolph had never betrayed his feelings by word or action. He had seemed a manly, quiet sort of chap, college bred, but somewhat old-fashioned in his ways, and absorbed in his research work. Janey had liked him too well to let him see much of her. Not until she and her father had been out West did he mention that he expected to meet Randolph. Then she was reminded that her father had been quite taken with the young archaeologist. It amused Janey.

"Dad might have something up his sleeve," she soliloquized. "I just don't quite get him lately."

Janey found him in the comfortable sitting room, reading a newspaper before an open fireplace. He was a well-preserved man of sixty, handsome and clean-cut of face, a typical New Yorker, keen and worldly, yet of kindly aspect.

"Good morning, Janey," he said, folding his paper and smiling up at her. "I see you've dispensed with at least some of your make-up. You look great."

"I confess I feel great," responded Janey, frankly. "Must be this Arizona air. Lead me to some lamb chops, Dad."

At breakfast Janey caught a twinkle in her father's fine eyes. He was pleased that she appeared hungry and not inclined to find fault with the food and drink served. Janey felt he had more on his mind than merely giving her a good time. It might well be that he was testing a theory of his own relative to the reaction of an oversophisticated young woman to the still primitive West.

"Randolph sent word that he could not meet us here," remarked her father. "We will motor out to a place called Mormon Canyon. It's a trading post, I believe. Randolph will be there."

"We'll ride into the desert?" asked Janey, with enthusiasm.

"Nearly a hundred miles. I daresay it will be a ride you'll remember. Janey, will you wear that flimsy dress?"

"Surely. I have my coat in case it's cold."

"Very well. Better pack at once. I've ordered a car."

"Are there any stores in this burg? I want to buy several things."

"Yes. Some very nice stores. But hurry, my dear. I'm eager to start."

When Janey went out to do her shopping, she certainly wished she had worn her coat. The air was nipping, and the wind whipped dust in her face. Flagerstown appeared a dead little town. She shuddered at the idea of living there. Limiting her errands to one store, she hurried back toward the hotel. She encountered Indians who despite their white man's garb were picturesque and thrilling to her. She noted that they regarded her with interest. Then she saw a Mexican boy leading several beautiful spirited horses. There was nothing else in her short walk that attracted her attention.

In a short time she was packed and ready for her father when he came to her room. He acted more like a boy than her erstwhile staid and quiet parent. The car was waiting outside.

"We're off," declared Mr. Endicott with an air of finality. And Janey bit her tongue to keep from retorting that he could speak for himself.

Soon they left the town behind and entered a forest of

stately pines, growing far apart over brown-matted, slow-rising ground. The fragrance was similar to that of Eastern forests, except that it had a dry, sweet quality new to Janey. Here and there the road crossed open ranch country, from which snow-clad peaks were visible. Janey wondered why Easterners raved so about the Alps when the West possessed such mountains as these. She was sorry when she could see them no more. Her father talked a good deal about this part of Arizona, and seemed to be well informed.

"Say, Dad, have you been out here before?" she asked.

"No. Randolph talked about the country. He loves it. No wonder!"

Janey made no reply, and that perhaps was more of a compliment than she usually paid places. The road climbed, but neither the steepness nor the roughness of it caused the driver any concern. Soon the car, entering thicker forest, dark and cool, reached the summit of a ridge and started down a gradual descent, where the timber thinned out, and in a couple of miles failed on the edge of the desert.

It was Janey Endicott's first intimate sight of any desert. She felt strongly moved; yet whether it was in awe or wonder or reverence or fear, or a little of each combined, she could not tell. The sum of every extended view she had ever seen, in her whole life, could not compare with the tremendous open space before her. First it was silver and gray, dotted with little green trees, then it sloped off yellow and red, and ended in a great hollow of many hues, out of which dim purple shapes climbed.

"That must be the Painted Desert, if I remember Randolph correctly," said her father. "It is magnificent. Nothing in Europe like it! And Randolph told me that this is nothing compared to the Utah country two hundred miles north."

"Let's go, Dad," replied Janey, dreamily.

From that time on the ride grew in absorbing interest for Janey, until she was no longer conscious of reflection about her impressions. The Little Colorado River, the

vast promontory of Kishlipi, the giant steppes up to the Bad-
lands, the weird and sinister rock formations stretching
on to an awful blue gulf which was the Grand Canyon; the
wondrous flat tablelands called mesas by the driver, the
descent into glaring sandy Moencopi Wash, and up again,
higher than ever, and on and on over leagues of desert,
with black ranges beckoning—these successive stages of
the ride claimed Janey's attention as had no other scenery
in her experience.

She was not ready for the trading post. They had reached
it too soon for her. It looked like one of the blocks of red
rock they had passed so frequently. But near at hand it
began to look more like a habitation. All about was sand,
yellow and red and gray; and on the curved knife-edged
ridge-crests it was blowing like silver smoke. There were
patches of green below the trading post, and beneath them
a wide hollow, where columns of dust or sand whirled
across the barren waste. Beyond rose white-whorled cliffs,
wonderful to see, and above them, far away, the black
fringed top of an endless mesa.

"What do you think of it, Janey?" asked Endicott, curiously.

"Now I understand why Phillip Randolph seemed such
a square peg in a round hole, as my friends called him,"
replied Janey, enigmatically.

"Humph! They don't know him very well," declared her
father.

They were met at the door of the post by the trader, John
Bennet. He was carrying some Navajo rugs. His sombrero
was tipped over one ear. He had a weather-beaten face, and
was a middle-aged man of medium height, grizzled and
desert-worn, with eyes that showed kindliness and good
humor.

"Wal, heah you are," he welcomed them, throwing down
the rugs. "Reckon we wasn't expectin' you so soon. Get
down an' come in."

Janey entered the door, into what appeared to be a colorful and spacious living room. Here she encountered a large

woman with sleeves rolled up showing brown and capable
arms. She beamed upon Janey and bade her make herself
"to home." Then she joined the others outside, leaving Janey
alone.

She looked around with interest. The broad window seat,
with windows opening to the desert view, appealed strongly
to Janey. Removing coat and hat she sat down to rest and
take stock of things.

The long room contained many Indian rugs, some of
which adorned the walls. On a table lay scattered silver-
ornamented belts, hatbands and bridles. Over the wide fireplace mantel hung Indian plaques, and on top of the
bookcase were articles of Indian design, beaded, and some
primitive pottery. A burned-out fire smoldered on the hearth.

At this point Mrs. Bennet came in, accompanied by the
trader, and Endicott, and a tall young man in khaki. Janey
had seen him somewhere. Indeed, it was Phillip Randolph.
Brown-faced, roughly garbed, he fitted the desert environ-
ment decidedly to Janey's taste.

"Miss Endicott, I reckon you don't need no introduction
to Phil here," announced Mrs. Bennet, with a keen glance
running over Janey's short French frock, sheer stockings
and high-heeled shoes.

"Phil? . . . Oh, you mean Mr. Randolph."

The young man bowed rather stiffly and stepped toward
her.

"I hope you remember me, Miss Endicott," he said.

"I do, Mr. Randolph," replied Janey, graciously, offering
her hand.

"It's good to see you out here in my West. I really never
believed you'd come, though your father vowed he'd fetch
you."

"Well, Dad succeeded, though I can't understand it,"
rejoined Janey, laughing.

"Mr. Endicott, did you-all have a nice trip out?" asked
Mrs. Bennet.

"I did. My daughter's rather doubtful yet, I fear."

"Now, isn't that too bad, Miss Endicott," sympathized

the genial woman. "I saw right off how pale you are. You'll get your health back in this desert."

"My health!" exclaimed Janey, almost indignantly. "Why, I'm absurdly healthy. I've been picked for a health poster. It's my father who is ailing."

"Excuse me, Miss," said Mrs. Bennet, embarrassed. "You see your father looks so strong—"

"It isn't his body that's weak, Mrs. Bennet," interrupted Janey. "It's his mind."

Here Phillip came to the rescue, as Janey remembered he had always done in New York.

"Mrs. Bennet, it's not a question of ill health for anybody," he explained. "Mr. Endicott was an old friend of my father's. I met him in New York. He wanted to come out West and get Miss Janey as far away from civilization as possible, to—"

"I'll say he's done it," interrupted Janey. "It must be a real knock-out to live here if you're crazy about miles of nothing but sand, rocks and sky, and you've committed some crime or other and want to hide."

Mrs. Bennet tried to control her amazement.

"Mr. Endicott, your rooms are not quite ready. Please wait here a little. . . . Pa, see that them lazy cowboys fetch in the baggage."

"Phil, where are the boys, anyhow?" asked Bennet, as his spouse bustled out.

"They were lounging in the shade when the car came up. Then they disappeared like jack rabbits in the sage. Sure they're going to be funny. I'll help you find them."

"Folks, make yourselves comfortable," invited Bennet, and left the room with the archaeologist.

Mr. Endicott sauntered over to Janey and gazed disapprovingly down upon her.

"Janey, I don't mind you calling me crazy or poking fun at me. But please don't extend that to my young friend Randolph. His father was the finest man I ever knew, and Phillip is pretty much like him. . . . Janey, you'll have to put your best foot forward if you want to appear well to

Phillip Randolph. He's not likely to see the sophisticated type with a microscope out here. In New York he had you buffaloed. You couldn't like him because you didn't understand him."

"Darling Father," replied Janey, smiling tantalizingly up at him. "Your name may be Elijah, but you're no prophet. I liked your young friend well enough to let him alone. But that was in New York where there are a million men. I don't know about out here. Probably he'll bore me to extinction. Can't you see he's as dry as the dust of this desert? He's living two thousand years behind the times. Fancy digging in the earth for things of the past. Well, he might dig up a jeweled corncob pipe and discover there were glamour girls in the old Aztec days."

"Janey, you're nothing if not incorrigible," returned Mr. Endicott in despair.

"Dad, I'm your daughter. I don't know whether you've brought me up poorly or I've neglected you. But the fact is all our educators and scientists claim the parents of the present generation are responsible for our demerits."

"Janey, I'm responsible for your conduct out here, at all events," declared Mr. Endicott, forcefully.

"Oh, you are! Well, my dearest Dad, I'm here all right—or else I've been drinking."

"Janey, there'll be no more of this drinking business."

"Dad, you've got me figured wrong. I admit my crowd hit the booze pretty strong. But I never drank. Honest, Dad."

"Janey, I don't know whether to believe you or not. But I've seen you smoke."

"Oh, well, that's different. Smoking isn't very clean, but it's a fashionable vice, and restful at least."

"How about all your men?" queried Endicott, evidently emboldened for the minute. "Lord! When I think of the men you've made idiots! Take that last one—the young Valentino who brags of being engaged to you."

Janey laughed merrily. "Dad, do you think that's nice?

Bert Durland is just too sweet for words; also he dances divinely."

"Durland is a slick little article. Like his social ladder-climbing mama. But I'll see that he doesn't dance or climb into your inheritance."

"To think you separated me from him!" cried Janey, pretending tragic pathos.

A slim young Indian girl entered. She was dark and pretty.

"Meester, your room ees ready."

"Thank you," said Endicott, picking up his coat and hat. "Janey, you've got me right. I did separate you from Durland. Also from a lot of other fortune hunters. That's why you're out in this desert for a spell. Except for Bennet and Randolph, whom you can't flirt with, there's not a man within a hundred miles."

Janey eyed her retreating parent, and replied demurely, "Yes, kind, sweet, thoughtful father."

Endicott went out with the Indian maid, and at the same moment a young man entered the other door, carrying a valise in each hand. He had a ruddy face, and was carelessly dressed in striped woolen shirt, overalls and top boots. He wore a big dusty sombrero.

When he spotted Janey his eyes popped wide open and he dropped one valise, then the other.

"Was you addressin' *me*, Miss?" he asked, ecstatically.

"Not then. I was speaking to my father. He just left the room. . . . You—sort of took me by surprise."

"Shore, you tuk my wind."

"Do you live here?" asked Janey with interest. This trading post might not turn out so badly after all.

"Shore do," replied the young man, grinning.

"Are you Mrs. Bennet's son?"

"Naw. Jest a plain no-good cowboy."

"My very *first* cowboy!" murmured Janey.

"Aw, Miss! I'm shore honored. I'll be yore—yore first anythin'. Ain't you the Endicott girl we're expectin'?"

"Yes, I'm Janey Endicott."

"An' I'm Mohave. The boys call me that after the Mohave Desert which ain't got no beginnin' or end."

As Janey broke into laughter another young man entered, also carrying a grip in each hand. He was overdressed, like a motion-picture cowboy, and he had a swarthy, dark face. He gave Janey a warm smile.

"Cowboy, reckon you can put them bags down an' get back for more," blandly said Mohave.

"*Buenas días, Señorita,*" greeted this one, dropping the bags and sweeping the floor with his sombrero. Janey was quick to see that Mohave suddenly remembered to remove his own wide headgear.

"Same to you," replied Janey, smiling as teasingly as possible.

"Miss Endicott, this here's Diego," said Mohave, apologetically. "He's a Mexican. He seen a Western movie once an' ain't never got over it. He's been dressed up all day waitin' for you."

"I'm tremendously flattered," returned Janey.

"Mees, thees are your bags I carry. I peeck them out weeth your name on."

"Now there, Buffalo Bill, you mustn't flatter me any more," replied Janey, coquettishly.

"Oh, Mees! Señor Buffalo Beel you call me. I have seen heem in the movies."

Here he drew two guns with an exaggerated motion-picture-drama style. "A-ha! Veelian! Een my power at las'! A-ha! Your time ees come. I keel you!"

He brandished both guns in Janey's face. In alarm she slipped off the window seat to dodge behind a table.

"Diego, you locoed cowpuncher, get on the job," ordered Mohave, forcibly. "Ray is comin'."

Diego evidently had respect for Mohave. Hurriedly sheathing his guns, and picking up his sombrero he recovered the two valises. Meanwhile Janey emerged from behind the table.

"Mees, Diego will act for you again," he announced grandly.

"Ye-es. Thanks. But please make it someplace where I can dodge," replied Janey.

Diego left the room, and Mohave, taking up his load, turned to Janey.

"Miss Endicott, don't trust Diego, or any of these other hombres. An' perticular, don't ride their horses. You'll shore get throwed an' mebbe killed. But my pet horse is shore gentle. I'll take you ridin' tomorrow."

"I'd love to go with *you*," returned Janey.

Then Mohave made swift tracks after Diego, just in time to escape being seen by a third cowboy, who entered from outside, carrying a trunk as if it had been a feather. He set it down. He was bareheaded, a blond young man, not bad looking, in size alone guaranteed to command respect. And his costume struck a balance between that of Diego and Mohave.

Janey gazed at him and exclaimed, "*Well!* Tarzan in cowboy boots, no less."

Ray stared, then walked in a circle to see whom she meant. But as there was no other man present he seemed to divine the truth, and approached her straightaway.

"Wal, for Gawd's sake!" he broke out, in slow sepulchral tones.

"Oh, yes, indeed, it's you I mean," returned Janey, all smiles. "I'll bet when your horse is tired you pick him up and carry him right home."

"Wal, for Gawd's sake!" ejaculated Ray, exactly as before.

"Are there any more verses to that song?"

"Wal—for Gawd's sake!"

"Third and last—I hope."

"First time I ever seen an angel or heered one talk," he declared.

"Please don't call me an angel. Angels are good. I'm not. I'm wild. That's why I've been dragged out West. Ask Dad, he knows. Say, that reminds me. I'm dying for a smoke. Dad's old-fashioned and I don't carry them when he's around. Could you give me a cigarette?"

Ray merely stared.

"Please, handsome boy! Just one little cigarette."

"Ain't got nothin' but the makin's," he finally ejaculated.

"Thanks. That'll do," replied Janey, receiving the little tobacco pouch he handed her.

It fascinated Ray to see Janey roll her own. He was so absorbed that he failed to note the entrance of a fourth cowboy, who was burdened with hatboxes and more grips. He was the handsomest of the lot. With his fine intent eyes straight ahead, not noticing Janey, he crossed the room and went into the hallway. Janey had watched him pass in a surprise that grew into pique. He had never looked once at her. He would have to pay for that slight.

"Wal! Yore shore some pert little dogie," remarked Ray, lighting a match for her.

"Dogie! . . . Say, Mr. Cowboy, explain what you mean!"

"A dogie is a calf or a colt that ain't got no mother."

"Where did you learn anything about me?" asked Janey, a bit wary.

"Shore any kid with a ma couldn't ever roll a cigarette an' smoke it like you do."

"Indeed! Ray, are you a desert preacher?" queried Janey, distantly.

"Sorry, Miss. Shore didn't mean to hurt yore feelin's. But it kind of got me—seein' you smoke like thet. Yore so damn —'scuse me, I mean yore so shore pretty that it goes agin my grain to see you up to dance-hall tricks."

"You don't like women to smoke?" returned Janey, curiously.

"Perticular, I don't like to see you smokin'."

"Then I won't," decided Janey, and walking to the fireplace she threw the cigarette down.

"Jes—jes 'cause I don't like you to smoke?" ejaculated Ray, rapturously.

"Jes 'cause you don't like me to."

"An' you'll forgive me fer talkin' like I did?"

"Surely."

"I'm askin' you to prove thet."

"How?"

"Go ridin' with me tomorrow," suggested Ray, breath-lessly. "You can ride my pet hoss. He's shore gentle. You don't wanna ride any of these hombres' horses. You might get throwed an' hurt. They're shore mean."

"I'd love to go with *you*," responded Janey, dreamily.

At this moment the handsome cowboy returned, and was again crossing the room, straight-eyed and hurried, when Ray hailed him. "Rustle now, you cowboy. Fetch them bags in."

Janey had taken a few steps forward. The cowboy glided round the table to avoid encountering her, and then bolted out of the room.

"Well, I never!" exclaimed Janey. "You'd think I was Me-dusa. He didn't see me. . . . He simply didn't see me! . . . Who is he?"

"Thet's Zoroaster. Mormon cowpuncher. Fine fellar, but awful scared of women. Ain't never seen any but Mormon girls. He'll never look at you!"

"Oh, he won't!" replied Janey, with a threat in her voice.

"Shore not. An' don't you ever talk to him. He'd like as not drop dead. Last year a girl from the East asked him to dance, an' he run right out of the hall. Didn't show up for a week."

"It's an awful chance to take, but that boy needs reform-ing," declared Janey.

Ray stared at her a moment before he took to his defense —"Wal, for Gawd's sake!"

Mohave came in with a sly grin on his ruddy face.

"Ray, Mr. Bennet is askin' fer you," he said.

"Where?" asked Ray, in both doubt and disgust.

"He's gone out to the post and wants you pronto."

Ray went out grumbling and Mohave approached Janey with evident profound satisfaction.

"Looks like you're goin' to be as popular as stickin' paper with flies," he said, meaningly.

"Mohave, after flies take to flypaper they struggle to get away. That's not a pretty compliment."

"Say! Did you know you called me Mohave?" he asked, in amazement.

Janey feigned surprise. "Did I?"

Then she was electrified at the entrance of still another cowboy.

"S-s-scuse me, f-f-folks, w-w-w-where's Ray?"

"Tay-Tay, he's gone to the post an' I wish you wouldn't—"

"Like h-h-hell he has," interrupted Tay-Tay.

"Bennet is lookin' fer him."

"L-l-last I saw of Bennet he was runnin' the car in the shed."

"Good. Then he won't be right back an' Ray'll have to find him."

Janey stood fascinated by Tay-Tay's struggle with words.

"B-b-b-bad I'd say! For you an' Ray! The cows are yore job, an' yore both locoed b-by this d-d-dame. It's g-g-goner rain like hell!"

Janey turned to Mohave. "Perhaps you b-b-better go. . . . Well, I hope to die if I'm not stuttering too!"

Here Diego, filling the doorway, struck a dramatic pose and fixed sentimental eyes on Janey.

"*Por último! Señorita mía!*" he said eloquently.

"Too many languages around here for me," returned Janey.

"Here's Diego to give a hand. I was jest tellin' Miss Endicott how you could ride. An' she's shore ailin' to see you round up the cows."

Diego's look of fiery pride slowly changed to one of suspicion; and Tay-Tay stared from him to Mohave. The next thing to happen was Ray shoving Diego into the room, and stalking after him, to transfix Mohave with menacing eyes.

"Wal, for Gawd's sake! So you was jest gettin' me out of the way. Said Bennet was lookin' for me. Wal, cowboy, he ain't."

"Don't you accuse me of no sneakin' trick," replied Mohave, flaring up.

"Bennet was askin' fer you. He's plumb forgot. He's gettin' absent-minded, you know. Ask Tay-Tay here if Bennet didn't send him lookin' fer you to fetch in the cows."

"S-s-smatter with you, Mohave?" retorted Tay-Tay. "B-B-Bennet didn't send me nowhere. I c-c-came fer myself."

"Tay-Tay, yore tongue's not only more tied since you seen Miss Endicott, but yore mind is wuss," complained Mohave.

Then followed a silence which Janey hugely enjoyed. What a time she was going to have! Wouldn't she turn the tables on her tricky father? Mohave backed away from the threatening Ray. The other boys edged nearer to Janey, who thought it wise to retreat to the window seat. The suspense of the moment was broken by the entrance of Zoroaster, who swung two pairs of boxing gloves in his hands. Behind him entered the Indian maid.

"Mees, your room ees ready," she announced, and retired.

Janey was in no hurry to follow. Something might happen here too good to miss.

"Thar you are!" announced Zoroaster, indicating Tay-Tay. He might be a Mormon, but he was certainly good to look at, decided Janey.

"W-w-what y-y-you w-w-want me for?" stuttered Tay-Tay, rebelliously.

"Yore time's come. I've been layin' fer you. An' right now we *can* have it out," returned the grim Mormon.

"W-w-why right now more'n another time?" asked Tay-Tay.

"Wal," spoke up Ray, "I reckon a blind man could see thet. Lope on outdoors, Tay, an' get yours."

Diego showed his white teeth in a gleaming smile.

"Geeve the gloves to Ray an' Mohave. They're lookeen for trouble."

"It's me who's lookin' fer trouble, an' after I'm through with Tay I'll take any of you on. Savvy?"

"B-b-but if I w-w-want to q-q-quit in the m-m-middle of a round I won't be able to say s-s-s-stop," replied Tay-Tay.

"Aw, yore jest plain backin' out before this lady. . . . Wal, who of you will put them on?"

Zoroaster looked from one to the other. They all appeared

to have become absent-minded. Janey had an inspiration, and rose, radiant, from the window seat.

"I will, Mr. Zoroaster," she said.

The Mormon cowboy's face turned redder than his hair. He was dumbfounded, and plainly fought to keep from running. But Janey's smile chained him. If she saw in the boxing bout an opportunity to get acquainted with Zoroaster, he evidently saw one to outdo the other zealous suitors for her favor. Awkwardly he thrust a pair of gloves at her.

"All right, Miss. You're shore showin' these hombres up. But I'll be careful not to hurt you."

Janey was athletic and, as it happened, was the best boxer in her club. Pretending unfamiliarity with boxing gloves she begged someone to help her put them on. All save Ray rushed to her assistance.

He stared, open-mouthed, and finally ejaculated, "Wal, for Gawd's sake!"

"There! Now, Mr. Zoroaster, give me a few pointers, please," suggested Janey, winningly.

"It's easy, Miss," he said, extending his gloved hands. "Keep one foot forward, an' lead with your left hand. Keep yore eyes on my gloves an' duck."

Janey affected practice while Zoroaster circled her. Plainly he was not a scientific boxer; and Janey who had had many a bout with the club instructor saw some fun ahead. Suddenly she ceased her pretense and went for Zoroaster, swift and light as a cat, and grasped at once that she could hit him when and where she pleased.

"Ride 'em, cowgirl. Oh, my!" cried Mohave.

"Thet's placin' one, Miss," shouted Ray, in great glee.

"S-s-s-soak him fer me," stuttered Tay-Tay, in delight.

"Señorita, you ees one grande boxer," declared Diego, dramatically.

Zoroaster's fear and amazement helped to put him at Janey's mercy. She danced around the transfixed Mormon, raining taps upon his handsome nose. Finally she struck him smartly with her left, and followed that up with as hard a right swing as she could muster. It landed square on Zoroaster's nose and all but upset him.

The cowboys, instead of roaring, seemed suddenly paralyzed. Janey, glowing and panting, turned to see what was wrong. Her father stood in the doorway, horrified, completely robbed of the power of speech. Zoroaster bolted out of the front door, followed by his cowboy comrades.

Janey's mirth was not one whit lessened by the sight of her father's face. Gayly she ran to him, extending the gloves to be untied.

"Weren't they something? I love 'em all, and that handsome red-headed devil best. Oh, bless you, Dad. I'll stay here forever!"

2

FROM THAT MOMENT events multiplied. Janey could not keep track of them. She was having the time of her life. And every now and then it burst upon her what really innocent fun it was, compared to the high pressure of life in the East.

She had disrupted the even tenor of the trading post. Bennet averred that something must be done about it. His cowboys had gone crazy. If they remembered their work it was to desert it or do it wrong. They manufactured the most ridiculous excuses to ride away from the ranch, when it chanced that Janey was out riding. When she was at home they each and every one fell victim to all the ailments under the sun.

Janey saw very little of Randolph during her first days at the post. He always left before she got up in the morning, and returned from his excavating work late in the afternoon. She met him, of course, at dinner, when they all sat at a long table, and in the living room afterward, but never alone. Janey was quite aware of the humor with which he regarded her flirtation with the cowboys. She did not like his attitude, and wasted a thought now and then as to how she would punish him.

On the whole, however, she was too happy to even remember her father's reason for fetching her out to the desert. The actual reasons for her peculiar happiness she had not yet analyzed.

It was all so new. She rode for hours every day, sometimes alone, which was a difficult thing to maneuver—and often with her father, and the cowboys. The weather was glorious; the desert strangely, increasingly impelling; the blue sky and white clouds, the vivid colors and magnificent formations of the rock walls had some effect she was loath to acknowledge.

When had she been so hungry and tired at nightfall? She went to bed very early because everybody did so; and she slept as never before. Her skin began to take on a golden brown, and she gained weight. Both facts secretly pleased her. The pace at home had kept her pale and thin. Janey gazed in actual amazement and delight at the face that smiled back at her from the mirror. Once she mused, "I'll say this Painted Desert has got the beauty shops beaten all hollow."

Her father had asked her several times to ride over to Sagi Canyon, where Randolph was excavating. But Janey had pretended indifference as to his movements. As a matter of fact, she was curious to see what his work was like—what in the world could make a young man prefer digging in the dust to her company? There was another reason why she would not go, and it was because the more she saw of Phillip Randolph and heard about him from the cowboys and Bennet—who were outspoken in their praise—the better she liked him and the more she resented liking him.

For the present, however, the cowboys were more than sufficient for Janey. They were an endless source of interest, fun and wholesome admiration.

In ten days not a single one of them had attempted to hold her hand, let alone kiss her. Janey would rather have liked them, one and all, to hold her hand; and she would not have run very far to keep from being kissed. But it began to dawn upon her that despite an utter prostration of each cowboy at her feet, so to speak, there was never even a hint of familiarity, such as was natural as breathing to the young men of her set.

First it struck Janey as amusing. Then she sought to break it down. And before two weeks were up she began to take serious thought of something she had not supposed possible to the genus Homo, young or old, East or West.

Janey did not care to be forced to delve into introspection, to perplex herself with the problem of modern youth. She had had quite enough of that back East. Papers, magazines, plays, sermons, and lectures, even the movies, had made a concerted attack upon the younger generation. It had been pretty sickening to Janey. How good to get away from that atmosphere for a while! Perhaps here was a reason why she liked the West. But there seemed to be something working on her, which sooner or later she must face.

One afternoon Janey returned from her ride earlier than usual, so that she did not have to hurry and dress for dinner. She had settled herself in the hammock when her father and Randolph rode in from the opposite direction. The hammock was hidden under the vines outside the living-room window. They did not see Janey and she was too lazy or languid to call to them.

A little later she heard them enter the living room. The window there was open.

"Janey must be dressing," said Endicott. "She's back. I saw her saddle. We have time for a little chat. I've been wanting to talk to you."

"Go ahead. I'm glad our ride didn't tire you. By the way, what did you think of my Sagi?"

"Beautiful but dumb, as Janey would say. Quietest place I ever saw. Why, it was positively silent as a grave."

"Yes. It is a grave. That's why I dig around there so

much," replied Randolph, with a laugh. Janey remembered that laugh, though she had heard it very seldom. It was rather rich and pleasant; and scarcely fitted the character she had given him. She had two sudden impulses, one to make them aware of her presence, and another not to do anything of the kind. Second impulses were mostly the stronger with Janey.

"Randolph, I'm very curious about you. What is there in it for you—in this grave-digging work, I mean?"

"Oh, it's treasure hunting in a way. I suppose an archaeologist is born. I seldom think of reward. But, really, if I discovered the prehistoric ruin I know is buried here somewhere it would be a big thing for me."

"Any money in it?" inquired the New York businessman.

"Not directly. At least not at once. I suppose articles and lectures could be translated into money. It would give me prestige, though."

"Hum. Well, prestige is all right for a young man starting in life but it doesn't produce much bread and butter. Do you get a salary, in addition to your remuneration for articles and lectures?"

"You could call it a salary by courtesy. But besides bread-and-butter fare of the simplest kind, it wouldn't buy stockings for a young lady I know," returned Randolph, and again he laughed, the same nice infectious laugh.

"Now you're talking," responded Endicott, with animation. "The young lady, of course, being Janey. . . . Randolph, we're getting to be good friends. Let's be confidential. Did you ever ask my daughter to marry you?"

"Lord, no!" ejaculated Randolph.

"Well, that's a satisfaction. It's good for a young man to have individuality. I'm glad you're different from the many. . . . May I ask—forgive my persistence; the awful responsibility of being this girl's father, you know—weren't you in love with her?"

There was quite a long silence in which Janey's heart beat quickly and her ears tingled. She had never really been sure of Randolph. That, perhaps, was his chief charm.

"Yes, Mr. Endicott," replied the archaeologist, constrainedly. "I was in love with Janey. Not, however, as those young men were in the East. But very terribly, deeply in love."

"Fine! . . . Oh, excuse me, Phillip," rejoined Endicott. "I mean—that's what I thought. That's why I liked you. These young lounge lizards play at love. They make me sick. Between you and me I've a sneaking suspicion they make Janey sick, too. . . . Now, Phil, here's the vital question. Is all that past tense?"

Janey made the discovery that she was trembling, and imagined it was from the shame of being an unwitting eavesdropper. How impossible now to call out! Yet she might have slipped away. But she did not.

"No. I never got over it. And now it's worse," said Randolph, not without a tragic note.

"Phil! By heavens, you are a loyal fellow. Would it surprise you to know I'm pleased?"

"Thank you, Mr. Endicott. But I fear that I'm more than surprised."

"See here, Phil, you want to be prepared for jars, not only from Janey, but also me. I'm her Dad, you know. . . . Listen, I brought Janey out to your desert with barefaced deliberate intent. To marry her to you and save her from that pack of wolves back there . . . Incidentally, of course, to make both of you happy!"

"My God!" gasped Randolph. He was not the only one who gasped. Janey in her excitement nearly fell out of the hammock.

"It's an honest fact, and I'm not ashamed," went on Endicott, getting earnest.

"But, Mr. Endicott—you do me honor. You are most wonderfully kind—but you are quite out of your head."

"Maybe I am. I don't care. I mean it. I love Janey and I'd go to any extreme to save her. Then I like you immensely. Your father was my dearest friend in college and until he died. I'd get a good deal of happiness out of putting a spoke in your wheel of fortune."

"Save her!" ejaculated Randolph.

"For God's sake, Randolph, don't say you think it's too late," appealed Endicott, in sudden distress.

No quick response came, and Janey's heart stood still as she waited for Randolph's answer. What did that fool think, anyway? She was getting a little sick with anger and fear when Randolph burst out: "Endicott, you're crazy. I—I meant—what did you mean when you said save her?"

"I meant a lot, my boy, and don't overlook it. . . . Tell me straight, Randolph. This is a serious matter for us all. Do you think Janey is still a good girl?"

"I don't think. I *know*," returned Randolph, ringingly. "Your question is an insult to her, Mr. Endicott."

"I wonder whether or not any question is that, in regard to young women in this age," went on Endicott, soberly. "I gave you credit for being a brainy clear-eyed fellow, for all your grave-digging propensity. I saw how you disapproved of Janey—her friends and habits."

"Yes, I did—deplorably so. But nevertheless—"

"Love is blind, my son," interposed Endicott. "You think more of Janey than she deserves. All the same I'm glad. That'll help us out. I regard you as an anchor."

"Mr. Endicott, I—I don't know what to say. I'm overwhelmed."

"Well, I dare say you've reason to be. But all the same you listen to me patiently. Will you?"

"Why, certainly."

"You were justified in being shocked at my question about Janey. But I wouldn't blame anyone for a pretty raw opinion of modern girls. I have it myself. . . . To be brief, they have gotten under my skin, if you know what that means. Janey's generation is beyond my understanding. They have developed something new. They are eliminating right and wrong. They have no respect for their parents, and so far as I can see very little affection. They have a positive hatred for all restraint. They will not stand to be controlled. They have no faith in our old standards. As a rule they have no religion. They wear indecent clothes, or I might say very few clothes at all. They dance all night, drown themselves in booze, pet and neck indiscriminately, and most of them go the limit."

"Mr. Endicott!" expostulated Randolph, somewhat taken aback by the elder man's outburst.

"Phil, I'm telling you straight. This is not my theory. I know. I've got this young crowd figured that far, at least. I have no patience at all with fatuous mamas and papas who claim the young people are all right. They are *not* all right. They are a fast crowd and the nation that depends on them and can't change them is slated for hell. These wiseacres who say there is no flagrant immorality are far off the track. Those who claim young women of today are no different from yesterday are simply blind. They *are* different, and I don't mean wholly the emancipation of women since the war. I was always for woman suffrage. . . . Well, I'm not concerned with the causes, as whether or not we parents are to blame. I've done my damnedest for Janey and it hurts to think maybe I've failed. I'm honest in believing I've not been a bad example for my child. But sometimes Janey makes me want to crawl into a dark corner and hide. . . . I'm concerned with the facts of what I'm telling you. I want to see Janey married to a good and straight and industrious young man. Janey says he doesn't exist. . . . Her mother was like Janey, though not so beautiful. She was willful, intelligent, bewildering. But she had no vices. . . . Now I take it Janey is about as fascinating as a young woman could be. Perhaps she is all the more so because of this complexity of modern times. She knows it. I wouldn't call Janey conceited. She's not really vain. She's rather a merciless gay modern young woman who takes pleasure in wading through a mob of men. If she heard her friends speak of a man who was not likely to fall for her, as they call it, Janey would yell, 'Lead me to him!' Despite all this I feel and hope Janey can be saved. Lord, fancy her hearing me say that! To my mind if she drifts with her crowd she'll never amount to anything. She would probably divorce one husband after another. I don't like the idea. Janey's mother

left her something which she will have control of in another year. And then of course she'll get all I possess,
which isn't inconsiderable. Her prospects then, and her
beauty, make her a mark for the men she comes in contact with, and their name is legion. I have tried to keep
her away from the worst of them. But it's impossible."

"Why impossible?" broke in Phillip, tersely.

"I gave up because when I'd tell Janey a certain young
fellow was no fit acquaintance for her I would only stimu-
late interest. She'd say, 'Dad, you think you know a lot, but
I'll have to see for myself'—and you bet she would."

"Then Janey wouldn't obey you?" asked Randolph.

"Obey!" echoed Endicott, in surprise. "Most certainly she
would not."

"Then indeed you are to blame for what she is."

"Ha! I'd like to see you or anybody else make Janey
obey."

"I could and I would," declared Randolph.

"My dear young Arizona archaeologist! May I ask how?"
returned Endicott, not without sarcasm and amusement.

"I'd take that young lady across my knee and spank her
soundly."

"Good Lord! You don't know what you're saying. . . .
Why, if I subjected Janey to such indignity she'd—she'd—
well, what wouldn't she do? Wrecking the place where it
happened would be the least. . . . Yet, oh—*how* I have
wanted to do that same little thing!"

"Mr. Endicott, your daughter is a spoiled child," asserted
Randolph, in a tone that made Janey want to shriek.

"Spoiled—yes—and everything else," agreed Endicott,
helplessly. "But with it all she is adorable. Have you noticed
that, Phil?"

"Why, come to think of it I believe I have," he answered,
with dry humor.

"Well, we are agreed on a few things, anyway. We can
dismiss her demerits by acknowledging that, and her intelligence, truthfulness, and other cardinal virtues which she
has in common with all the young people today. It may be

that they are too advanced for us of the older generation
to understand. It might be that something wonderful will
come of such a paradox. But I can't see it, and my problem is to check Janey's mad career. . . . Ha!—Ha!"

"If I may presume to advise you, Mr. Endicott, you are
undertaking a perfectly impossible task," said Randolph.

"No! Why, Phil, I am sometimes damn fool enough to believe Janey might do all I ask just because she loves me. I
know she does. But I always put things to her in a way that
makes her furious. So I've quit it. . . . This is my last
card—my trump."

"This?" asked Randolph, with curiosity.

"This trip, and the plan I've decided upon. Here it is!
I'm going to marry Janey to you."

There was an absolute blank silence. Janey felt what a
shock this must have been to Randolph. It was no less a
shock to her.

"Now—now I know what's the matter," said Randolph,
finally, in a queer voice.

"What?"

"You really *are* out of your mind!"

"Well, that may be," returned Endicott, with good humor.
"But I'll stand by my guns. I've sense enough to understand
that you will at first indignantly refuse such a proposition.
Won't you?"

"I certainly do," replied Randolph, bluntly.

"Randolph, no young man who knew and loved Janey
could refuse for any other reason than he thought it preposterous. . . . That she didn't care two straws for him?"

"Exactly. In my case one straw."

"The only weakness in my proposition is the hope, the
dream, that Janey might love you someday. You must remember I know her as I knew her mother. Janey, too, is
capable of the most extraordinary things."

"It surely would be that for her to—to— Oh, Endicott,
the idea is ridiculous," returned Randolph, beginning in
bitterness and ending in anger.

"Hear me out. If you don't I'll think you, too, are just like the rest of this generation. . . . I base my hopes on this. Janey likes you—respects you. She makes all manner of fun of you, but underneath it there's something deep. At least it's deep enough to keep her from adding your scalp to her belt. . . . You'll forgive me, Phil, for saying that my fancy-free girl would learn to care for you—under favorable circumstances."

"What are they?" queried the archaeologist.

"Never mind details. But I mean the things that make a man. I'll swear I don't believe Janey has ever met a real man. . . . Well, to go on. I save my conscience in this case by believing she could care for you. And my plan is simply to give Janey a terrific jar—and then nature, with such a favorable start, will do the rest."

"Believe me, it would have to be a terrific jar, all right," said Randolph, with another of his resonant laughs.

"Believe me, it *is*. And it's simply this. Be as nice as pie to Janey. Then at an opportune time just throw her on a horse and pack her off to one of your ruins in the desert. Kidnap her! Keep her out there a little while—scare her half to death—let her know what it is to be uncomfortable, hungry, helpless. Then fetch her back. She'd have to marry you. I would insist upon it. . . . Then we'd all be happy."

"Mr. Endicott, the only sane remark you've made is that epithet you applied to yourself a few moments ago."

"It is a most wonderful opportunity. You are ambitious. This would make you."

"No."

"I will make you a most substantial settlement. You will be independent for life. You can follow up your archaeological work for the love of it. You—"

"*No!*"

"Now, Phil, I can apply that epithet to you. May I ask why you refuse?"

"You—I— Oh, hell! . . . Endicott, it's because I really *love* Janey. I couldn't think of myself in such a case. If I did

I'd—I'd be as weak as water. . . . Why, Janey would hate me."

"Don't be so sure of that," replied Endicott, sagely. "You can't ever tell about a woman. It's a gamble, of course. But you have the odds. Be a good sport, Phil. Even if you lose you'll have gained an experience that you'll remember a lifetime."

"Mr. Endicott, you're taking advantage of human nature," replied Randolph, with agitation. Janey could hear him pacing the room, and she felt sorry for him. It pleased her that he had refused. But she knew her father, his relentless ways, and she held her breath.

"Certainly I am," agreed Endicott, growing warmer. "Phil, look at it this way. Consent for Janey's sake!"

"But man, I can't believe that wonderful girl is going to hell. I *can't*."

"Naturally. You're in love with her. To you she's an angel. All right. Think of it this way then. You admitted she was adorable. You just said she was wonderful. You know how beautiful she is. Well, here's your chance to make her yours. Maybe it's a thousand-to-one shot. Remember, you'll do her good in any case. And you've that one chance in a thousand. Her mother was the most loving of women. Why, Phil, if Janey loved you—you would be entering the kingdom of heaven. She might."

"My—God!" gasped the young man.

"I am her father. I worship her. And I am begging you to do this thing."

"All—right. I—I'll do it," replied Randolph, in a queer strangled voice. "It will—be my ruin. But I can't resist. . . . Only, understand—I couldn't accept money."

"Fact is, I didn't think you would," replied Endicott, quickly. "And your refusal makes me sure you are the right man. Come, shake on it, Phil. I'll be forever grateful to you whether we win or lose."

Janey heard him rise and cross the room. Taking advantage of this she slipped out of the hammock and ran round to the back of the house, and entering the long corridor she arrived at her room in a more excited and breathless state than she had ever been in all her life. Closing the door she locked it and then relaxed against it, with a hand over her throbbing breast.

"If that wasn't the limit!" she exclaimed, and succumbed to conflicting emotions, among which such rage as she had never felt assumed dominance.

Not long afterward her father knocked on the door. Janey did not answer. He knocked again, and called anxiously.

"Janey?"

"Yes."

"Dinner is ready. We're waiting."

"I don't want any," she replied.

"Why, what is the matter?"

"I've a headache."

"Headache! . . . You? Never heard of the like before."

"Maybe it's a toothache."

"Oh!" he returned, and discreetly retired.

When Janey's anger had finally subsided so that she could think, she found she was deeply wounded. Things for her had come to a very sad pass indeed, if her father could go to such extremes. But were they so bad for her? How perfectly absurd! There was not anything wrong with her. Yet all the same an awakened consciousness refused to accept her indignant assurance. She knew she was the pride and joy of her father's life. He was a trying parent indeed; nevertheless she could not seriously say he had neglected her or given her a bad example. He was just thick-headed, and too much concerned about her affairs. Janey, however, dodged for the present any serious thought concerning her friends and acquaintances at home. They were as good as any other crowd.

Randolph! She could overcome her shame and resentment enough to feel sorry for him. What chance had he against her father, especially if he was genuinely attracted to her? Janey blushed in the loneliness of her room. Randolph had saved his character, in her estimation, by scorning her father's opinions, by resisting his subtle attack, by refusing any consideration of a material gain in his outrageous proposals.

Then Janey happened to remember what Randolph had said about spanking her. In a sudden fury she leaped up and began to pace the little room. There was not very much in the way of disgust, contempt, amazement, pride, wrath, that did not pass through her mind. What an atrocious insult! He had been in earnest. He talked as if she were a nine-year-old child. Her cheeks burned. She refused in the heat of the moment to answer a query that knocked at her ears.

"Oh, I won't do a thing to Phillip Randolph!" she said, under her breath, and as she said it she caught sight of her face in the mirror. When had she looked like that? Only the other day she had fancied she wore a tired bored look. At least she was indebted to Randolph for a glow and a flash of radiance.

A hundred thoughts whirled through her mind. One of them was to run off from her father and punish him that way. Another was to actually be what he feared she was or might become. The former appeared too easy on him and the second unworthy of her. It stung her acutely that she was compelled to prove to him how really different she was. But revenge first! She would show them. She would play up to their infamous plot. She would walk right into their little trap. Then—she would frighten her clever parent out of his wits. And as for Randolph! She would reduce him to such a state of lovesick misery that he would want to die. She would be ten thousand times herself and everything else she could lend herself to. She would help him on with the little scheme, make him marry her; and then, when he and her father were at the top of their bent and ridiculously sure of her so-called salvation, she would calmly announce to them that she had known all about it beforehand. She would denounce them, and go home and divorce Randolph.

The next morning Janey saw Randolph and her father ride away on their horses, evidently well pleased with themselves over something. Then she went late to her breakfast, finding it necessary to play the actress with the solicitous Mrs. Bennet. She would have to be a brilliant actress, anyway, so she might as well begin. She might develop histrionic ability, and make a name on the stage.

She did not ride that morning. Part of the time she spent in her room, and the other walking in the shade of the cottonwoods.

After lunch Janey tried to read. All the books and magazines she had appeared to be full of humor or tragedy of the younger generation. One after another she slammed them on the floor.

"This business is getting damn serious," ejaculated Janey.

All the preachers, editors, physicians, philosophers, were explaining either how horrible the young people were, or else how misunderstood, or abandoned by money-mad parents to their dark fate. Even college boys and girls were writing about themselves. Something was wrong somewhere; and as the thought struck Janey she found herself reaching for a cigarette. With swift temper she threw the little box against the wall. She would have to quit smoking—which meant nothing at all to Janey. She could quit anything. She remembered, however, that in accordance with the plan to revenge herself upon her father and Randolph, she must smoke like a furnace. So she took the trouble to pick up the cigarettes. Still, she did not smoke one then.

The afternoon slowly waned. It had been an upsetting day for Janey. She had changed a hundred times, like the shifting of a wind vane. But the thing most permanent was the stab to her pride. Not soon would she get over that hurt. She did not realize yet just why or how she had been so mortally offended, but she guessed it would come to her eventually.

For the first time in years Janey missed her mother. Was she self-sufficient as she had supposed? She certainly was not, for she fought an hour against rather strange symptoms, and then succumbed to a good old-fashioned crying spell.

3

THAT EVENING a little before suppertime, when Randolph walked into the living room, Janey made it a point to be there. She had adorned herself with a gown calculated to make him gasp. She perceived that he had difficulty in concealing his dismay. The day of mental stress, without the usual exercise and contact with the open, had left her pale with faint purple shadows under her eyes. Janey thought she could take care of the rest.

"I'm sorry you were indisposed," said Randolph, solicitously. "I see you haven't been out today. That's too bad."

"It has been a lonely, awful day," replied Janey, pathetically.

"I hope you haven't been very ill. You looked so—so wonderful yesterday. You're pale now. No doubt you've overdone this riding around with the cowboys."

"I guess I'm not so strong as Dad thinks I am. But I'm really not tired—that is, physically."

"No? What's wrong then?"

Janey transfixed Randolph with great melancholy eyes. "I'm dying of homesickness. This place is dead. It's a ruin. You could dig right here and find a million bones."

"Dead! . . . Oh, yes, indeed, it is rather quiet for a girl used to New York," he returned, plainly disappointed. "I rather expected you would like it—for a while, and, really, you seemed to be enjoying yourself. I know your father thinks you're having the time of your life."

"I was. But it didn't last. Nothing happens. I imagined there'd be some excitement. Why, I can't even get a kick out of a horse," complained Janey.

"Take care about that," said Randolph, seriously. "Bennet has seen to it that you've had only gentle horses. I heard him rake the cowboys about this. None of their tricks!"

"Mr. Randolph," returned Janey, sweetly explaining, "I didn't mean that kind of a kick. I'd like a horse to run off with me—since there's no man out here to do it."

Janey was blandly innocent, and apparently unconscious of Randolph's slight start and quick look. She was going to enjoy this better than she had expected.

"I—I daresay the cowboys—and all Westerners—couldn't understand you, Miss Janey," rejoined Randolph. "They will exert themselves to amuse you—take care of you. But never dream—of—how—"

"That a New York girl requires some stimulant," interposed Janey. "Oh, I get that. These nice dumb cowboys! I thought they were going to be regular fellows. But, do you know, Mr. Randolph, not a single one of them has attempted to kiss me!"

"Indeed! From what I know of them I think that'd be the last thing they'd attempt. They are gentlemen, Miss Endicott," said Randolph, rather stiffly.

"What's that got to do with kissing a girl?" retorted Janey, hard put to restrain her laughter. "It'd be fun to see their line of work. And in the case of that handsome Zoroaster—well, I might let him get away with it."

Randolph stared at her incredulously, with infinite disapproval.

"Outside of yourself, Mr. Zoroaster is the only good-looking man around the place. And as you don't seem to be aware of my presence here, I'd rather welcome a little attention from him."

"Miss Endicott!" ejaculated Randolph. "You are complimentary—and rather otherwise, all in one breath. It is you who have not been aware of *my* presence."

"What could you expect?" queried Janey, with a bewildering confusion. "I might flirt with a cowboy. But I couldn't —well—throw myself at a man of your intelligence and culture. All the same I've been hoping you'd take me around a little. To your ruins and interesting places. And maybe

amuse me in the evenings, or at least do something to kill
the awful monotony. In New York you seemed to like me.
I daresay Dad has talked about me—queered me with you."

Randolph had been reduced to a state of speechlessness.
He actually blushed, and there leaped to his eyes a light
that made them very warm and appealing. At this point
Mr. Endicott came in. He looked unusually bright and
cheerful, but at sight of Janey his smile faded.

"Janey, dear, you look sort of down," he commiserated,
kissing her. "I forgot you had a headache or something."

"Dad, I've just been complaining to Phil. But he doesn't
care whether I'm sick or homesick, or what."

"Phil!—Homesick?—Why Janey!" exclaimed Mr. Endicott, quite taken aback.

"Dad, will you let me go home?" she asked, mournfully.

"Janey!"

"Don't look like that. What do you think anyway? You've
dragged me out to this dead hole. Nothing happens. You
said Phil would be tickled pink to run around with me."

"I didn't say anything of the kind," declared her father,
turning a little pink himself.

"Oh, I mean words to that effect," replied Janey, airily.
"But, as you've seen, he has studiously avoided me—as if I
was a pestilence. Left me to the mercy of these cowboys!"

"I'm sure there is a misunderstanding," returned Mr. Endicott, divided between doubt and exultation.

"There certainly is," added Randolph, emphatically. "I
hope it isn't too late for me to correct it."

"I'm afraid so," said Janey, with eyes on him. "Else how
could I *ever* have told you?"

"Nonsense," spoke up her father. "Janey, you must be a
little off your feed or something."

"Dad, I'm not a horse or a cow—and I would like a little
fruit salad or a lobster." Suddenly she clapped her hands.
"I've an idea. Perfectly delicious. Let me send for Bert?"

"What? That last faint gasp of the Durland family?"

"Dad, I'd have a perfectly glorious time riding around
with him."

"Humph! I don't believe it. You don't know what you do want."

"Please, Daddy. Bert would at least amuse me."

"He would. And us, too. But no, Janey. I can't see it," declared Endicott.

"Very well, Father," agreed Janey. She never called him "Father" except in cases like this. "I've done my best to please you. The consequences will be upon your head."

Endicott grunted, gave Janey a baffled glance and stepped out the open door to view the afterglow of the sunset. Randolph was perturbed. Janey enjoyed the assurance that her new line had been effective. No man could resist subtle flattery!

"Miss Janey—if you—if I—if there *has* been a misunderstanding—let me make it right," began Randolph, with a sincerity that made Janey feel villainous. "Frankly, I—I didn't think you cared two straws about my work, or the ruins—or me either. So I never asked you. You remember I used to try to interest you in the desert. Indeed there is much here to interest you—if you will only see. Suppose you ride out with me tomorrow."

Janey fixed sad eyes upon his earnest face.

"No, Phil. I told you—it's too late. You'd never have thought of it, if I hadn't gone down and out. I'm sorry, but I can't accept solicited attention."

"You're very unkind, at least," rejoined Randolph, vexed and hurt. "You've scarcely looked at me, since your arrival. Now you complain of my—my neglect. I tell you—to accuse me of indifference is perfectly ridiculous."

Then the little Indian maid called them to supper. When Endicott followed them in and caught a glimpse of Randolph's face he threw up his hands, then he laughed heartily. Janey understood him. It was a return to good humor and the hopelessness of ever doing anything with her. His mirth, however, did not infect Randolph, who scarcely said another word, ate but little, and soon excused himself.

"Say, honey, what'd you do to Phil?" inquired Endicott, genially.

"Nothing."

"Which means a whole lot. Well, tell me."

"I let him know I *did* like him very much—that his indifference has hurt me deeply—and that *now*—"

"Ah! I see. Now, in the vernacular of your charming crowd there's nothing doing," interrupted her father. "Janey, dear, if I were Phil I'd be encouraged. I remember your mother. When I was most in despair my chances were brightest. Only I didn't know it."

"Dad, I *did* like Phil," murmured Janey, dreamily.

"It's too bad you don't any more. . . . What are you going to do tomorrow?"

"Perhaps I will feel well enough to ride a little."

"Good. I'm motoring to Flagerstown. I'll be back before dark, I think. I've got important letters and telegrams to send."

"You won't let me wire for Bert Durland?" asked Janey.

"Janey, don't always put me at a disadvantage," returned Endicott, impatiently. "You know I'd let you have anyone or anything—if you convinced me of your need. But, darling, you know Durland would bore you to death. Be honest."

"I suspect he might—after he got here," acknowledged Janey, demurely. "But, Dad, just think of the fun the cowboys would have out of him. And he'd make Phil perfectly wild!"

"Aha! You've said it, my daughter," declared Endicott, clapping his hands. "I had a hunch, as Bennet says. . . . Well, Janey, you must excuse me. I've got to spend the evening writing. You can have a nice quiet hour reading."

"Hour! I can't go to bed for hours."

"Janey, you look perfectly wonderful, ravishing—and—well, indecent in that flimsy white gown. It'd make a first-rate handkerchief for one of these man-sized Westerners. But it's wasted on the desert air."

"Yes, I'm afraid my desire to look well for Phil was wasted," returned Janey. "Men are no good. You can't please them."

"Perhaps the emancipation of women has peeved us," remarked Endicott, slyly.

Janey was curious to see if Randolph would come back to the living room. She hoped he would not, for he appeared to be giving her a taste of something different in masculine reactions. She talked to the Bennets about the cowboys and Randolph, learning more and more for her amusement and interest. They regarded the archaeologist as one of the family and were immensely proud of his work. It might have been gold hunting, for all the store they put on it. Janey began to gather some inkling of the importance of Randolph's discovery of the pueblo claimed by scientists to have existed there centuries past. She began to hope for his success.

Randolph did not appear again and the Bennets retired early. Janey was left to her thoughts, which she found pleasant. Soon she went to her room, and to bed. Though she would not admit it to her father, the quiet of the night, the comfortable feel of wool blankets, the black darkness appealed strongly to her.

What few words and glances it had taken to upset Phillip Randolph! If Janey had not been so outraged her conscience might have given her a twinge. Deep within her dwelt a respect for honesty and simplicity. The idea she had given Randolph—that she had expected and hoped for a little attention from him—had completely floored him. After all it was not much of a deceit. She had expected more than a little. There was something warm and sweet in the thought of his really caring for her like that. Janey believed that no real woman of the present or of the future would ever feel otherwise than stirred at a man's honest love. It was in the race, and the race's progress toward higher things depended upon it. Janey made the mental observation that the world had not progressed very much lately.

Next morning she again delayed going into breakfast purposely to miss Randolph and her father. Janey put on her riding clothes, taking her time about it.

After breakfast the only one of the cowboys around the corrals was Ray.

"Mornin'," he greeted her. "When did you come back to life? Us boys figgered you was daid."

"Me? Oh, I never let anybody get tired of me," responded Janey. "Can I have Patter saddled?"

"I reckon, but I cain't see what for. That cayuse is no good. He's got a mean eye when he rolls it. Now my little roan—"

"Ray, you boys can't fool me any longer about the horses. They're all good. Please saddle Patter for me."

While Ray went to fetch the horse Janey walked into the trading post, always and increasingly interesting to her. Bennet was selling supplies to the Indians. Janey liked to hear the low strange voices. One of the Indians was nothing if not frankly admiring. He was a tall, slim, loose-jointed individual, wearing corduroys and moccasins, a huge-buckled and silver-ornamented belt, a garnet-colored velveteen shirt, and a black sombrero with a bright-braided band. He had a lean face like a hawk, dark and clear, and piercing black eyes. Janey had been advised not to appear interested in the Indian men—that they misunderstood it, and had been known to give Eastern women some rude shocks. As usual Janey disregarded advice.

She noticed when she left the post that the Indian sauntered out to watch her. Janey thought if Phil Randolph would act that way, she would be highly gratified. Patter was saddled waiting for her, a fine little bay mustang.

"What's Smoky followin' you for?" queried Ray, gruffly.

"Smoky, who's he?"

"Thet blamed Navey."

"Oh, I see. I don't know, Ray. I certainly didn't ask him to. It's quite flattering, though. But not complimentary to you boys."

"Wal, Miss, if you excuse me I'll say thet's not funny an' you ain't ridin' out alone," said Ray.

"Indeed. Ray, you can be most disagreeable at times. It spoils a perfectly wonderful man. I *am* going to ride alone."

"Nope. If you won't listen to me I'll tell Bennet."

"Aren't you just inventing an opportunity to ride with me?"

"Reckon not. I don't care particular aboot ridin' with you, after the deal you gave me last time."

"What was that, Ray? I forget."

"Wal, never mind. . . . Now this Indian Smoky is a bad hombre an' it's really because he's not all there. He's not to be trusted. He might foller you around jes' curious. But if you got too nice to him things might happen. If he annoys you he'll be a daid redskin damn quick."

"Thank you, Ray, I'll say that's talking," responded Janey. "But tell me, what do you do to white men out here, when they insult Eastern girls?"

"Wal, Miss, white men—that is, Westerners *don't* insult girls from anywhere," returned Ray, forcefully.

"But they do. I've heard and read of lots of things— Suppose now just for example you were to kidnap me and pack me off into the desert. What would happen to you?"

"If I didn't get strung up to a cottonwood I'd shore be beat till I was near daid. . . . But, Miss Janey, you needn't worry none about me. I've learned to fight my natural instincts."

Janey laughed merrily. Some of these cowboys were full of wit and humor.

"Ray, I'll compromise this ride with you," said Janey. "I want to surprise Mr. Randolph at his work. So you take me out and show me where he is. But you must wait some little distance away— But won't I be taking you from your own work?"

"Boss's orders are that I look after you, Miss Janey," said Ray, with emphasis on the personal pronouns. "I'll throw a saddle an' be heah pronto."

They rode out along the fenced ground, where Bennet kept stock at times, and came upon Tay-Tay, Diego and Zoroaster digging postholes. If there was anything a cowboy hated more than that, Ray declared he did not know what it was. The trio doffed their sombreros to Janey, and grinned because they could not help it, but they were galled at the situation.

"Reckon that's fair to middlin'," declared Ray, eying the postholes. "But you ain't diggin' them deep enough."

Zoroaster glared at Ray and threw down the long-handled shovel. Diego wiped the sweat from his face.

"Say, are you foreman on this ranch?" he asked, scornfully.

"G-g-g-go along w-w-w-with you or you'll g-get h-h-h-hurt," stuttered Tay-Tay.

"Wal, as I don't care to have Miss Endicott see you boys any wuss than you are now reckon I'll move along," drawled Ray.

Janey gave each in turn a ravishing smile, intended to convey the impression that she wished he were her escort rather than Ray. Then she trotted Patter out on the desert after Ray.

They climbed a gradual ascent to the level of the vast valley and faced the great red wall of rock that loomed a few miles westward. She rode abreast of Ray for a couple of miles, talking the while, then, reaching uneven ground, she had to fall behind on the rough trail. Ray halted at a clump of cedars.

"Reckon this is as far as you'll want me to go," he announced. "Follow the trail right to where it goes into the canyon. You'll see a big cave in the wall. That's the old cliff dwellin' where Mr. Randolph is diggin' around."

"Thank you, Ray. Will you wait for me?"

"Wal, not if you're ridin' back with him," returned Ray, reluctantly. "But I want to be shore aboot it."

"I think you'd better wait. I'll not be long."

Janey had not ridden a hundred paces farther before she forgot all about Ray. The trail led down into a red-walled wash where muddy water flowed over quicksand, which she had to cross. She had already crossed this stream at a different point, though not alone. Here she had to use her own judgment. She made Patter trot across; even then he floundered in the quicksand and splashed muddy water all over

Janey. Once he went in to his knees and Janey's heart leaped to her throat. But he plowed out safely. It was this sort of thing that so excited and pleased Janey. All so new! And being alone made it tenfold more thrilling. The dusty trail, the zigzag climb, the winding in and out among rocks and through the cedars, with the great red wall looming higher and closer, the dry fragrance of desert and sage, the loneliness and wildness, meant more to Janey this day than ever before. Not for anything would she let Phil Randolph and her father into the secret that she was actually learning to love Arizona. The beauty and color and solitude, the vastness of it had called to something deep in her. First she had complained of the dust, the wind, the emptiness, the absence of people. But she had forgotten these. She was now not so sure but that she might like the hardship and primitiveness of the desert.

Presently she rode out of the straggling cedars so that she could fully see the great wall. Janey threw back her head to gaze upward.

"Oh—wonderful!" she exclaimed. "I thought the New York buildings were high. But this!"

It was a sheer red wall, rising with breaks and ledges to a cedar-fringed rampart high against the blue sky. The base was a slope of talus, where rocks of every size appeared about to totter and roll down upon her. Then Janey discovered the cave. It was the most enormous hole she had ever seen, and she calculated that Trinity Church would be lost in it. The upper part disappeared in shadow; the lower showed a steep slope and ruined rock walls, which Janey guessed were the remains of the cliff dwellers' homes. She was being impressed by the weirdness of the scene when she heard a shout and then spotted a man standing at the foot of the cave. It was Randolph. He waved to her and began to descend the slide of weathered rock. As he drew nearer to her level Janey saw that he had indeed been working. How virile he looked! She quite forgot the object of her visit; and almost persuaded herself that if he was particularly nice she would climb up to see him at his work.

"Howdy, Phil," she called, imitating the trader, as nearly as possible. It struck Janey then that Phil did not appear overjoyed to see her.

"Is your father with you?" he asked.

"No. He went to town."

"I hope to goodness you didn't ride up here alone," he said.

"Sure I did. And a dandy ride it was."

"Janey!" he ejaculated.

"Yes, Janey!" she returned.

He did not grasp any flippancy on her part.

"Why did you do it?" he asked, almost angrily.

"Well, come to think of it I guess I wanted to see you and your work," she returned, innocently.

"But you've been told not to ride out alone—away from the post."

"I know I have, and it makes me sick. Why not? I'm not a child, you know. Besides, there aren't any kidnapers about, are there?"

"Yes. Kidnapers and worse. . . . Frankly, Miss Endicott, I think you ought to have a good stiff lecture."

"I'm in a very good humor. So fire away."

"You're a headstrong, willful girl," he declared, bluntly.

"Phillip, you're not very kind, considering that, well—I relented a little, and rode out here to see you," she replied, reproachfully.

"I am thinking of you. Somebody has to stop you from taking these risks. The cowboys let you do anything, though they have been ordered to watch you, guard you. If your father can't make you behave somebody else must."

"And you've got a hunch you're the somebody?" inquired Janey, laconically.

"It seems presumptuous, absurd," he answered, stubbornly. "But I really fear I am."

"We're both going to have a wonderful time," said Janey, with a gay laugh. "But before you break loose on this reforming task let me confess I came alone only part way. I left Ray back down the trail at that gully."

"You did! . . . But you told me—you lied—"

"I wanted to see how you would take it," she said, as he hesitated.

Randolph sat down on a slab of rock and regarded her as one baffled.

"That's the worst of you," he asserted. "A man can't quite give you up in despair or disgust. There always seems to be something wholesome under this damned frivolity of yours."

"I'm glad you are so optimistic," returned Janey.

"No need to ask you how you are feeling," Randolph observed. "Yesterday you were pale—drooping. Your father was really worried. And I . . . But today you look like a sago lily."

"Sago? That's the name of your canyon, isn't it? And what kind of a flower? Is it pretty?"

"I think it the most exquisite in the world. Rare, rich, vivid. It blooms in the deep canyons in summer. I daresay you'll not stay long enough to see one."

"Phil, I never guessed you could be eloquent, or so good at blarney," she said, studying him gravely. "I'm beginning to believe there are unknown possibilities in you for good —and maybe evil, too."

"Sure. You can never tell what a man may do—or be driven to."

"Aren't you going to ask me to get down and come in?" she asked, archly.

"You must pardon my manners," he said, rising.

Janey slipped out of the saddle without accepting the hand he offered, and leading Patter to a near-by cedar she tied the bridle to a branch.

"I want to see your cave."

"It's pretty much of a climb."

"I suppose yesterday will stump you for some time," she replied. "Can't I have an off day once in a while without being considered a weakling? Come on, let's go."

Janey soon found that it was indeed a climb. Distances deceived her so strangely here in Arizona. There was a trail up to the cave, but it wound steep and rough, with many high steps from rock to rock. She was glad to accept Randolph's hand; and when they surmounted the slope she was breathless and hot. Randolph held her hand longer than necessary.

"Oh-h—Gee!" panted Janey, flopping down on a rock in the shade. "Some—climb."

"You made it without a stop," returned Randolph, admiringly. "Your heart and lungs are sure all right—if your mind is gone."

"Mr.—Randolph!"

"That's your father's assumption," said Randolph, dryly. "I don't exactly share it."

"Maybe I am—just a healthy—moron," laughed Janey, removing her sombrero. "Wouldn't it be fine—if the desert and *you*—developed me into a real woman?"

"Morons don't develop," he replied, ignoring her intimation.

Janey now took stock of the archaeologist's cave. It was an amazing cavern. She sat at the lower edge of the slope of its back wall, yet the vaulted roof, far overhead, reached out into the canyon. A dry, dusty, musty odor, not unpleasant, permeated the place. The debris from the walls and slopes was red and yellow. Far up Janey discerned the remains of walls. In the largest section a small black window, like a vacant eye, stared down at her. It gave her a queer sensation. Human eyes had gazed out of that window ages ago. She saw a trench near her, with pick and shovel lying where Randolph had thrown them.

"Mr. Randolph, were you in the war?" asked Janey, suddenly.

"Yes, a little while. Long enough to learn to dig. That's about the only real good the service did me," he replied, somewhat bitterly.

"You should be grateful. My friends who went to France

came back *no* good. You certainly seem free of any injury."

"I am, I guess, except a twist in my mind. I only knew
of it recently—last winter in fact."

"Indeed. And how does it affect you?" asked Janey,
doubtfully.

"I think it developed a latent weakness for beauty."

"In nature?"

"Oh, no. I always had that. It must be in—woman."

"*Any* woman. Well, that is no weakness. It's a very com-
mendable thing, and gives you a kinship with most men."

"Miss Endicott, I didn't say in any woman," returned
Randolph, sharply.

"Didn't you? Very well, it doesn't matter. . . . Now,
show me around the place and tell me all about your
work."

Randolph had something on his mind. He did not seem
natural. It was as if he had been compelled to be someone
he was not. Janey half regretted that she had not encouraged him to tell more about the woman he had a weakness
for. So far she was inwardly elated with the success of her
machinations.

"You wouldn't make much of a hit as a guide for lady
tourists," remarked Janey, after Randolph had shown her
the several trenches he had dug, some bits of pottery, dry
as powder, and the ruined walls.

"On the contrary, I was a decided success for the party
of schoolteachers who visited me here last summer," declared Randolph.

"Oh. Then I have some inhibitory effect upon you," remarked Janey.

"Probably. I don't seem to care a—er—anything about
archaeology, geology, theology, or any other kind of ology,"
returned Randolph, ruefully.

"I'm sorry. I must not tax your mental powers so severely," said Janey.

"You think you're being sarcastic. But as a matter of

fact you have taxed all my powers to the limit. Powers
of patience, resistance, faith—and I don't know what all—"

"What a dreadful person I am!" interposed Janey, really
in earnest. "Please, if you can't forget it, at least you
needn't rub it in. . . . Where do you expect to uncover this
buried pueblo? Dad said you had set your heart on discovering it."

"You don't care two whoops for any ruin—unless it is
the ruin of a man."

"Maybe I didn't at first. But I do now. Can't you credit
me with change or growth or something worthwhile?"

"I don't know what to think about you," he returned, almost dejectedly.

"Assuredly you don't. Well, I'm quite capable of coming
out here and finding that ruin for you."

"Please don't. I'm perfectly miserable now," he retorted,
grimly. But there was a light in his eyes that belied his
words. Janey knew he was saying to himself he must not
have faith in dreams.

"It would mean so much to you—finding this pueblo?"

"Yes. There's only one thing that could mean more."

"I don't suppose I'd look very well digging around in this
dirt," mused Janey. "But as you haven't any use for me in
up-to-date evening clothes perhaps you might like me all
dusty and red and hot. So here goes."

Janey began to clamber down into the deepest trench,
and when she got up to her shoulders she grasped the pick.

"Miss Endicott, can't you be serious?" burst out Randolph. "You're not a bit funny. And that talk about me—"

"I'm serious about making you admire me, at least,"
laughed Janey, brandishing the pick.

"Please come out of there. You're just soiling your
clothes."

"Nope. I'm going to dig," rejoined Janey, nonchalantly.
"*Quién sabe?* I may have to marry an archaeologist someday."

"Come out of there," called Randolph, peremptorily.

Janey began to dig in the red earth. She dragged up

stones, and presently what looked very much like a human bone.

"Ugh! I declare. What's that thing?" ejaculated Janey.

"It's a legbone, of course. You're digging in a grave. I told you that."

"You didn't," retorted Janey.

"Never mind about that. You come out of there."

"Mr. Randolph, you might send me to my own grave, but you can't make me get out of this one."

As she brandished the pick again he reached down to grasp it. Janey held on. Randolph slipped his grip down the handle until he caught her gloved hands. Whereupon he forced the pick from her and dragged her, not at all gently, up out of the trench.

He let go of her rather abruptly, probably because of the look she gave him; and Janey's impetus, being considerable, caused her to stumble. It was a little downhill on that side. She fell right upon Randolph who caught her in his arms. The awkwardness of her action made Janey more indignant than ever. Her sombrero fell off and her hair covered her eyes. She raised her face from his shoulder and sought to catch her balance. Suddenly, Randolph bent to kiss her full on the lips.

4

JANEY BROKE AWAY from Phil and started back. For a moment she was too conscious of unfamiliar and disturbing agitations to remember that she had adopted the role of actress.

"Janey!—Miss Endicott!" stammered the young archaeologist. "I—I didn't mean that. I must have been out of my head. Forgive me!"

"Now you've done it!" exclaimed Janey. She was not sure yet what he had done, but it was certainly more than he felt guiltily conscious of.

"I was beside myself," said Randolph, hurriedly. "You must believe me. I—I had no such intention. I'm—I'm as —as shocked as you are. . . . You fell right into my arms. And I—I did it involuntarily."

"You may tell that to the marines," replied Janey, recovering, and getting back to the business of her part.

"You won't believe me?" he demanded, getting red in the face.

"Certainly not," returned Janey, coldly, as she smoothed her disheveled hair. "I wouldn't put it beyond you to treat every girl that way—especially if she was fool enough to visit you alone out here."

He glared at her in mingled wrath and distress.

"I never kissed a girl before!" he asserted, stoutly.

"Well!" exclaimed Janey, in simulated contemptuous doubt, when really she was thrilled with what seemed the truth in his eye and voice. "You must have a poor opinion of my intelligence. If you had come out like a man and told me straight that you couldn't resist such an opportunity and were glad of it, I might have forgiven you. It's nothing to be kissed. But you've pretended to be so self-righteous. You've scorned my young men friends. You've deceived me into thinking highly of you—respecting you. And I honestly believe I did like you. . . . Now I'm quite sure I ought never ride out alone."

Randolph groaned. Then he leaped into the trench and seizing the pick he began to dig with great violence, making the stones fly and the dust rise. Janey spoke again, but either he did not or would not hear her. Whereupon she recovered her sombrero and turned to find her way down the slope. She had just reached the rough part, and was searching for the trail when she heard Randolph behind her.

"I quite forgot. I can't let you attempt getting down here alone," he said.

"Mr. Randolph, I'd fall and break my neck before I'd let you help me," returned Janey, loftily.

"I warn you not to fall again within my reach," he declared, grimly.

Janey started down, aware that he followed closely. She was glad she had her face turned away from him. When she got to the broken sections of rock she performed apparent feats of balancing which would have put a tightrope walker to shame. She would sway this way and that, and almost fall. Then she leaped the fissures, and took some chances of hurting herself. But she descended the jumble of rocks safely, and then the rest of the slope with ease. Randolph had halted about a third of the way from the bottom, and when Janey looked over the saddle of her horse she saw him sitting on a stone, watching her.

"Good-by, wild woman," he called.

"Good-by, cave man," she retorted.

Mounting she rode away without looking back, which was an act that required will power. Once in the cedars, out of sight and alone, she reveled in the unexpected turn and success of her venture. Randolph was simply an honest boy, very much in love, and at the mercy of his feelings. He had helped along her little plan by placing himself at a disadvantage. How astounded he had been, then furious at himself and her! Janey remembered that he had winced when she said it was nothing to be kissed. Well, she had lied in that. It was a great deal to be kissed, as she began to realize now. She had chosen to lead him to believe kissing was merely a casual and familiar thing in her young life, when in reality she had not been nearly as indiscriminate in her games as she had let on.

Janey believed she was angrier than ever with Randolph, a great deal more so now than at her father. Yet there was a tempering voice she would not listen to. It was piercing her armor to some extent when she rode right upon Ray, so abruptly that she was surprised. That ended her meditations, for Ray appeared curious and keen about her visit to the archaeologist. It did not occur to Janey to tantalize Ray, or to stop and torment the cowboys at their fence-post digging. By the time she was again at ease in her room she realized the cowboys had begun to fade out of the picture. Janey did not regret it, though she wondered at herself. Naturally, however, if a girl was going to be abducted against her will, and maltreated, and finally married, she must be quite interested in the man who was daring to do all this.

At lunch she was outspoken about her visit to Randolph's cave. The Bennets were much pleased. Plain indeed was it that they were fond of Randolph and proud of his archaeological work.

"Wal, if you liked that Sagi hole you shore ought to see Beckyshibeta," remarked Bennet.

"Beckyshibeta! My, that's a jawbreaker," replied Janey, with a laugh. "What and where is it?"

"Beckyshibeta means cow water. It's Navajo for a water hole. I never saw it when it wasn't muddy an' shore tastin' of cows. Reckon it's about sixty miles by trail, nearer across country. Wild rocky place where the Indians seldom go. Phil thinks they've a reason for avoiding it, same as in the case of Nonnezoshe, the great Rainbow Bridge. He has a notion there might be a buried pueblo at Beckyshibeta. There are cliff dwellin's still in good state of preservation, an' many ruins. We seldom recommend Beckyshibeta to our visitors. It's far off. The cowboys hate the rocky country because they have to pack hoss feed and water. An' shore there are places interestin' enough near at hand, an' comfortable for camp. But before you an' your father leave you want to see both Nonnezoshe an' Beckyshibeta."

"I'm sure I'd love to," responded Janey.

She did not meet the cowboys again that day until after supper when she walked out to see the sunset, and to look for her father. This was always an attractive hour at the post. Indians were riding up and departing; the picturesque cowboys, mostly through with work for the day, were lounging about on the bales of wool and blankets. The moment Janey arrived they became animated as one man.

Janey did not take much notice of them, despite their
transparent acts and words. Strolling a little way she halted
at the hitching rail to watch the pageant in the gold-and-
purple West.

"Mighty cool evenin'," remarked Mohave, in a voice that
came clearly to Janey.

"Say, fellars, did anythin' hit you in the eye, kinda like
a chunk of ice?" drawled Zoroaster.

"S-s-s-some of y-y-y-youse hombres has done s-s-s-some-
thin'," stuttered Tay-Tay, belligerently.

"Our gracious Señorita is in one of her grand moods,"
Diego said.

"Aw, you punchers are locoed," added Ray, scornfully.
Cain't you tell when to get off and walk?"

Janey moved on out of earshot of her loyal cavaliers. It
was the first time she had not paid attention to one or all
of them. What had happened to her? But she soothed both
conscience and concern with former arguments.

In the west the bulge of desert waved black as ebony
against the intense gold flare of sky. Above this belt, a
broken reef of purple clouds appeared beaten upon by contending tides of silver and rose. Through a ragged rent
the sinking sun sent shafts of radiant light down behind
the horizon.

In the east the panorama was no less striking and beautiful. The desert sent its walls and domes and monuments
of red rock far up into the sky of gorgeous pink and white
clouds.

Janey drew a deep full breath. Yes, Arizona was awakening her to something splendid and compelling. How vast
and free and wind-swept this colored desert! She had
learned to recognize a faint fragrance of sage, which came
only in a north breeze. It was sweet and cool now in her
face. Then up over a near-by ridge appeared a black sil-
houette of an Indian and mustang, wild and lonely. Next
the hum of a motorcar broke her absorption. No doubt it
was the trader's Studebaker returning with her father.

"Look here, peaches," quizzically remarked her father,

when they had gotten indoors. "Anyone would think I'd been absent a month. What's the bright idea?"

"Oh! Did I make such a fuss over you—as that?" asked Janey, merrily.

"You sure did. Fact is you never welcomed me like that, even on my returns from Europe. . . . Have you been lonely and blue again? Is that why?"

"Not today," returned Janey. "No, I was just happy and unconscious of it, Dad. . . . I guess maybe I did miss you a lot."

"Well, you can bet I'm glad, whatever it is."

Janey left him in the dining room, too hungry for conversation. Then she delved a little into her mind. She had absolutely forgotten her new role. She was supposed to be very angry with her father, but she wasn't. She had not been in the least lonely for him or homesick. In reality she had skipped about ten years of her life and had met him as a child. Janey's deductions took her back through the eventful day at the tilt with Phil, and then she got no further. It was rather confusing. But at length she assuaged her wounded vanity by accepting her remarkable fine spirits as due to the way she was turning the tables on Phil and her father.

"Maybe I'm kidding myself," murmured Janey, with a snicker. "Ye Gods! Could I have been so happy because *he* kissed me?"

Janey was wholly at ease again when her father joined her in the living room. He was full of his trip to town, and claimed the ride in—looking the opposite way to that in which they had come—was even more beautiful. Telegraph communications from New York had been eminently satisfactory.

"How's your day been?" he asked, when he had concluded about his own.

"Mine? Oh, rich, immense," replied Janey.

"I hope you haven't played any more hob with these cowboys."

"Oh, dear, no. I've scarcely seen them, but once or twice.

. . . I did take Ray, and rode out to see Phil's cave. Surprised him. I left Ray below a little way and went on alone."

"You did!" exclaimed Endicott, surprised and pleased. "That was nice of you. What did you think of Phil's cave? I've been there, you know."

"An awful hole! Just suits him to a 'T.' He's a cave man. Don't you overlook that, darling Papa."

"Cave man? Phil Randolph! Why, he's the gentlest and mildest of men."

"Not so you'd notice it. At least for me," replied Janey, giggling. "No, Dad, you're vastly mistaken in Phil's character. He's a bad hombre."

"Did you quarrel?" Endicott probed, his curiosity overcoming his doubt of her.

"Oh, we scrapped as usual. He wasn't at all tickled to see me. Made some idiotic remarks about being a lover of beauty in woman—*one* woman. Naturally I kidded him, and when he got wise to that he was sore. Well, finally, to prove my interest in his old cave I climbed down in one of his graves. I took the pick and began to dig. Do you know, Dad, he didn't like that a bit."

Endicott let out a hearty laugh. "Janey, you are incorrigible. No wonder he wasn't tickled to see you. Why, he wouldn't let even me dig in one of those holes. Said I might break a piece of precious pottery. Besides in your case he wouldn't like you to soil your clothes and blister your hands."

"I should think he would have liked that," returned Janey. "Once he called me fastidious and elegant. Another time one of the idle rich. He held my hand once and had the nerve to say it was a beautiful useless thing. Well, to go on, he ordered me out of the grave. I paid no attention to him. Then he took hold of the pick, pulled me up till he could reach me. Next he yanked me out. Gentle? You should have seen him. But he let go of me too quick and I stumbled. Like a ninny I fell into his arms. Did he gently set me upon my feet? I should snicker not. This paragon of yours, this nice quiet gentleman, grabbed me and kissed me smack on my mouth—as I never was kissed in my whole life!"

Whereupon Janey's father exploded with mirth. Recovering and seeing her face he apologized contritely.

"Janey, it's just too good," he added. "I think a lot more of Phil for having the nerve to do it. I wonder, now, did *that* make you so happy?"

"Rot!" exclaimed Janey, with hot cheeks. "It wasn't nerve in him. He just went loco. Then he swore he'd never kissed any girl before. Fancy that? . . . Well, I've told you. I don't quite know what to do about it."

"I shall congratulate Phil on punishing you properly."

"I don't take punishment easily," said Janey, with menacing hauteur.

"Lord. Be easy on the poor chap, Janey."

Bennet interrupted them at this point and asked if they would require any or all of the cowboys for any especial trip the next few days.

"I want to drive some cattle out, an' reckon this is about the best time," he added. "I've got some tourist parties comin' soon, an' the boys will take them to Nonnezoshe. After that the rains will be here."

"Thanks, Bennet. We can do very well without the cowboys," returned Endicott, brightly. Janey guessed why her father felt so chipper about that news.

"Do you have a rainy season here on this desert?" inquired Janey, aghast.

"Nothin' to concern you, Miss," replied the trader. "Reckon you'll like the thunderstorms, the clouds an' rainbows. But for us the rains are sometimes bad, because the washes get full of water an' quicksand, so we can't move the stock."

"Thunderstorms? I love them. It will be great to be out in one here," said Janey.

Janey was lying in bed reading when she heard Randolph come in and go to his room. The hour was rather late for him. She wondered if he had gone supperless.

Next morning when she went in to breakfast her father and Randolph were there. If Janey had expected him to be downcast or embarrassed she had reckoned without her host. He was neither. He greeted her as if nothing unusual had occurred and he gave her a cool steady stare. Janey's quick intuition grasped that Randolph had burned his bridges behind him. It did not seem likely that her father could have had much to do with this late decision in Randolph. Janey had bidden him good night at his door, and he was not an early riser. So she concluded Randolph had fought out something with himself and the die was cast. It stirred Janey as had nothing she could recall. She was ready, even eager for the adventure.

"When is Bennet sending out the cowboys?" inquired Randolph.

"Today," replied Endicott, with a meaning glance at his young friend. "It'll be terrible for Janey to be left without anybody to pick on. Phil, suppose you knock off work and stay home to amuse her."

"Very happy to," returned the archaeologist. "I'm sure I can think up something that will amuse even the blasé Miss Endicott."

"You needn't concern yourself about me," said Janey, spiritedly. "And I'll have you know I'm not blasé. Did you ever see me look old or bored?"

"Certainly not old, but bored—yes, indeed, and with your humble servant, myself."

"You don't bore me any more, Phillip," replied Janey. "You have become a mystery. Your possibilities are unlimited."

"Much obliged," rejoined Randolph, with nonchalance. "I hope I can live up to your idea of my development."

"When will you start amusing me?" asked Janey, with a provoking little smile.

"There's no time like the present."

"Very well, begin. You have only to be perfectly natural."

"That is what I thought. So I need not exert myself. After

breakfast come with me for a walk. I know where to find
some horned toads."

"How far is it?"

"Quite near. In the big wash over the ridge. But I advise you to change that child's dress for something comfortable and protecting."

"Goodness! This is a tennis skirt and blouse."

"Who'd guess it," returned Randolph, dryly. "Be ready in
about an hour."

Janey went to her room. Phillip had been quite businesslike. She had fancied he would take her for a long ride
someday, which would give him better opportunity to make
off with her. Surely he would not attempt the abduction
while on a short stroll near the post. But she felt uncertain
about him. She had best be prepared. To this end she considered what it would be best to wear. If she donned riding
clothes and boots, which she heartily wanted to do, it would
rouse Randolph's suspicions. Outside of that all her clothes
were unsuitable for the kind of a jaunt she was likely to
have. She gave Randolph about one day and one night
before fetching her back to the post. That, however, was
long enough for his purpose, though she remembered her
father hinting otherwise. Janey searched among her things,
and finally found an old woolen outing skirt, absurdly
short. It would have to do. She selected the heaviest stockings she could find, which were thin at that, tennis shoes,
a blouse with high collar and long sleeves. She put on a
soft felt hat and gloves. Then as an afterthought she slipped
a vanity case into the pocket of her short sport coat, and
tried to choose the things she would need badly, in case
she were kidnaped. But pocket space was limited. Thus
equipped, and full of suppressed mirth, yet not free from
other agitation, she sallied forth to meet Mr. Randolph.

Janey knew she had occupied more than an hour, but she
was surprised to find he was not waiting for her. Nor was
her father anywhere in sight. "Something's up—I'll bet,"
soliloquized Janey. She went out to see the cowboys ride

away with Bennet. They were a disconsolate lot, and gazed at her from afar.

Upon her return to the house she met Randolph. His boots were dusty, and his face heated from exertion. He looked too grim and tense for a little walk. Unless he meant to propose to her! Or else carry out her father's plan. Janey knew it was one or the other; and she trembled. But Phil seemed too concerned with himself to note that she was not wholly at ease. And in another instant Janey regained composure.

"Here you are," he said, as he met her. "Glad you're a little more sensibly dressed."

"I thought maybe you'd have me digging round in the sand after horned toads," she replied.

"Daresay you'll be digging round for more than that before we get back."

He led her out the side exit of the yard, where the foliage of peach trees and the house obscured their departure from anyone who might have been looking from the post.

"Horned toads are really one of the wonders of the desert," he said, as he walked briskly out toward the rise of ground. "They have protective coloration. It is very difficult to see them. They are beautiful, with eyes like jewels. At rare times when angry one will emit blood from its eyes."

While he talked he was leading Janey up the ridge. Then in a few moments they were over and going down on the other side, out of sight of the post. He talked horned toads until he had exhausted his fund of natural history, then he switched to desert scenery. Janey knew he was only marking time, endeavoring to absorb her so that she would scarcely notice the distance they had come and that it was still far to any break in the floor of the desert. She helped him by listening intently. It was a full ten miles to the wash.

"Phil, didn't you say it was only a little walk?" she asked, innocently.

"Why, yes. Isn't it?"

"If you'd ask me I'd say it was long. Where do we go

from here?" returned Janey, gazing down into the sandy void. There was no trail she could see, though in the sand just below she discerned horse tracks. Randolph jumped down off the bank to the slope, which was several feet under the level.

"Come," he said, and Janey detected a slight change of tone.

"Gee. I can't get down there," she replied, fearfully.

"If you won't let me lift you down, why, slide."

"Slide!—Mr. Randolph, I'm not a baseball player."

Quick as a flash, then, he reached for her, clasped her knees and lifted her so that she fell over his shoulder.

"Oh!" cried Janey, in genuine surprise. How powerful he was! She might have been a sack of potatoes. He carried her several strides down before Janey began to protest and squirm. She would have kicked if her legs had been free. At any rate her struggle and the steep soft slope of sand caused Randolph to lose his balance and fall sidewise. Janey rolled off his shoulder and sat up. Randolph stumbled to his feet, and seeing her sitting there wide-eyed and blank he burst into laughter. Janey could not help following suit.

"Mr. Randolph, is this how you hunt horned toads?" she asked sternly.

"No. But why did you overbalance me? I could have packed you down to the bottom."

"My position was scarcely dignified. In the future if it is necessary to pack me, as you call it, please give me a moment to prepare."

"All right. Come on. Let's see if you're any good on seven-league boots," he said, and strode down with giant steps.

Janey tried to imitate him, succeeded admirably, and reached the bottom of the wash in good time.

"My shoes are full of sand," she announced, and sat down to remove them.

"Don't let a little thing like that fuss you. It may happen again."

"You're quite gay, all of a sudden," remarked Janey, as she shook the sand out of her shoes.

"Yes. Why not? It's something to see Miss Janey Endicott as she is this morning," he responded, eying her with a glint of admiration.

"I suppose you mean me in this short skirt," she returned, calmly. "But you needn't look. It was the only old thing I had."

Soon she was following him down the wash. It appeared to be quite deep, with a dry stream bed of rock and gravel at the bottom. Desert plants grew sparsely along the banks. Randolph did not look back nor speak, and he walked a little too swiftly for Janey who lost a few paces. Presently they turned a corner, and Janey spotted what she had been expecting—two saddled horses. Later she saw another animal carrying a pack.

Janey plodded on, pretending not to see them. How foolish! Nevertheless she was aware of a palpitating heart, of a rush of blood, of prickling skin. A quick glance up showed Randolph had halted beside the horses. Janey strove to find wits and nerve to meet this situation as she had planned. Where was her anger? It had oozed out of her trembling finger tips. But that was only momentary. Sight of Randolph rallied her courage. She would deceive him, punish him and her father if it took all the spirit and endurance she could muster.

"Whose horses?" asked Janey, as she reached Randolph, and sat down on the slope of sand. She did not look at him directly. "It's pretty warm—for a short walk. When do we hunt horned toads?"

As he did not answer she glanced up at him. Assuredly he was tense and altogether too pale. Janey suddenly realized that despite what he had undertaken he was afraid of her and of the outrageous indignity he had been persuaded to attempt. That acted as a spur to her. It was the stimulus she needed.

"What's the matter, Phil? You look strange. Your eyes!

You're staring at me. It's the second time. I can't complain of lack of attention right now."

"Better late than never."

"Come here, Mr. Archaeologist. I won't hurt you," said Janey, beckoning.

"You want me? Over there?"

"Ah—huh!"

"You're taking a chance. I've become a—a bad man," he returned, doggedly, as if he needed to convince himself.

"Since when? Since that episode at the cave? Well, if you repeat that your end will be near. . . . I asked you whom these horses belonged to?"

"They're mine."

"Yours!—What are they doing here—saddled? Surely we don't need this outfit to hunt horned toads."

"Janey, that about the toads—was a lie," he returned, haltingly. "It was a trick to get you away from the post."

"A trick? How thrilling! Well, now you've so basely deceived me and got me here—what are you going to do with me?"

"I've—kidnaped—you," he declared, huskily.

Janey laughed merrily. "Oh, I remember. You were to amuse me. Fine, Phil! I suppose you planned a little ride and picnic for me. But my dear man, I can't ride in this skirt."

"You can't walk, so you'll have to ride," he returned.

"*Have* to! Say, Phil, this is getting to be more than a joke. I can stand a lot of fun. But horseback in this knee-high skirt? Nothing doing!"

"It's not a joke, Janey. I'm in deadly earnest. You're going with me willingly—or otherwise."

"Indeed! Isn't that sweet of you? Lovely little all-day party, eh?"

"We will not return tonight."

"*Mr.* Randolph!" she exclaimed, coldly.

That was the crucial moment for Phillip Randolph. His face paled.

"Are you drunk or mad?" she added, icily.

"Both! Drunk with your beauty—mad for love of you," he replied, hoarsely.

"It would seem so," said Janey. She turned her back upon him and started to walk away. Then he seized her by the shoulders, whirled her round and forced her back to the shade.

"If you run it'll only be the worse for you," he warned, releasing her.

"You beast!" cried Janey, wheeling. "Let me go."

Randolph confronted her, and when she tried to get by he put his hands on her shoulders and gave her a good hard shove. Janey staggered backward. The sand was soft and deep. She lost her balance and suddenly fell on the slope, thus losing coat and sombrero. This was most undignified. Yet Janey wanted to laugh. She sat there, blazing up at him, in a gathering might of wrath.

"Beast or anything you like," said Randolph, darkly. "But you go with me, if I have to throw you on that horse."

"Father will beat you for this."

"No doubt. But it will be too late."

"And the cowboys will do worse."

"Yes. But I shall have queered you with them."

Janey got to her feet and stepped close to Randolph. There was now a dangerous gleam in his eye—a wild dark light. He had gotten by the most difficult part for him—the announcement of his intention. Janey saw that he did not expect any serious trouble with her. How she would fool him!

"Don't you dare lay a hand on me again," she said, passionately.

"I hope it won't be necessary. But you get on this horse."

"No!"

"I tell you—"

Janey rushed to pass him, yet was not quick enough. He caught her arm. As he swung her around she gave him a terrific slap on the side of the face. Randolph dropped her arm. His hand went to his cheek which was as red as fire. It seemed realizataion was upon him, augmenting shame

and fury. Janey realized that but for her blow he might
have betrayed himself and given up this outrageous affair.

"You—you struck me," he said, hoarsely, and suddenly
snatched out and caught her left arm.

"Sure I did, Mr. Hoodlum," rejoined Janey. "And I'll do
it again. Did you think you'd get away with this so easy?
There!" And she struck him quick and hard, this time with
a tight little fist.

"Wildcat!" shouted Randolph, roused to battle, and then
he closed with her. Janey was strong, lithe, supple as a
panther, and she fought him fiercely. It was no longer pretense. The rough contact of his hands and her own violent
action brought her blood up, gushing and hot. He was endeavoring to subdue her and she was struggling to get
away. At the same time she beat and tore at him with all
her might. She scratched his face. She got both hands in
his hair and pulled. Naturally the fight could not last long,
for he was overpowering her. When he got his left arm under her right and around her waist to grasp her left he
had her nearly helpless. Then he put his other arm under
her knees and lifted her.

His hair stood up like the mane of a lion; his face was
bloody from the scratches. his eyes gleamed with fire.

"My God!" he panted. "Who'd have—thought it in you."

"Let me down!" cried Janey, straining and writhing.

"Will you get—on that horse?"

"No—you wildween boob!"

"Boob?—Ha! Ha! You've hit it," he replied, wildly. "Very
well—my Eastern princess—take this from the Western
boob."

He bent his head and kissed her quickly—then again,
crushing his hot lips on hers.

"I'll—kill- you!" gasped Janey, when she could speak.

"Kill and be damned. I wish you would," he returned,
passionately. Then he surrendered to the contact and possession of her. Clasping her tight he rained kisses on her
lips and neck. Janey felt the wet blood from his scratched
face on her cheek. Her muscles grew rigid. She was like

bent steel about to spring. Suddenly she sank limp. His
passion had overcome her where his strength had failed.
But Janey did not lose her wits. It was as if she knew she
had to keep playing her part. Yet her collapse and the shaking of her relaxed body had nothing to do with reasoning.
He had surprised her into the primitiveness of a savage.
The change in her reaction struck him, and he released
her.

Janey slipped down, as it chanced, to her knees. The thing
could not have happened better.

"I—I—understand now," gasped Janey. "You mean—
to—"

"My God!" cried Randolph, staggering back, in horror.

"Phillip," went on Janey, piteously. "I—I'm not the girl
I—I've made you believe. This is as much—my fault—as
yours. But have mercy. Don't be a brute."

"Shut up!" shouted Randolph, his face changing to a
dusky red.

He backed against a stone and sat down, to cover his face
with his hands, deeply and terribly shaken.

Janey sank back herself, to rest a moment, and to straight-
en her disheveled apparel. Her rage had died a sudden
death. She was still conscious of disturbing unfamiliar sensations, which, however, were gradually subsiding. Much
had happened that had not been down on the program. She
realized that Randolph had not intended even the least
insult, let alone the assault on her. And certainly in her
plan Janey had not dreamed of making him think she believed him capable of more. Even at that troubled moment Janey realized that more could come of this incident
than had been expected. Both of them were trifling with
deep and unknown instincts. They might pass from jest
to earnest. But Randolph had not the slightest inkling of
Janey's duplicity.

"You've blood on your face," said Randolph, suddenly.

"Yes, it's yours. If I had my way I'd have your blood on
my *hands*," returned Janey, murderously.

"Wipe it off," he ordered, getting up.

Janey produced a wisp of a handkerchief.

"Where is it?" she asked.

"On your cheek—the left one. Here, let me rub it off. That inch-square rag is no good." He had a silk scarf, which he used to remove the blood from her cheek. He applied considerable force, and his action was that of a man trying to remove a stain of guilt.

"You scratched me like—like a wildcat," he said, harshly.

"Did you expect me to purr?" she returned, with sarcasm. Then she rose to her feet. "You tore my sleeve half off. I hope you happen to have a needle and thread."

Ignoring her facetiousness he picked up her coat and sombrero, and handed them to her.

"Get on that horse," he ordered.

5

WITHOUT COMMENT and as one subdued Janey went up to the horse and mounted. Her skirt slipped halfway above her knees. She stood in the stirrups and pulled it down, but at best it was so short that it exposed several inches of bare skin above her stockings.

"Is this supposed to be a movie or a leg show?" she asked, bitingly.

"I can't help it if you've no decent clothes," he replied.

"Why didn't you suggest I wear my riding clothes?"

"I didn't think of that. But you'd have suspected something."

"Me? No. I'm much too stupid. If I had been capable of thinking I'd have known you were a villain. . . . To force a girl to ride a horse with her dress—this way!"

"I don't care how you look," he flashed, hotly, stung at her retort. "At that you don't look *much* worse than usual."

He picked up Janey's coat, which she had dropped, and hung it on the pommel, and draped it over her knees.

"That'll keep you from sunburn, at least."

"You're very thoughtful and kind, Mr. Randolph," said Janey, sweetly. "And may I inquire our destination?"

"Start up the wash," he rejoined, gruffly. "You take the lead."

"Want to watch me, eh? You think I might run off? I note you've given me a plug of a horse that probably never ran in its life."

"You might do anything, Miss Endicott," he said.

"What wonderful trust you have in me!" exclaimed Janey. Whereupon she rode on up the deepening gully. Randolph followed her, leading the pack horse.

So the great adventure was actually on! Janey could not have believed it but for the bruises she had sustained in the fight with Randolph, and her torn blouse, and this ridiculous skirt that had begun to have resemblance to a ballet dancer's.

After she had taken stock of her physical state she delved a bit into the mental. She found she was still trembling ever so slightly. Her heart beat high. And her mind was racing. She was stirred by bitterness toward her father, and resentment toward this man who had been led to believe she was no good and needed this kind of a lesson. They thought they had her number, mused Janey, defiantly. Pretty but vain! Intelligent, yet too languorous to think or work! Adorable, though probably immoral! Modern, still there were hopes!

An alarming thought struck her which she had experienced vaguely before. It was barely possible that these accusations were justified. Janey swore, and refused to listen to such a treacherous voice.

Something more pleasant to dwell upon was a genuine pity for Randolph. He had been a perfectly straightforward, fine and promising young man until he met her father. He was now in line to become a first-rate villain. No doubt when Janey finally divorced him there would be no hope

whatever. She decided, in order to make it impossible that
he ever could recover, she would delay the divorce proceeding for a time—and meanwhile be very sweet and sor-
rowful and might-have-been-loving to him, so that he would
be abjectly crushed.

Her meditations on this phase of the experience were decidedly pleasant. And it was most agreeable to be on horseback again. She had been rather unjust to the horse, for he
was turning out to be docile, easy-gaited and willing. He
had struck into a trail which wound up the gorge.

The walls were perceptibly higher and changing their
character somewhat. The sand slopes were disappearing.
Presently this wash turned at right angles and opened into
a canyon. It was deep, yellow-walled, and rugged, and
through the center of it meandered a thin stream of water.
Janey believed this creek was the Sagi, which she had
crossed a number of times above. But she had not seen this
canyon. The very sight of it was exciting and disturbing.
There was sure to be quicksand. Janey hoped she would
have some narrow escapes, so that she would find out what
Randolph was made of. If no risks came along naturally
she would make some.

The sand in the creek bed, however, was disappointingly
solid. In the next hour Janey crossed this water a dozen or
more times, without a mishap. Her horse was a much better judge of places than she. Meanwhile the canyon grew
wider and deeper.

It also grew hot. Janey began to feel the burn of the sun.
And as the movement of the horse often jolted her coat
from its protective service her knees began to get red. This
was a novelty, and she was divided between concern and
a satisfaction that she could presently show Randolph more
objective proofs of his cruelty.

Unobtrusively, at moments when the trail made a short
turn, she saw Randolph in the rear. He did not look in the
least like a bold bad man. He drooped. Apparently he did
not see her, let alone watch closely against any attempt
she might make to escape. Perhaps he was disgusted now

and hoped she would run off. This was embarrassing. Janey
did not want to escape. She was getting a tremendous kick
out of being kidnaped. But she would not let him know that.
She considered the advisability of attempting to get away.
It did not strike her favorably. If Randolph did not or
would not catch her, there would be something of a different predicament. She would be lost, unless she could go
back as they had come.

Janey rejected the idea. Too much risk! And she adopted
another, equally feminine, and very much better. When a
turn of the trail hid her from Randolph's sight she selected
a soft place in the sand and slid off her horse, careful to
make it look as if she had fallen.

Presently she heard the hoofs of Randolph's horse pad-
ding closer. Then Janey made herself look as much like a
limp sack as she could. From under the brim of her sombrero she saw him come into sight. He gave a violent start.
Leaping out of the saddle he ran to her. His action, his
look were unaccountably sweet to Janey. It was hard to
close her eyes.

Evidently he stopped to gaze down upon her a moment,
for there was a silence, then he knelt to lay a hand on her
shoulder.

"Now, what's the matter?" he inquired, with more doubt
than sympathy.

Janey stirred and sat up.

"I fell off my horse," she said.

"What for?"

"Guess I got dizzy or something. You must have hurt me
internally. Or I wrenched my side—anyway I had a terrible
pain."

"That's too bad. I'm sorry. I never calculated on *any*
weakness, physical or mental." He was studying her face
with deep inscrutable eyes, and despite his words he was
not sympathetic.

"Weak! Why I'm bordering on nervous collapse right
now," returned Janey.

"Yes, I observed how weak you were—physically," he

said. "You could probably throw me in a catch-as-catch-can wrestling match. And when you hit me on my nose—with your fist—well, you came very near being alone for a while."

Janey gave him a searching look. "Will you take me back to the post?"

"Certainly not."

"But if I'm hurt or ill."

"You're going to Beckyshibeta in any event."

"Beckyshibeta? Why, that's a long way, you told me."

"Sure. It's far away, and lonely too, believe me. No one will find us there."

"How long do we—do you mean to keep me prisoner there?"

"I have no idea how long it will take for you to change —or die."

"Oh! . . . Very well, you can bury me at Beckyshibeta," concluded Janey, getting up wearily.

She refused his proffered assistance, and made a fine effort at mounting, as if some of her bones were broken. And she rode on, thinking that the weak-sister stuff would not work with Phil Randolph. She must slowly recover her strength and become a veritable amazon. Perhaps some accident would occur that might be calculated to frighten even her, though she could not imagine what it could be. Then she would try the clinging vine. Even Phil Randolph would fall for that. But it must be something over which a modern girl could safely lose her nerve. A terrible storm or a flood! Janey prayed for both. Phil Randolph must be reduced to a state of perfect misery.

Janey rode on, gradually recovering her poise in the saddle. The canyon opened wide, with the walls far away. There were flats of green grass and cedar groves to cross. In one place she saw several deserted hogans. Indians had lived there. She had a desire to peep in at the dark door, facing the east.

The trail came to a point where it forked. Janey waited for Randolph to come up.

"Which way, Sir Geraint?" she inquired.

"Left," he said. "And I don't think you're a bit like Enid. She was meek. Besides she was Geraint's wife."

"Well, Geraint drove Enid ahead, so she would encounter all the risks and dangers first. No doubt the similarity of our ride to theirs ends right there."

"The only danger here, Miss Endicott, is the one I'm incurring. And it's too late to avoid that."

Danger! What did he mean? Perhaps the wrath of the cowboys, for it was certain they could not have been let into the secret. How would they take this stunt of Randolph's? Janey began to wonder why she had not thought of that before. True, they had ridden away with a herd of cattle, but they must return sooner or later, and find out. Here was a factor her father had not considered. Even if he did have to tell them she knew the cowboys, especially Ray, would not stand for it. On the other hand, perhaps Randolph had meant the danger to be love of her. And he had said it was too late to avoid it. She was very glad, and if it were actually true she would see to it that he suffered more and more.

They took the left-hand fork of the trail and entered an interesting canyon, which narrowed until the crumbling walls seemed ready to tumble down upon her. Soon the trail became so rough that Janey had to pay heed to it and have a care for her horse. The ascent increased until it was steeper than any Janey had ridden. As she climbed, the trail took to a zigzag course up the slope and often she could look directly down upon Randolph, who was not having the best of luck with the pack animal.

Presently it took Janey's breath to gaze down and she quit it. The trail sometimes led along a ledge so narrow that she wondered how the horse could stick to it. But he never made a misstep or a slip, and appeared unconcerned about the heights. Janey christened him Surefoot.

At last the trail led up to a level again, from which Janey gazed back and down at the red slope, the huge rocks, the slides of weathered stone, the cedars, and the winding dry stream bed at the bottom. Janey had to look awhile to locate Randolph. It was no trail for a pack horse, or rather the horse was not one for such a narrow steep obstructed trail. Randolph was walking, dragging at the animal. When he finally reached the summit he was red-faced and panting.

"I note the way of a transgressor is hard," observed Janey.

"Why—didn't you—run off?" he asked.

"I'd only have got lost. Besides I think it'd be unwise to leave the commissary department. Also I have an absorbing desire to see what is going to happen to you."

"That'll be nothing compared to what's coming to you," he returned, as he mounted again. "Oh, by the way, how is that internal injury I gave you?"

"It's better. But I can bear it for your sake, Phil. I want so much to help you make a success of this cradle-snatching stunt."

"Say, you flatter yourself," he retorted.

"Well, yes, I'm not exactly an infant. But I'll be good practice for you, so that later, when the tourists come, you may be able to manage some of the girls pretty well."

"Would you mind riding on, and not talking so much," he said, with asperity.

"I certainly wouldn't have waited for you, if there'd been any trail. But it's disappeared."

"Ride straight toward those red rocks," he returned, pointing.

Janey did as she was bidden, glad to be able once more to let her horse look out for himself, so that she could attend to the surroundings. The sun was slanting westward, toward a high wall that ran away to the northward. The desert stretched level ahead of her, with a horizon line matched by red rocks. Not far in front, a growth of purple brush began to show sparsely and to thicken in the distance. It was very fragrant and beautiful. Presently Janey recognized the fragrance of sage.

Huge clouds had rolled up, and except in the west they

were black and stormy. Dark curtains hung down from them to the floor of the desert. They must be rain. The afternoon was hot and sultry, without a breath of wind. By and by the clouds hid the sun and turned duskily red.

Janey was somewhat surprised to have Randolph catch up and pass her.

"Better trot your horse, if you're not too weak to hang on," he said. "It's going to storm and we must reach the shelter of the rocks."

"How lovely! I hope it rains cats and dogs," she returned amiably.

"Don't worry. You'll be scared stiff when night comes, if it does."

Janey was about to laugh at him scornfully, but happened to remember that she really was afraid of storms.

"Are desert storms bad?" she inquired, anxiously.

"Terrible. . . . You can't see. You get half drowned. Rocks roll down the cliffs and floods roar down the washes."

"How lovely! . . . I imagine one of your brilliant ideas to keep me interested."

Surefoot had an easy trot, for which Janey was devoutly thankful. She had begun to realize that she was not made of leather. And the faster gait had a businesslike look of getting somewhere.

Meanwhile the sun disappeared wholly behind massing clouds, and thunder rolled in the distance. Drops of rain began to fall, and the warm air perceptibly cooled. Janey put on her coat; and was once more reminded of the annoying brevity of her skirt. What a picture she must make! How her riding friends would have howled to see her mounted in this rig! She wondered what Randolph would do if it rained heavily. Janey had a sneaking suspicion that he would let her get as wet as if she were under Niagara. But after all a warm rain would not be such a hardship. Thunder and lightning, however, made her nervous, even indoors.

The storm quartered slowly across the desert, a wonderful sight to eyes used to close walls and crowded streets.

Janey breathed deeply. The sage fragrance seemed to intoxicate her. The misty rain felt sweet on her hot cheeks. The growing breeze brought a breath of wet dust.

Randolph was trotting his horse at as fast a clip as the pack animal could keep up. Janey set Surefoot to a lope. Then she experienced an exhilaration. She was astounded that she was not thinking about the possibility of being wretchedly wet and uncomfortable.

It turned out, however, that they beat the gray pall of rain which moved behind them across their trail. Randolph led her down among the strange scrawled rocks Janey had seen for so long into the shelter of a shelving cliff. Clumps of cedar and patches of sage dotted the slope in front, and, opposite, a high wall of rock shut out the horizon.

"Throw your saddle," ordered Randolph, practically, as he dismounted.

When Janey had accomplished this Randolph was at hand to hobble her horse and turn him loose.

"If there isn't a water hole in this canyon there sure will be one pronto," he said.

"You think it will storm?" she asked, dreamily.

"Storm? You're to see your first real storm. Say, are you any good at camp work?"

"You mean chopping sticks, cooking stuff and washing dishes?"

"Well, not exactly. We don't chop sticks, etc. But you have grasped my meaning."

"I'm perfectly helpless," Janey assured him, which was a lie.

"Fine wife you'll make," he replied.

"Mr. Randolph, I'm used to being waited upon," said Janey, elevating her chin. "And I didn't coax you to fetch me on this—this camping trip."

"Ye Gods!" he expostulated, spreading his hands wide. "I know that . . . But I didn't figure on what we're up against."

"You should combine study of weather conditions with your archaeological and girl pursuits."

"Damnit!" he returned, doggedly. "I can't get rid of the idea that you'd be a thoroughbred—a real sport in any kind of a situation."

Randolph turned away then, unconscious that he had brought delight to Janey's heart. She hoped she had deserved what he had said. And there appeared to be signs that she would be tested to the utmost. She decided, however, to allow him to labor under doubts for a while longer.

Finding a seat where she could lean against the wall Janey watched her captor with interest. He unpacked with swift hands. Then he strode to the cedars and fetched back an enormous load of firewood, which he threw down with a crash. His next move was to start a fire, and wash his hands. Following this, with a speed and facility that astonished Janey, he mixed biscuit dough in a pan. There were several canteens full of water, and a number of canvas sacks, all bulging. He had two small iron ovens in the fire and a coffeepot If Janey had been blind she would soon have been pleasantly aware of steaming coffee and frying bacon. Presently Randolph straightened up and glanced in her direction.

"Of course you can swear you'll starve to death. But you won't do it. And you can save your face by not making the bluff. . . . Will you have supper?"

"Yes, Professor Randolph, I'm hungry. And besides, I'm curious to see if you can cook. You have such varied accomplishments."

He brought her supper and laid it on the level rock beside her. Janey had told the truth about being hungry, but she did not tell him how good everything tasted. The hot biscuits, well buttered, were delicious. And when had she tasted such coffee? For dessert she had a cup of sliced canned peaches. And altogether the meal was most satisfying. Janey was ashamed to ask for more, but she could have eaten it.

Meanwhile the afternoon had waned, and twilight shadows were filling the hollows below. A steady rain set in. The campfire lighted up the shelving roof of the cliff. Janey walked to and fro, round the corner of projecting wall, and explored some of the niches. She felt pretty tired and sore. Her knees burned from their exposure to the sun. Her cheeks felt pleasantly warm.

Randolph was packing loads of firewood. He did not appear to mind the rain, for he certainly was wet, and did not take the trouble to put on his coat. It was seeing him in a different light. Janey remembered a good many of her friends and acquaintances, who could dress and talk and dance and grace social occasions in the great city, who she doubted would have been her selection for service and protection in the desert.

She walked to the campfire and held her hands to the blaze. The night air had begun to have a little chill. The hot fire felt pleasant.

"You got your hair wet," said Randolph, disapprovingly.

"So I did," replied Janey, with her hand to her head.

"Well, there isn't very much of it, so it'll dry quickly. . . . You must have had beautiful hair once."

"Once?"

"Yes, once. Women have sacrificed for fad and comfort. The grace, the glamour, the exquisite something natural to women disappeared with their long hair. It's a pity. Why did you want to look like a man?"

"Look like a man? I *never* did."

"Why did you cut your hair then?"

"To be honest I don't know. My reasons would sound silly to you. But as a matter of fact women are slaves to fashion. They used to be slaves to many things—men, for instance. But we've eliminated that."

"I wonder if women are eliminating love also?" he inquired, gloomily.

"They probably are, until men are worthy of it."

Randolph stalked off into the darkness, and stayed so long that Janey began to be anxious. Surely he would not leave her alone. It was pitch dark now; the rain and wind were augmenting; the solitude of the place seemed accentuated. Janey gazed out into the dark void, and then

back at the caverned cliff. There might be all kinds of wild
animals. Snakes and reptiles. It was delightful for a woman
to be alone on occasions, but here was one when there
seemed need of a man. To her relief Randolph emerged
from the gloom, packing another load of firewood.

"Are you going to stay up all night?" he asked. "Tomorrow will be the hardest day you've had. You need sleep and
rest."

"Where am I supposed to get them?"

"I made your bed up there," said Randolph, pointing to
a ledge. "It's easy to climb up from this end. You'll be
dry. . . . I'll spread my tarp and blankets here by the
fire."

Janey did not show any inclination to retire at once. She
was tired enough, but did not choose to be sent to bed like
a child. She stood by the fire until she was thoroughly dry.
Then she sat down on a stone just the right distance from
the red crackling logs. Randolph stood on the other side,
looking down with his hands outstretched. He seemed to
have the burden of the world upon his shoulders. Then he
turned his back to the fire, and stood that way for a long
time. The wind whipped in under the shelving rock, cool
and damp; the rain pattered steadily outside; the fire sput-
tered and cracked; the fragrant smoke blew this way and
that. At last Randolph turned again to face the fire. And
he looked more troubled than ever.

"Mr. Randolph, you seem gravely thoughtful for a man
who has accomplished his purpose," observed Janey.

"I was just thinking," he replied, giving her a strange
glance, "how pleasant a picnic it would be—if we were
good friends."

"Yes, wouldn't it?" returned Janey, flippantly.

"Very unreasonable of me, I know. I didn't and couldn't
expect you to enjoy being dragged off this way. But being
here made me think how—how wonderful it would be if—
if—"

He did not conclude the sentence and his closing words
were full of regret. Quite evidently he felt that he had

sacrificed a great deal to her father's whim. Janey had an uneasy consciousness that sooner or later he would betray her father and explain this unheard-of proceeding. She did not want Randolph to do this and must prevent it coming about. The only way, she repeated to herself, was to give him such a hard time that he would carry the thing out through sheer anger and disgust. As an afterthought Janey reflected that she could correct the terrible impression she was likely to give him. But suppose she could not! She dismissed that as absurd.

"I'd prefer you had kidnaped me in a limousine," she said lightly. "I'm used to being whisked off—and kept parked in some outlandish place."

"Good God!" he ejaculated. "I've begun to believe your father!"

"What did he say?"

"Never mind. But it was enough. . . . And—will you oblige me by keeping your—your habits to yourself."

Janey tittered. "If that isn't just like a man! A lot of thanks I get for trying to make it easy for you."

"Make what easy?" he asked, belligerently.

"Why, this stunt of yours. . . . Now you've got me off on your old desert I should think you'd be glad to find I'm not—well, an innocent and unsophisticated little gal."

"Janey Endicott, you're a liar!" he almost shouted at her, starting up, bristling. Then he wheeled and strode off into the darkness along the cliff wall.

He left Janey with a heart beating high. In spite of her bald remarks he was struggling to keep alive his ideal of her. Janey thought she might go too far and stab it to death. But the truth was that her father had grossly misrepresented her, and that she had aided and abetted it by falsehood. Love was not easily killed, certainly not by a few lies. She would carry on. And the revelation of her true self to Randolph would be all the sweeter. Gazing into the opal heart of the campfire Janey lost herself momentarily in a dream, from which she awakened with a start. A coyote had wailed his dismal war cry. It made Janey shiver.

She left the campfire, and climbed up the slanting rough rock to the ledge where Randolph had made her bed. What a nice snug rock, high and dry! Janey would feel reasonably safe when Randolph came back. She sat down on the tarpaulin covering her bed, and her sensation roused the conception that it would not be a feather bed or a hair mattress by an exceedingly long shot. Suddenly she realized she would have to sleep in her clothes for the first time in her life. How strange! Then without more ado she took off her coat, made a pillow of it, and removing her shoes she slipped down into the blankets, stretched out and lay still.

The bed consisted of two thicknesses of blankets and the canvas under and over them. Hard as a board under her! Yet what a relief, warmth and comfort the bed gave! The fire cast flickering fantastic shadows upon the roof of this strange habitation. Gusts of wind brought cool raindrops to her fevered face and the smell of wood smoke. Above the steady downpour of rain she heard a renewed crackling of the fire. Rising on her elbow she saw Randolph replenishing it with substantial logs. The night gave Janey satisfaction. She dropped back, laughing inwardly. Phil Randolph was in quite a serious predicament.

Janey settled herself comfortably to think it all over. But she did not seem to be able to control her mind as usual. Her eyelids drooped heavily and though she opened them often they would go shut again, until finally they stuck fast. A pleasant warmth and sense of drowsy rest were stealing over her aching body. She had a vague feeling of anxiety about snakes, tarantulas, scorpions, but it passed. She was being slowly possessed by something vastly stronger than her mind. The rainfall seemed to lessen. And her last lingering consciousness had to do with the fragrance of smoke.

Janey half roused several times during the night, in which she rolled over to try to find a softer place in her bed. But when she thoroughly awoke it was daylight. The rain had ceased. Sunrise was a stormy one of red and black, with a little blue sky in between. When she sat up with a groan and tried to straighten she thought every bone in her body was broken. She sat on her bed and combed her hair, and slyly cleaned her sunburned face with cold cream. Over the edge of rock she spotted Randolph, brisk and whistling round the campfire. Whistling! Janey listened while she put on her shoes. Then she got to her knees. Never had she had so many sore muscles. The arm Randolph had wrenched was the worst.

"Hey, down there," called Janey. "What was the name of that robber baron who ran off with Mary Tudor?"

Randolph stared up at her, almost laughing.

"Bothwell, I believe," he replied, constrainedly.

"Well, good morning, Mr. Bothwell," added Janey.

He returned her greeting with the air of a man who had almost forgotten something unpleasant. He did not whistle any more, and eyed Janey dubiously as she limped and crawled down the slope to a level.

"How are the eats?" she asked, brightly.

"I was just about to call you," he said. "Breakfast will be ready soon as the coffee boils."

"What kind of a day is it going to be?"

"Bad, I fear. It's let up raining, but I think there'll be more."

"Gee, how sore I am! You nearly broke my arm. And that slabstone bed finished me."

"I hope the internal injury is better," he rejoined dryly.

"Oh, that. I guess that was hunger, or else a terrible pang of disappointment to find you such a monster. . . . Call me when you're ready to give me something to eat."

Janey walked about to stretch her limbs. The overhanging sky was leaden and gray, except where a pale brightness had succeeded the ruddy sunrise. She heard a roar down in the canyon and concluded it was running water. Little muddy streams were coursing down the shallow ditches. Beyond the cliff she saw water in sheets running off the rocks above. The cedars were green and fresh; and the sage had an exquisite hue of purple. Janey ventured to the edge of the cedar grove; and saw down into the canyon where a red torrent swirled and splashed. She recalled hearing the trader tell of sudden floods pouring down the dry washes. This was one of them; and she understood now why heavy storms impeded desert travel.

A shout turned Janey's footsteps campward. Randolph had breakfast ready, and it was equally as appetizing as the supper the night before.

"Evidently you're not going to starve me into submission, anyway," she observed.

"I don't know about submission, but you'll be starved into something, all right," he declared.

"Do we have to cross this canyon?"

"We do, and pronto, or we won't cross at all."

"Why, there's a regular torrent."

"Not bad yet."

"Then we must hurry?"

"Yes. If we rustle along—and are lucky—we may make Beckyshibeta tonight."

Not for anything would Janey have importuned Randolph to turn back. But the serious nature of desert travel under unfavorable conditions now dawned upon her; and her mood of levity suffered a side-tracking. She had no more to say. Hurrying through breakfast she proceeded to assist Randolph with the camp chores. He objected, but she paid no attention to him.

"Where are the horses?" she asked, suddenly.

"They'll be near somewhere. They're hobbled, you know, and wouldn't stray from good grass. I'll fetch them in."

He was absent so long that Janey began to worry. At last he showed up, riding his horse bareback, and leading the other two. Surefoot looked fat. Janey undertook the job of saddling him. As she swung up the heavy saddle she observed Randolph watching her out of the corner of his eye. When her horse was ready she turned to Randolph. He was loading the pack animal. Janey had watched the cowboys throw what they called the diamond hitch—an intricate figure-eight knot that held the pack on—and she now saw Randolph was as expert as any of them. Nevertheless some assistance from her was welcome to him. He made only one remark, which concerned the way she pulled on the rope. When the pack was on tight Randolph saddled his own horse.

"I've left my chaps out for you to wear," he said, indicating a pair of worn leather chaps lying on a rock.

"How can I wear chaps in this dress?" asked Janey.

"I don't know. Stuff your skirt down in them. Reckon there's not much to stuff."

Janey overlooked his retort, and picking up the chaps she stepped into them. They were too long and too large. From the expression on Randolph's face she gathered that she must be a peculiar-looking object.

It was when Janey tried mounting her horse that she came to grief. The chaps were stiff and heavy, and she could not reach the stirrup with her foot. Randolph offered to lift her up, but she declined. Finally she made a violent effort, a sort of spring. She missed the pommel with her hand and the stirrup with her foot, and fell flat. Janey scrambled up quite enraged. If there was anything she hated it was to look clumsy. Randolph's face had a strained look. He was holding in his laughter.

"I—I suggest you try to mount from the rock there," he said.

"I'll get up here or die," replied Janey, furiously.

Next time she lifted her left foot with both hands and got it in the stirrup. Then she leaped, sprung from her right foot, and, catching pommel and cantle, she dragged herself up into the saddle.

"Not so bad for a tenderfoot," observed Randolph. Whereupon he rode off, leading the pack horse.

Janey followed down the slope of wet red earth, by some scrawled rocks, into the canyon. They rounded a corner to come upon the muddy swift stream. It was silent here, but from below came up a dull roar. Janey had never seen such dirty-looking water. It was half silt. What a terrifying place to venture into!

Randolph crossed a flat sand bar, and urged his horse into the water. He spurred, and yelled, and dragged at the pack animal. They set up a great muddy splashing. Janey gathered that the more speed used here, the easier and safer the crossing. Her heart simply leaped to her throat. Randolph's horse went in to his flanks. What a tremendous but clumsy struggle the two animals made! Janey almost lost sight of them in the splashing. They reached shallow water, heaved up, and waded out safely on the bar opposite. Randolph halted his horse and turned to look. For a moment he merely looked.

"Well, Central Park," he called, in a tone that challenged Janey.

"Coming, fossil hunter!" she replied, defiantly.

Surefoot naturally would rather have turned back. Janey had to kick him to start him at all. And then she could not make him go fast enough. He splashed in to his knees, slowed up, and began to flounder.

"Come hard," yelled Randolph.

Janey urged her horse with all her might. It was too late for good results. Surefoot struck the deep water at too slow a gait, and the current carried him off his feet. Janey's distended eyes saw the red flood well to her hips. How cold, angry, strong. Randolph rode madly down along the opposite bank, yelling she knew not what. In the presence of real peril Janey's sense and nerve rose to combat her terror. She kept her seat in the saddle. She pulled Surefoot diagonally downstream. He was half swimming and half wading. Fifty yards below where Randolph had crossed, Janey's horse struck shallow water and harder bottom and made shore just above a place where the stream constricted between steep banks, and began to get rough.

Randolph had waded his horse in to meet hers.

"You should have ridden in fast," he said, almost harshly. But the fact that his face was white caused Janey to forgive his rudeness.

"You told me a little late," replied Janey, coolly.

"I apologize. I—I thought you would follow suit," he returned with an effort.

Janey did not need to be told what a narrow escape it had been. She effectively concealed her real feelings.

"Pray don't apologize. I didn't expect much courtesy from you," she said, evenly.

The blood leaped to Randolph's pale cheek and he stifled a retort. Then he rode back to the pack animal and took up the halter again. Janey rode on behind him, pondering over the possibilities of this eventful day.

6

FIVE HOURS LATER, and fifteen miles farther on over this awful desert, Janey had experienced sensations never before known to her except by hearsay.

She had been wet to the skin for hours. It was not rain but a deluge. She had forded so many gutters and wastes and gorges that she could no longer remember the number. She had fallen off her horse into the mud. She had been compelled to dismount and climb up steep wet sand slopes, where every step seemed the last one before she flopped down to die. She had been pulled across raging creeks by Randolph, and rescued from certain death at least twice. And the wonder of it all was that she had kept the true state of her misery and terror from her captor. She vowed nothing would ever make her show yellow and crawl—to give this man and her father the satisfaction they craved. She would prove one thing anyhow—that a modern girl could have more nerve than all the old-fashioned women put together. Lastly she was unable to decide whether she would end by passionately hating Randolph or loving him.

Certainly he could not have planned such opportunities as had come up. He treated her almost precisely as if she had been a young man. Indeed it was because of this in two instances that she had nearly drowned. Yet he was amazingly cool, indifferent to her and danger as well. But when necessary, he had the quickness, the judgment and strength to drag her to safety.

The rain let up now and then, so that Janey could see the desert. If it had ever been level, it was no longer so. It was turned on end, broken into ragged pieces, upheaved and monumental, a wild world of walls, cliffs, rocks, canyons.

There was not a dry stitch on her, and she appeared to be red mud from head to toe. Sand and water were mixed inside her shoes. When Randolph trotted his horse, or dismounted to descend into some gully and climb out, Janey, following suit, grew hot and breathless from the unusual exercise. When they rode slowly, which fortunately was not often, she grew cold. And now she began to get hungry.

She remembered she had wrapped up a piece of meat and a biscuit, and deposited it in her pocket. With dismay she found the biscuit wet and soggy. But she ate it anyhow. Then the piece of meat. She had never before known anything to taste so good. And she reflected on how little she had ever appreciated food. A person must starve to realize that.

The rain poured down again, so thick and heavy that Janey could only dimly discern the pack horse scarcely fifteen paces ahead. Janey's saddle held a pool of cold water. It rained down inside her chaps into her shoes. What a miserable sensation that was! It pelted her back and ran in a stream off the brim of her hat. Patiently she waited, praying for a lull. But none came. And her state became one of utter wretchedness. All she asked now was to live long enough to choke her father and murder Randolph.

Janey was to learn something undreamed of—the latent endurance of a human being. She managed to stick on her horse, to keep up without screaming. But she knew another gorge, if they encountered one, would be her finish. She would just fall off her horse and sink out of Randolph's sight. Maybe that would touch the indifferent brute!

No more canyons were met, however, though the rock walls grew mountainous. All at once Janey seemed to realize the dull gray light was darkening. The day was ended, and the storm appeared to increase in fury. At times the great walls afforded protection, but largely they rode in the open. Surefoot now kept on the heels of the pack horse. When Randolph at last halted, Janey had an overpowering sense of huge black walls, and a roaring of wind or water.

"It's been some rotten day," said Randolph, as he reached to take her from the saddle.

Janey could see his face dimly in the gloom. When she tried to get out of the saddle, she simply slid off into Randolph's arms. He carried her a few steps and set her upright on a rock.

"You're a game kid, anyway," he muttered, as if speaking to himself. Then he disappeared. Janey found she could lean back against a wall, which she did in unutterable relief. Evidently they were under some kind of shelter, for it was dry. She smelled dust that had never been wet. The blackness above was split by a pale band, which must have been the sky. Sound of wind and water filled the place with hollow roar. She was very cold, miserable, inert and hungry. If she could only sleep or die! Her wretchedness was a horror. She could scarcely lift a hand. Every bone in her body seemed broken, every muscle bruised. And she was so wet she felt she would liquefy into a stream of water!

Suddenly a light pierced the blackness, and she heard a crackling. Randolph's figure showed in a dim flare. He had kindled a fire. Wonderful man to find dry wood in a deluge! She saw a blue-gold blaze leap up through a tangle of brush and sticks. In a moment the place was illumined by a roaring fire. It had a subtle effect upon Janey. She saw sheer walls of rock on three sides, and a black void on the other.

Randolph approached her, and drew her to the fire.

"Get dry and warm. It'll make a difference," he said, and he placed one of the canvas packs for her to sit upon. But Janey, weak as she was, stood up to the blaze, extending cold trembling hands.

"It feels good," she replied.

Indeed she wanted to walk into that blazing pile of sticks. What had she ever known about a fire? Of its singular beauty, its power to cheer, its wonderful property to warm cold flesh! It was the difference between death and life. She understood the barbarians who first invented, or found it. She knew now why she loved the sun.

Her wet clothes began to steam. She turned from one side to the other, as long as she could stand the burn.

"Sit down and let me pull off the chaps," suggested Randolph.

When he had accomplished this task, which was not easy, in view of the fact that Janey had to hold desperately on to the pack to keep from being dragged off, she felt almost as if she were undressed. The short skirt of woolen material had shrunk and wrinkled until it was a spectacle that made Janey shriek with laughter, despite her woes. Randolph laughed with her, but evidently avoided looking at her. After wringing the water out of her skirt as best she could, Janey approached the fire, standing as close as she dared. She turned round and round, sat down upon the pack until she rested then repeated the performance. It was amazing how quickly her clothes dried. And equally amazing was the effect upon her spirits.

Meanwhile Randolph was cooking the meal so quickly that Janey thought there must be very little firewood left.

"What's the rush?" asked Janey. "Looks as if we'd have to stay here tonight anyhow."

"Aren't you hungry?"

"Famished."

"Well, that's reason enough."

"You're awfully good to me. . . . Where are we?"

"Beckyshibeta."

"So soon!" exclaimed Janey, gazing around her. The flare from the fire showed yellow walls, dark caverns, cracks; and in front a space of rock-strewn ground leading to dimly outlined trees, and then a blankness.

"So it was your life's ambition to fetch me here?" Janey said incredulously. "Gee, men are queer! You might have accomplished much more by taking me to the Waldorf Astoria!"

"Any man could do that," replied Randolph. "At least you'll remember this trip."

"I'll say I will!"

The rain had ceased and the wind had lost its force. Janey heard a low, dull rumble. Randolph informed her it was thunder and that they were in for an even worse storm.

"But we're safe and dry, unless we get flooded out. That's happened here before."

"Indeed! Interesting place."

"Are you dry?"

"Just about, I guess. And burned to a crisp."

"Come to the festal board, then," he concluded.

The wants of primitive peoples must have been very few. Shelter, warmth, food, and something to wear. Yet what cardinally important wants these were! Janey was so grateful for the first three wants that she almost reconciled herself to the lack of the last. She reflected that if her skirt shrunk any shorter she would have to don Randolph's chaps permanently or else look like one of the chorus girls in the Follies. She did no care after all. It would only add to the sum of Randolph's iniquity.

Janey was thinking along that line, and eating prodigiously, when something happened. All went dazzlingly, blindingly white. She lost her sight. Deep blackness again, then an awful terrific crash. The great walls seemed to be falling. Janey screamed, yet did not hear her own voice. A tremendous boom and bang resolved into concatenated

thunder, which rolled away, leaving Janey weak and paralyzed with fear.

"W-what was—th-that?" she faltered.

"Just a little lightning and thunder," he replied. "They'll
get bothersome presently, when the streaks of lightning
come down like the rain. Better finish your supper. Then
you can crawl under your blankets and shut out the
flashes, anyhow."

Janey's appetite had been effectually checked, but she
swallowed the rest of her meal, every moment dreading
another earth-riving crash. But it did not come at once. She
had surprise added to dread. The stillness and darkness
became most oppressive.

"Where's—my bed?" asked Janey, rising.

"I haven't unrolled it yet," replied Randolph, jumping
up.

Just then a sudden silver-blue blaze struck Janey blind.
She stood as one stricken, every muscle, nerve, and brain
cell in abeyance to the expected crash. Such a shock came
that it knocked Janey flat. And when she became conscious
of sound again a mighty rumble of thunder boomed at the
walls. Randolph was trying to lift her. Janey opened her
tight-shut eyes and clung to Randolph. He had got her to
her knees when another white flash and awful clap made
her collapse in his arms.

Randolph carried her a few steps back and put her down.
But she still clung to him.

"It's only a storm—just lightning and thunder," he was
saying, most earnestly. "We're safe. We can't be struck or
hurt. There's only one danger—that of being caught in a
flood. But it'd have to rain a long time. . . . Janey, don't
be such a child. Why—"

His assurances did not compose Janey. She knew it, too.
She had been worn out physically. And from childhood she
had always dreaded a storm. That fear had been born in
her. And never had she seen or heard anything to compare
with this lightning and thunder. They were blinding, deaf-
ening, nerve-racking and absolutely stunning. That was why

Janey had her face on Randolph's breast and clung to him
with all the strength she had left. She was aware that he
tried to disengage himself—that he kept on talking, but
both action and voice augmented her terror. They would
come again, and she wanted to be hidden, to be held. They
did come, and Janey, even with her eyes shut and face
pressed hard against Randolph's breast, saw the intense
white light. Then followed the stupendous crash. The earth
shook under her. The whole world seemed full of staggering sound. It clapped back and forth from wall to wall, and
rolled away like a mountain of stone.

Janey had a last lingering recollection of the part she
had meant to play, of a wicked hope for this very opportunity.

"Y-you've taken m-me from m-myself," she faltered.

Randolph's reply was drowned in another explosion. But
Janey felt him take her closely in his arms and hold her
tightly. Then it seemed the storm broke into incessant flash
and crash, until there was no darkness or silence again.
That period, long or short, was the worst Janey had ever
experienced. When the storm passed she was dazed. But
she felt Randolph lay her down and cover her with blankets.
And that was the last thing she knew.

When she awakened the sun was shining somewhere, for
she saw a gold-crowned rim of lofty wall. She remembered
instantly where she was and how she had gotten there. Yet
the place was as weird and magnificent as any dream.
Great walls and columns of colored stone rose above her.
Only a narrow strip of blue sky could she see. She heard
a sullen roar of waters and smelled wood smoke.

"So this is Paris—I mean Beckyshibeta," murmured
Janey, wonderingly. And she tried to rise so that she could
look about her. But with the movement such a pang shot
through her body that she fell back, uttering a sharp little
cry. She was so cramped and stiff that the slightest sudden
effort caused pain. Whereupon she moved her aching limbs
very cautiously and stretched her sore body likewise.

Janey was swearing softly to herself when she discov-

ered her muddy shoes on a rock beside her bed. She did
not recall taking them off. Randolph had done that. Her
coat, too, was under her head. Then she ascertained with
relief that these two kindly services constituted the extent
of Randolph's activities as lady's maid.

She heard a step grate on rock. Randolph appeared to
gaze anxiously down upon her.

"Did you call?" he asked, quickly.

"I just squealed," she replied, gazing up at him, careful
to draw the blankets close to her chin.

"Good morning," he went on, as an afterthought.

"Good morning," returned Janey, sweetly.

"How are you?"

"I'm not sure, but I think I'm dead."

"You're sure a live and handsome corpse," he said, bluntly. "Lord, I wonder if anything could mar your beauty."

His tone was one of exasperating resignation, as well
as reluctant admiration. To Janey it was like a drink of
wine.

"Phil, are you calling on the Lord?"

"I sure am."

"Well, I think it's sacrilege!"

"In extreme cases the most degraded of men might naturally express himself so. I own it was silly of me. I can't
expect to be saved," he said solemnly.

"You shouldn't expect mercy either, from the Lord—or
me."

"Probably you'll be more inclined to be merciful if I
fetch you a nice hot breakfast," he said tentatively.

"Yes. Your cooking is your one redeeming virtue."

"Thanks," he replied, and turned to go.

"Phil, wait," she called. "What did I do last night?"

"Do? Why, nothing in particular."

"I remember being knocked flat by a stroke of lightning.
That must have dazed me, for the rest seems a sort of dim
horror."

"It was a bad electric storm even for this desert. No wonder you were shocked. You see it's very much worse when

you're walled in by cliffs. The echoes crack from cliff to
cliff—truly terrific."

"Was I frightened?"

"Rather."

"Did I scream or—say anything?"

"You told me I had taken you from yourself."

"Heavens! . . . What did I *do*?" she exclaimed, intensely
curious.

"I fear it would embarrass you."

"No doubt. That's why I insist. I want to know."

"Well, I picked you up, intending to carry you up here,
where it's more sheltered. But you grabbed me—hid your
face—and hung on as if for dear life. So I just held you
till the storm was over."

"Indeed! . . . Did the storm last long?"

"Hours."

Janey gave him an inscrutable glance and smile.

"I presume you would have a storm like that every
night."

"Yes. I would—if I had the power," he said, intensely.

"You would be worse than cruel," she rejoined, gravely.
"My mother was a very highly organized and sensitive person, inordinately afraid of lightning and thunder. I was
prematurely born after a storm. . . . One of the recollec-
tions of my childhood is that mother used to take me into
a dark hallway during a storm."

"I'm sorry I said that," he replied, and left. Presently he
fetched up her breakfast and retired rather hurriedly, without speaking again. Janey struggled to a sitting posture,
and applied herself diligently to the ham and eggs, toasted
biscuit, well buttered, and coffee. Truly Phillip Randolph
was astounding. Where did he get fresh eggs? Of course he
had fetched them. But how? Perhaps he believed that the
way to a woman's heart lay through her stomach.

Janey had intended to stay in bed and rest. But one
look over the bulge of rock up at lofty golden rims and
down into a wilderness of bright green canyon put idleness
out of the question. She would explore Beckyshibeta if she

had to drag herself around. Consulting her little mirror she saw that her face had been sunburned, but not unbecomingly so. And the other sunburn, even if it did hurt, did not matter, any more than her shriveled and shrunken garments. There was no danger of any critical and supercilious woman seeing her. Suppose Bert Durland's mother could see her in this outfit! Janey giggled. It would be priceless. Nevertheless she did not care for that catastrophe.

She got up groaning. Muscles and bones were no doubt essential to the human frame, but this morning she would rather have dispensed with them. She was weak, lame, sore and burned. The band of sunburn above her knees was particularly annoying.

"Ooooo!" moaned Janey, as she drew herself erect. "Why did I leave home?"

Finally she wore off the stiffness to the extent of being able to walk; then she laboriously climbed down to a level and gazed about her. The place appeared to be simply an enormous cavern with a dome higher than that of the Grand Central Station, which was going some, Janey admitted. It opened on a level bench that extended out over a green canyon, perhaps half a mile wide and twice as long. How refreshing and colorful the different kinds of foliage! It contrasted beautifully with the red and gold of gorgeous colossal cliffs that sheered up as if to the very sky. A sullen roar of water greeted Janey's ears. She heard the twitter of birds in the cedars and cottonwoods. All appeared bright and clean, with a warm sun shining after the storm. Thin waterfalls were dropping over the cliffs, and at the apex of the canyon, its upper end, a heavy torrent was tumbling down over the broken masses of rocks.

These were Janey's first impressions and sensations. She walked out of the shade into the sunshine. Every step was an effort, but resulted in a wonderful reward in an enlargement of her view of the weird and magnificent surroundings. The stone walls were higher than any New York skyscraper. They were full of great caverns and hollows near their base, and above were cracked and stained and covered with moss, with niches and ledges where green growths grew. Janey stood spellbound. Beckyshibeta! What a marvelous place! It was majestic, grand, and increased in beauty and wonder as she grasped its true perspective. The canyon stunned her too, with its shut-in solitude.

"Oh, glorious!" murmured Janey. "I had no idea it was like this. He never said so. Mr. Bennet didn't lead me to expect much. But this!"

Janey sat down in the sun, and time was as nothing. She might have been there minutes or an hour. It was long, however, for cramped muscles told her so. She breathed it all in. Her eyes feasted. Something seemed transformed within her. What had she missed all these idle years? Never, except in a highly colored romance or two, had she read of such places as this, and she had believed them merely fiction. But no pen, no brush could do justice to the truth of Beckyshibeta.

Janey felt that she would be unutterably grateful to Randolph always. Still she could not let him know. Where was he anyhow? For a kidnaper who had made off with a victim, he was certainly elusive.

She went in search of him. Owing to her crippled condition and the awesome nature of the place, Janey did not make much progress. She got around an immense corner of wall, below the cavern he had chosen for their camp, and found another cave higher and larger than the first. It was full of the ruins of sections of wall that had fallen. Janey threaded slow passage between blocks of rock and over weathered slides to another projecting corner which she thought hid the mouth of the canyon. The roar of water grew louder. Her way was so beset with obstacles that she was long in reaching her objective. But at last she got around the corner.

If she had gazed and gaped before, what did she do now? All the details she had seen were here repeated and magnified. In addition, a wicked red stream went brawling down in a series of rapids. The canyon opened into a larger one, bewildering to Janey's eyes.

Next she spotted Randolph digging with a pick. He stood just round the jutting point of wall, and it had been the cracking of his pick that attracted her attention. Janey made her way to him. Strange he did not see her! He was shamming or absorbed, not improbably the latter. He dug like a man who had found the foot of the rainbow.

Janey hailed him with: "Hey, there, subway digger!"

Randolph was startled. He whirled and dropped his pick. Janey did not need to be told that he had actually forgotten her.

"Why—Miss Endicott—you—I—" he stammered.

"Fine morning on the avenue," she returned.

"It is fine," he said, recovering himself, and reaching for the pick.

"Phillip, you forgot me, didn't you?"

"I'm afraid I did."

"Left me alone to be eaten by grizzly bears or run off and get lost or anything!"

"There are no bears. And you can't run off until the creek falls. Nor can anybody get across to frighten you."

"Very well, but that doesn't explain your leaving me alone."

"No, it doesn't. To be honest, I just plain forgot you."

"Can you beat that! . . . You're a fine kidnaper. As you evidently didn't intend to maltreat me, I certainly expected to be taken care of, amused and instructed. And you forget me!"

"I always forget everything, when I come to Beckyshibeta," he replied, apologetically. "Everything except that here, somewhere in these caverns, is buried the lost pueblo of Beckyshibeta. I know it. I have read the signs. . . . I daresay if I had run off with Cleopatra or Helen of Troy, I'd have forgotten."

Janey was impressed again by his singular simplicity and passion. The man seemed so keen, so sincere, so strong and hopeful that she almost wished that he would find the treasure upon which he set such store.

"I'll find Beckyshibeta for you," she said, impulsively.

He stared, then laughed. "I suppose that'd be woman's revenge. To heap coals of fire upon my head. To flay me with remorse. . . . But, fun or no fun, please don't find Beckyshibeta for me."

"Why not? It seems to be your driving passion. Most men I know are driven by other motives. Money, power, fame."

"Beckyshibeta would give me all these. But I've never thought of them."

"Then why don't you want me to find it?"

"I'm quite mad enough over you now. If you found Beckyshibeta, I—"

"Oh. So that's it? That would be a calamity."

"I agree with you. Therefore be careful not to go digging around these caves. As to that, you stay in camp and stop following me."

"I'll follow you if I want to—but I don't," retorted Janey.

"I don't approve of you running around here," he said, severely. "I thought you'd rest all day."

"Take me back," returned Janey, imperiously.

"You found your way here alone. Now go back and stay there," he ordered.

Janey did not know whether to swear or laugh at him. He was most decidedly in earnest. It might be well to save the profanity for a more fitting time. So she laughed.

"My Lord, I go," she said. "When will it please you to return to our castle?"

"I'll be along later," he rejoined, quite oblivious to her levity. "You can fix yourself some lunch."

Whereupon Janey left him to his explorations and turned back, pondering the interview. Every encounter with Randolph left her unsatisfied, but she could not figure out why. It took her a good half hour, resting frequently, to retrace her steps; and all this while she divided her thoughts between Randolph and Beckyshibeta. At last she reached camp and found a comfortable slab. She was exhausted, yet the exertion had been good for her.

"Dad was not such a damn fool, after all," soliloquized Janey. "I like Phillip Randolph. . . . It's up to me to find

out why. I'm sorry Dad picked *him* to run off with me. Because I want to hate him and foil him utterly. But thank
the Lord I've finally run into one man who isn't drunk with
alcohol, money or women."

Janey found resting so good that she went back to her
blankets, and did such an unheard-of thing as to fall asleep
in the daytime. When she awoke it was the middle of the
afternoon. She felt better. Randolph had not returned. The
fact that he stayed away from her, on any pretext, astonished Janey. She was unaccustomed to that in men in
her society. She had scarcely believed that he would re-
main away all day. "He's gone on me, I don't think," she
told herself, emphatically. She was puzzled, piqued, amused,
resentful, and something else she did not quite realize yet.
It was, however, having a salutary effect.

Janey contented herself with watching the changing
afternoon lights in the canyon; and toward sunset, which
came early, owing to the high walls, she thought she had
been transported to some enchanted world. She saw the
top of a distant mesa turn bright gold; exquisite rays of
indescribably pure and beautiful light streamed down over
the rims; in the distance, far through the gateway of the
canyon, she saw purple of so royal a hue that she exclaimed
in delight; walls were shrouded in pink haze, and near at
hand the amber air seemed to float over the soft green
foliage.

"I'm glad to be here," sighed Janey. And she began to
discover hidden depths in herself. It might be possible that
she could be self-sufficient for a while. There was something incalculably strong working against the habit of
mind that had been hers. Clothes, luxury, amusement, idleness, the theater, the dance, the ever-present necessity of
unlimited money, the attention of men—these were most astonishingly unnecessary here. Janey shook off the spell.
Beckyshibeta was only a hole in the rocks. Beautiful,
strange, wild, yes, but it was not a place to change one's
soul. And she resented the awakening, insistent tearing at
her mind.

The sun had set and the sky was full of rosy clouds when Randolph returned, dusty and tired, wiping his tanned face. He seemed different to Janey, or she saw him with different eyes. There was something proven about him.

"How's my fair prisoner?" he asked.

"If I'm better in body and mind, I can't thank you for it," she replied.

"*Quién sabe?*" he returned. "Do you like Beckyshibeta?"

"This terrible shut-in lonely hole in the rocks? Heavens!" she ejaculated, languidly.

"Janey, be honest," he said.

"Why, Phillip, honest is my middle name," she averred.

"No. It might be game, but it's not honest. You are as crooked as a rail fence—mentally. . . . Please be honest *once*, Janey."

"Why?" she inquired, curious, in spite of her frivolity.

"Because I have always connected you somehow with Beckyshibeta. Strange, but it's so. I believed you would like it—be inspired, perhaps softened."

"Phillip, am I hard?"

"Hard as these rocks."

"You are not flattering."

"Maybe not. But I'm honest," he said, stoutly.

"No, you're not. You're not straight about this stunt of yours. Dragging me off here!" And she bent penetrating eyes on Randolph.

"You will find me honest in the end," he replied, the dark red blood staining his cheek.

"Ah-huh," returned Janey, doubtfully.

"Are you going to be honest or not?" he inquired, sharply. "I still have faith left in you—enough to believe you're not utterly lost to—to the dream of glory of nature."

"Ain't nature grand?" rejoined Janey, with simpering impudence.

"Janey Endicott, if you don't *love* Beckyshibeta, I shall despise you," he declared, hotly.

There was no doubt about this, Janey saw. Randolph was at war with the world—backing his faith in her against the materialism and paganism of the modern day. It thrilled Janey—quite robbed her of her contrariness.

"Phillip, I'd like to make you despise me, but I can't honestly. I do love Beckyshibeta and I am *glad* you dragged me here," she said, with a rich note in her voice, and turned away her face.

"Thank you. That will help," he replied, with emotion.

Janey watched him go down to the creek with the water bucket. It would hardly do, Janey considered, for her to think seriously about him just then. But she realized she must, sooner or later, have a reckoning with herself. For the present, she must stick to her part, and not let any earnestness or eloquence of Randolph's betray her into honesty again.

Randolph returned whistling. Besides the brimming bucket, he carried a log of wood big enough to crush most men Janey knew. She leisurely approached the camp and watched him swing an ax. He started a fire, put on the oven, and then went for more wood. This time he brought such a big load that Janey objected.

"You'll break your back," she said in alarm. "Phillip, you may not be the most desirable of companions, but you're better than a cripple. Please be careful."

"Say, I'm not half a man. You ought to see an Indian pack in firewood. He fetches a whole tree. . . . But come to think of it, if that causes you concern, I'll try a big load next time."

Janey did not answer this. She sat down close by and watched him get supper.

"Phillip, how long will our supplies last—grub, as the cowboys call it?" she asked.

"I packed enough for three weeks, but did not allow for your unsuspected capacity. I daresay, if I stint myself, it'll last ten days."

"And then what?"

"Sufficient unto the day. We can subsist on rabbits, or I can ride to an Indian camp over here and get more. Or— we can return to the post."

"What! You'd take me back there—to face my father, the Bennets and the cowboys, knowing me ruined, disgraced?" she exclaimed.

"Sure, I will," he replied, cheerfully.

"Phillip, if any other man had done this thing to me, and fetched me back—what would you do?"

"Do? A whole lot. I'd kill him."

"Exactly. But it's all right for *you* to do it?"

"Janey, my intentions are honorable."

"Do you imagine you can make the cowboys believe that?"

"I confess I'm a little worried on that score," he replied, ponderingly. "As a rule cowboys are obtuse and inclined to be bullheaded. Then they were so absurdly infatuated, and each of them thought he owned you. Stupid, conceited jackasses! Still they had ample encouragement."

Janey relapsed into silence, the better to enjoy the ever-increasing humor of this situation, and the deliciousness of another sentiment that seemed hard to define. Presently Randolph began to talk, as if she were the most interested of comrades, as indeed, if the truth were admitted, she was.

"I followed another blind lead today, all to no avail. Eight hours of digging for nothing. How often have I done that here! But I know Beckyshibeta is buried here somewhere. If I only had unlimited time! But the department insists on definite rewards, so to speak. I have to find things—bones, pottery, stone utensils and weapons. In short, I am forced to explore where they tell me to and not where I want to. Elliot, head of our department, was out last year. I think I told you. Awful pill—Elliot! He's only a surface scratcher. Well, he belittled my theory. He said there was little sign of ancient pueblo here at Beckyshibeta. . . . And so I can get only snatches at work here."

"Suppose we tell Elliot to go where it's hot," suggested Janey.

"I wish I could. But I must have bread and butter, and some clean clothes occasionally," he returned.

"Phillip, do you always expect to be poor?" she asked.

"I hope not. I have my dream. But I suppose I really always will be."

"Too bad. But I don't know. Money is a curse, they say. Personally, I don't see it. . . . Do you know I am rich?"

"No. Your father, of course. But are you, too?"

"Yes, disgustingly rich. My mother left me several hundred thousand dollars when she died."

"Good Lord!" ejaculated Randolph. "Your father never told me that."

"Well, it's true. And Dad tells me it has nearly doubled. You see I can't touch the whole principal until I'm twenty-five. I have only the income from it—fifty thousand or so a year—and I confess, I'm broke half the time. I'm always borrowing from Dad."

"Janey, are you honest, now?"

"Assuredly. I certainly wouldn't string you about money."

"Damn him, anyway," declared Randolph, forcefully, with a violent gesture.

"Who? Dad?" she asked, innocently.

But Randolph did not answer and there was an immediate change in his demeanor. He prepared supper in silence, and remained glum during the eating of it. She partook heartily of the good meal, and then left Randolph to himself. By this time the early twilight was creeping under the walls and it would soon be night. Janey strolled a little on the edge of the bank. She saw one lone star come wondrously out of the paling pink. Fair as a star when only one was shining in the sky! She had read that somewhere. Wordsworth, perhaps. What would he or Tennyson or Ruskin make out of Beckyshibeta? There was nothing in Europe to compare with the canyon country. Janey felt proud of that.

As it grew dark she returned to the campfire. Randolph had disappeared. She looked into the opal heart of the embers and saw beautiful disturbing visions there. Then she climbed up the rock to her bed.

As she sat down on it she was surprised to find it high

and soft. Upon examination she discovered a foot layer of
cedar boughs under it. How fragrant! Randolph must have
done that right after supper. He was a paradox. He had
handled her roughly, had driven her to the limit of endurance, yet he was thoughtful of her comfort. But the new
bed certainly was a relief and a joy. Janey sighed for some
soft woolly pajamas. But she had to sleep in her clothes.
After removing her shoes, she decided she would take off
her stockings, too.

She crawled in between the blankets, and knew in her
heart she would not have exchanged them for silk sheets.
Weary, aching as she was, she could not wish it otherwise.
She had never actually experienced rest. She had never
been sufficiently aware of comfort, ease. They had been
habits, with no reason for them. Here they served a wonderful blessing, a reward.

Where had Randolph gone? It had upset him to learn
she was rich. Janey could not figure out just why. No one
would take him for a fortune hunter. It would be more
embarrassing, of course, to compromise a wealthy girl
than a poor one, simply because marriage would not have
such a sacrificial look. Every hour of this adventure had
enhanced its romance, augmented its possibilities for delight as well as pain. What would the new day bring?

7

JANEY HAD BEEN ALONE all morning. For several hours she
had welcomed the solitude. She had not seen Randolph,
who had called to her that he was leaving her breakfast on
the fire. If anything she was more stiff and sore than ever,
but the pangs wore off more quickly with the use of her
muscles. About noon she began to feel relief.

She simply could not get over Randolph leaving her to her own devices. Beckyshibeta was more to him than she was. That both irritated and pleased Janey. But of course she would not stand for it. So she set out to hunt him up.

The day was lovely, although when she emerged into full sunshine, which was seldom, it was hot. The fragrant smells of summer wafted down into the canyon, mingling the sweetness of sage with wild flowers and fresh green verdure. The creek had run down and was no longer a roaring torrent. Janey thought she could wade in it if she wanted to. It would have been nothing for a horse.

When she walked away from camp under these magnificent walls, she became somebody else. She grew pensive, dreamy, absorbed and happy. No use to deny her feelings! Only she did not want Randolph to see them. A confusing thing, too, was the fact that under their spell she had to force herself to be true to her old inclinations. Therefore she refused to realize, or at least to seek to understand, the elevating power of this strange canyon wilderness. She could not help sensation. She had to see, to feel, to smell the place, and even to taste the sweetness of the dry desert air.

By the time she had worked her way round the second jutting wall, where Randolph had been digging, she was warmed by the exertion and free of stiff joints. In truth she felt fine. Randolph had abandoned this cavern. So Janey went on, to encounter the most difficult and hazardous climbing over rocks that the kidnaping escapade had led her to. There was a thrill in it. How gratified she felt to surmount the last rock pile! She discerned Randolph about on a level with her. But the canyon jumped off deep below him and zigzagged in wonderful hair-raising ledges beyond.

Randolph did not see Janey. She had opportunity to approach him by way of a dangerous ledge before he would be aware of her presence. High places did not bother Janey. She was level-headed and cool, and reveled in taking risks. When she got about halfway to him, however, she had to

halt. She was getting in trouble and faced inclines that
made even a girl of her bravery quail. So she sank down
to rest and gaze.

The canyon opened wide. It was much vaster and wilder
than that part of Beckyshibeta where Randolph had pitched
the camp. Janey felt something pull at her heartstrings.
Was not this desert fastness simply marvelous? But to look
down now made her shiver. She had been aware of the
gradual height she had attained. Below, a hundred feet
or more, spread a slope of talus, a jumble of broken rock
that fell roughly down to the green thicket. She almost forgot Randolph and her mission in a realizing worship.

Randolph's pick, ringing steel on stone, brought Janey
back. She discovered a ledge above her where no doubt
Randolph had crossed to the wide area beyond. Coming to
a narrowed point, she got on hands and knees, and began
to crawl out. She knocked some loose rocks off the ledge.
They rattled down. Janey swore. Randolph heard the rat-
tling and turned to look up.

Flinging aside his pick he ran forward to the end of
the bench.

"Stop!" he shouted.

Janey obeyed, more from suggestion than anything else.
She gazed across the void at Randolph.

"Howdy, Phil," she called, gaily.

"Didn't I tell you not to follow me?" he said, angrily.

"I don't remember."

"Yes you do."

"All right, then I do."

"You turn round very carefully and go back," he ordered.
"Be careful. . . . You'll turn my hair gray!"

"That'd make you very handsome and distinguished
looking," replied Janey.

"Go back!" he shouted, sternly.

"Not on your life!" retorted Janey, and started to crawl
again. She was approaching the narrowed part. It might
have daunted her before, but now she could have managed
a more hazardous place.

"*Stop! Turn back!*" thundered Randolph.

This was pouring oil upon the flame.

"You go to the devil!" cried Janey, and kept on crawling. She passed the risky point without a tremor or a slip, and presently, reaching the bench, she stood up before Randolph in cool triumph.

"If you do that again, I'll—I'll—" he choked.

"That was a cinch," replied Janey, coolly. "My stockings are thin, though, and the rock hurt my knees."

She rubbed them ruefully, quite unabashed by Randolph's staring.

"You'll fall and kill yourself," he stormed.

"No, nix, never, not little Janey. I did tumbling in my class at college. That little jaunt across there was just an exercise in co-ordination, that's all."

"I tell you it was extremely dangerous," expostulated Randolph.

"We'll always disagree, Phil. I imagine life together for us will be one long sweet hell."

"No it won't. I might have entertained such an idiotic idea once, but it's dispelled."

"We needn't discuss the future now. I've begun to reconcile my—myself to this and you. Don't spoil it. . . . Did you have a nice dig this morning?"

"Come. I'll help you back over this ledge. Then you go to camp and stay there," he said, peremptorily.

"No, I won't. I want to be with you."

"Very sorry, but I don't want you here."

"Why? I'll sit still and watch you, and be quiet."

"No."

"Please, Phil," she pleaded.

"I couldn't work with your big eyes mocking me. You make me remember I'm only a poor struggling archaeologist."

"But you brought me here."

"Yes, and I'd—I'm damned sorry for it. Someday I'll tell you why I did it."

"Are you repudiating your—your, well, your interest in me?" she queried, with hauteur.

"Call spades, spades," he returned. "You mean my love for you. No, I don't repudiate that. I'm not ashamed of it, though it has made me a fool."

"Oh! Then there's another reason why you brought me to Beckyshibeta?" she went on, gravely. It seemed to Janey that there was no use in trying to stall off the inevitable. Things tumbled over one another in a hurry to drive her. Pretty soon she would get sore and face them.

"Yes, there's another, and of *that* I am ashamed. But come, get out of here and leave me in peace."

"Mr. Randolph," said Janey, now haughtily. "Has it occurred to you that I ought not to be left alone—entirely aside from my loneliness?"

"No, it hasn't," he returned, clenching his hands, and gazing helplessly down at the river.

"Well, you're rather dense. Some Indian or desperado—anybody might come. They could get across now, I think."

"No one ever comes here. At least, very seldom, and then I know they're coming. You're quite safe. And certainly you don't want my society."

"It is rather dreadful. But I'll stand it awhile. I'll stay here until you get ready to go back to camp," replied Janey, airily, and she promptly sat down.

Randolph took her hand and pulled at her.

"Come," he said, trying to control his temper.

"Let go, or we'll have another fight," she warned. "The other time I didn't hit below the belt or bite."

He gave up. "Very well, if you're that mulish, stay. But look here, you spoiled brat—if you cross this dangerous place again you'll be sorry."

"Why will I?" asked Janey, immensely interested.

"Because you'll get what you should have had—long ago and many a time."

"And what's that, teacher?"

"A damned good spanking."

Janey could not believe him serious, yet he looked amaz-

ingly so. But that was only temper—a bluff to rout her utterly. It was so preposterous that she laughed in his face.

"Mr. Randolph, pardon my laughing, but you are so
crude—so original," she said, and here the Janey Endicott
of Long Island spoke in spite of her.

Perhaps nothing else she could have said would have
stung him so bitterly.

"I have no doubt of it. All the same, I meant what I said.
We are in Arizona now. And if you can't see the difference
between real life and modern froth, I'm sorry for you. Most
of America is too far gone for a good, healthy spanking. It
has, I might say, a vastly different kind of interest in a
young woman's anatomy. But among the few pioneers left
in the West, thank God, there are parents who are still
old-fashioned. I'm not a parent. All the same I can make
myself into one, and give you damn well what you need."

He strode away to his work leaving Janey for once at a
loss for words. It took some moments for Janey to recover
her egotism. Randolph must be having hallucinations. She
would put him to the test presently.

Sauntering closer to the middle of the wide bench, where
he was plying his pick, she found as restful a seat as appeared available. It would tantalize him to have her so
near, watching, as he called it, with her mocking eyes. She
confessed to herself, however, that her interest in his work
was growing keenly sincere. She truly wanted him to find
Beckyshibeta.

"Phillip, how will you know when you strike this buried
pueblo?" she asked, suddenly. "What will it be like?"

"I'd know the instant I struck my pick in it," he replied,
with surprising animation. Randolph evidently was quick to
recover from anger or slight.

"You would, of course, but how would I know?"

He gave her a depreciating glance.

"Well, judging by the intelligence you've shown lately,
you never would know a pueblo. Not if you fell into a kiva!"

"Ah—huh! Gee, I'm a bright girl. . . . What's a kiva?"

"It's a deep circular hole in the ground, covered by a roof, with an entrance. Used by the cliff dwellers—"

Janey interrupted him. All she had to do was to ask a question of an archaeological nature and he forgot everything else.

"Then if you disappear suddenly I'm to search for your remains in a kiva? Very appropriate end for you, I'd say."

Randolph went back to work and though Janey pestered him with questions he apparently did not hear them. She grew provocative. He gave no heed. Then she called him mummy hunter, grave robber, bone digger and like names. Finally, she resorted to "cradle snatcher," but that glanced off his thick hide, too.

"Say," she concluded in disgust, "if I offered to kiss you, would you talk?"

"Yes," he flashed, swiftly facing her with a gleam in his eye.

"Oh! Well, I withhold the offer, but I'm glad you're not altogether a dead one."

"Janey Endicott, you're an unmitigated fraud," he returned. "Also, you are a teaser."

"I don't like the sound of that last word. Where did *you* hear that?"

"It's a term I heard in New York. I gathered that it was applicable to a young woman who enticed with false smiles and words and suggestions. Who allured with all feminine —I should say female—powers and never gave a single thing she promised."

"Phillip, you are calling a turn on all women from Eve to Mata Hari. . . . Say," she burst out suddenly, "I'll bet you a new saddle to a pair of gauntlets that I make you swallow your slight."

"You're on Miss Endicott," he declared. "I'll enjoy riding that saddle, and remembering this winter, while you are back in New York—"

"Doing what?" she interposed, as he hesitated.

But he dropped his head and returned to his interrupted digging.

"I'll finish it for you," she added with scorn. "While I am idling, flirting, dancing, sleeping away the beautiful sunrise hours, wasting money, drinking—and worse!"

She saw him flinch, then his jaw set, but that was all the satisfaction she got. Janey had an unreasonable longing to hear him passionately deny at least some of these vices for her. But he did not. He believed them—perhaps now thought the very worst of her. This was what she had desired, yet most inconsistently, she would have preferred him to defend her as he had to her father.

Janey let him alone for a while, although her contemplative gaze often returned from the lofty crags and wonderful walls to his strong, stooping figure, and his tireless labor.

When the enchantment of the canyon began once more to lay hold of her, with its transforming magic, she had recourse to a very devil of perversity and provocation. Studying the ledges and slopes of all this great section of ruined wall she at last noted a narrow strip where even a goat might have had difficulties. It led toward another projecting corner of red wall, beyond which another and larger level beckoned with a strange spell. Janey studied the place a long time. She had reason to believe that Randolph had not worked any farther than where he now stood. She yielded to an unaccountable impulse to gain that level.

Rising, she took occasion to stroll around in front of Randolph, then up to the edge of the amphitheater and in the direction of a rounded wall which led toward the objective point.

The ring of Randolph's pick ceased. Janey missed it with infinite satisfaction.

"Janey, where are you going?" he demanded. "Didn't I—"

She crossed the rim of curved wall and gained the near end of the narrow strip. How fearful the depth below looked.

"Hold on!" yelled Randolph, his boots thudding over the rock.

Then Janey turned. "Don't dare come another step!" she cried, more than defiantly.

Randolph halted short, perhaps a matter of fifty steps from her.

"Please, come back."

"I'm going across to the next bench."

"Janey! That is worse than this other place. I have never risked beyond where you are now. Honest. It is more treacherous than it looks."

"I don't care."

"My God, girl, if you should slip! Have you no sense?"

"You'll have only yourself to blame."

Randolph struggled as if resisting a temptation to leap. He was silent a full moment. Janey saw his expression and color change.

"You damned little fool!" he roared, at last. *"Come back!"*

"Nothing doing, Phil," she taunted.

"Come back!" The stentorian voice only inflamed Janey the more.

"Say, how'd you get like that?"

Randolph started for her and strode halfway round the curved rim wall before he halted. Janey backed upon the narrow strip, an exceedingly risky move, but her blood was up and she had no fear. He saw and stopped as if struck.

"Janey, darling," he called, with an importuning, almost hopeless, gesture.

This, strangely, came near being Janey's undoing. She wanted to obey him. Never could she be driven, but she was not tenderness-proof. Her sudden incomprehensible weakness roused her to fury.

"Philly, sweetheart, you've kidnaped the wrong woman!" she screamed at him.

Randolph deliberately wheeled and went back to the bench. Facing her then he called out: "Go and be damned. You'll find out you can't fly. And you'd better stay over there, for if you ever come back, you'll pay for this."

Thus inspired, Janey turned to the narrow strip. It would not have frightened her if it had been a beanpole

across Niagara. Sure as a mountain sheep she stepped, and
never got down on hands and knees until she reached the
knifelike edge. Over this she crawled like a monkey. She
stood up again and ran the rest of the way. Gaining the
bench she went for a peep round the vast corner of wall.
The most wonderful of all the caverns opened before her.
It was stupendous, overpowering. How marvelous to come
back again and explore! Whereupon she retraced her steps.

Randolph remained as motionless as a statue watching
her. On the return, Janey exercised coolness where at first
she had been daring. She crawled most of the way and
never looked down into the abyss once. Breathless and hot
she rested a moment before taking to the rim wall, then
walked across that to where Randolph stood waiting. She
saw that he was white to the lips, but he wheeled before
she could get a second look at his face. It seemed silly to
follow him, but she did, wondering what he would do or
say. He led the way back toward camp.

Janey had not anticipated this. Had she gone too far?
Had she hurt him irretrievably? And now that it was over
she reproached herself. What a spiteful vengeful little fool
she was! Still this was the part she had set herself to play.

She had difficulty in keeping up with Randolph. She kept
up on the easy level ground, but over the rock slides she
fell behind. It seemed a long way back to camp. Excitement
and exertion had told on her. When the last corner of wall
had been passed Janey thought she was pretty well all in.

Randolph had his back to her. How square his shoulders
—rigid! He pivoted on his heels, to disclose terrible eyes.

"Janey Endicott, do you remember what I told you?" he
demanded.

Swift as his words came a sensation of sickening weakness. Like a stroke of lightning it had come. She imagined
she had been prepared, but she was not. She had mis-
judged him, underestimated his courage. Her subtle mind
grasped at straws.

"Re-member?" she faltered, trying to smile. "About being
—mad about me?"

"Mad *at* you!" he replied, grimly.

Then he seized her before she could move a hand. Surprise and fear inhibited her natural fighting instinct. Randolph lifted her—carried her.

Suddenly he sat down on the flat rock and flung her over his knees, face down. All her body went rigid. A terror of realization and horror of expectation clamped her mind. He spanked her with such stunning force that it seemed every bone in her body broke to the blow. The pain to her flesh was hot, stinging, fierce. The shock to her mind exceeded the sum of all shocks Janey had ever sustained. She sank limp over his knees. Smack! Harder this time. Her head and feet jerked up. Her teeth jarred in their sockets. Again! *Again! Again!*

Janey all but fainted. Intense fury saved her that. She rolled off his knees to the ground and bounded up like a cat. A bursting tearing gush of hot blood ran riot in her breast.

"I'll—kill—you!" she panted, low and deep.

Randolph was somewhat shaken at her fury, when she blazed so fiercely, her fists clenched, her breast swelling.

"Once in your life, *Miss* Endicott!" he said, huskily. "It's done. You can't change that. And *I* did it. I shall have that unique distinction among your acquaintances."

Janey tried to fly at him, to scratch his eyes out, to beat him before murdering him. But she let him pass. She felt her legs sag under her. Blindly then she groped and crawled up to her bed, sank under the blankets and covered her face. The tension of her body relaxed. She stretched limp, palpitating, quivering. That numb dead sensation gradually gave place to burning smarting pain. The physical suffering at first had precedence over the chaos of her mind. Hot tears streamed down her cheeks. And she lay there panting, slowly succumbing, her spirit subservient to her tortured flesh.

It was dark when she had to uncover her head to keep from suffocating. The bright shadows of a campfire flickered on the stone above her.

"Janey, child," called Randolph, like a fond parent, "wash your face and hands and come to supper."

Her blood leaped and boiled again. Rising on her hand, she was about to give passionate vent to all the profanity she had ever heard, but as she saw Randolph moving round the fire she stilled the impulse. She sank back under a compulsion she had never known. Was she beaten—whipped —cowed? No! She had only been preposterously shamed and humiliated by an educated ruffian. Her pride had been laid low. Her vanity was bleeding to death. Janey writhed in her bed, only to be made painfully aware again of the maltreated part of her anatomy. The instant there was a possibility of her returning to the old Janey Endicott, that burning pain had to recur. What a strangely subduing thing! Her mind had no control over it or the whirling thoughts it engendered.

She composed herself at last, in as comfortable a position as she could find. Again Randolph called her to supper. Eat! She would starve to death before she would eat anything he had prepared. How terribly she hated him! The revenge she had planned seemed nothing to her wild ragings now. Mere killing would not be enough. Death ended all sufferings. He must be made most horribly wretched. He must grovel at her feet and bite the very dust.

These bitter thoughts had their sway. They did not have permanence. All of a sudden Janey discovered she was crying. To realize that, to fight it and fail, added to her breakdown. She cried herself to sleep.

Her eyes opened upon azure blue sky and gold-tipped wall. Consciousness came as quickly as sight. Her impulse was to shut out the beautiful light of day. She was ashamed to face it. But slowly she moved the blanket aside. Listening, she soon ascertained that Randolph was not in camp. Peeping over the rock she saw a smoldering fire, and the steaming coffeepot and oven on it.

Janey got up. If she had needed anything to remind her of the insufferable outrage she had sustained, she had it in sudden pains, more excruciating than any she had yet en-

dured. The ape! He had not realized his strength. Maybe
he had, though. How coldly and calmly he had gone about
the beating! To wait until they had come all the way back
to camp! In the light of another day his offense seemed
greater.

There was her breakfast on the fire. Janey remembered
that she had sworn she would starve before she would
touch Randolph's food again, but she did not see any
sense in that now. As a cook she was not a genius.

"If there was a mantelpiece here it's a cinch I'd eat my
breakfast off it this morning," she said, mirthlessly.

Dark, brooding thoughts attended the slow meal. Afterward it occurred to Janey to wash the few utensils Randolph had left for her use. There was a pan of hot water
at hand. This she did and not without an almost conscious
gratification. Then she stared awhile into the fading red
coals of the fire. Next she walked in the sun, and could
not shut out a sense of its warmth, of the sweet songs of
wild birds, of the fragrance of sage and canyon thicket, of
the glorious light under the walls.

What was she going to do? There were a thousand things.
But first, and of absolutely paramount importance, was the
fact dawning upon her that she had to repeat the fool-
hardy act of yesterday. A new vague sweet self raised soft
voice against it, but was howled down by Janey Endicott
proper. She had to show Randolph that this so-called cave-
man dominance of the past, as well as the masculine su-
periority of the present, were things abolished, obsolete,
blazed out of the path by modern woman. This was no part
she was playing. She had ceased to be an actress. That
fun, that desire to turn the tables upon her father and
Randolph had vanished in the night.

Randolph was at work higher up than the day before and
close to the amphitheater around which Janey had crossed
to the next bench.

She walked right past him, casually glancing in his direc-

tion. How could he guess that her heart was beating fast
and that contending tides of emotion warred within her?

If she ever saw a man surprised it was then. The last
thing Randolph would imagine was that she would come
back. What sweet healing balm to Janey's crushed vanity!
He leaned on his pick and watched her. Would he order
her back? Would he plead with her again?

Janey was not foolish enough to underestimate the risk
of this slanting narrow trail. This time, her nerve and
caution, and lightness of foot, balanced the audacity of
yesterday. She crossed without a slip.

Randolph stood leaning on his pick, watching. Not a
word had come from him! She could guess, of course, that
he was completely routed, and probably furious. But was
he disappointed? That she was an irresponsible child!
Janey tossed her head. What did she care? Something hot
seared her and she accepted it as hate.

Once round the huge buttress of wall, out of Randolph's
sight, she forgot him. Here was an amphitheater that
dwarfed the Coliseum at Rome, and it was set against a
background of magnificent forbidding walls. How silent!
Janey felt that she was alone in a sepulcher. Her steps
led her high, so high she marveled and thrilled, and trembled sometimes at the gigantic fissures and the leaning
cliffs.

Suddenly she spotted what appeared to be little steps cut
in the rock. She was astounded, could not believe her eyes.
But there they were, one after another, worn, scarcely dis-
tinguishable in the smooth stone. They had been cut by
hand. Intensely absorbed, Janey mounted them, forgetting
the fear of high places and crumbling walls.

Presently she lost the little steps. She halted, breathless
and flushed. Evidently she had climbed far. Before her
spread a level bench most wonderful in its location and
isolation. To look back and down made her gasp. How
would she ever descend?

Her quick eye grasped at once that this wide protected
bench could be reached only by the slope up which she had

climbed. Suddenly it dawned upon her that the predominating feature of this place was its inaccessibility. These little steps had been cut by cliff dwellers! Her heart beat faster than ever. She had discovered something. If Randolph had known of this place surely he would have told her.

Janey began to explore. In the smooth rock she found round polished holes where grain had been ground centuries before. She found the stone pestles lying as if a hand had laid them aside only yesterday. She found the edge of a wall buried in debris. Little red stones, neatly cut and cemented! High up she sighted a cliff dwelling pasted like a mud wasp's nest against the shelf of rock. She had thought this amphitheater level, but it was not. It began to look as if a great space had been buried by avalanche or the weathering processes of ages. It would take days to explore it.

Janey stepped into a hole up to her knee. It appeared to her the ground had given way under her. Pulling her leg out she was overcome to discover that she had stepped through a roof over something. Carefully she brushed aside the dirt and dust. She found poles of wood, close together, and as rotten as punk.

"Ah—huh! That's something," she ejaculated.

The hole made by her foot stared at her like a black eye. It spoke. Janey began to thrill and shake. She dropped a little stone in it. No sound! She tried a large stone. She heard it strike far down. Then this was a kiva. Well? Then Janey's mind bristled into action. "Beckyshibeta!" she whispered, in awe.

She sat down, suddenly overcome. She had discovered the ancient pueblo for which Randolph had been searching so diligently. It stunned her. How strange! What luck! There seemed a destiny in the willfulness that had led her to this place. It must be more than chance.

Then she remembered boasting to Randolph that she would find Beckyshibeta for him. She had done so. She had not a single doubt. And suddenly her joy equaled her amazement and transcended it. What a perfectly wonderful thing for Randolph. She was so happy she laughed and cried at once. It was not a delusion. Here opened the black mysterious eye of a kiva.

Janey was consumed with only one desire. To tell Randolph! She climbed, she ran. The little steps cut in the stone slope had no terror for her now. In bad places she sat down and slid, unmindful of her dress or skin. Yet how long it took to get down. Once on the bench below she could not go fast. It was too rough. And at that she got more than one knock from a rock. At last she got round the last corner of wall, out of breath, panting so that she had to rest a moment.

Randolph was there, digging, digging, digging. Presently he would have something to dig for. With her breast heaving, Janey watched him. The moment was somehow rich, sweet, beautiful, far reaching and inscrutable. Then she cupped her hands and called through them piercingly.

"Mr.—Randolph."

He heard her, for he straightened up, looked, and then resumed work with his pick.

"Come! Come over!" called Janey. He looked again, but did not reply.

"Phillip. Come over!"

Here he quit his labors and leaned upon his pick, evidently nonplused.

"Phil! Please come!" shrilled Janey.

"No. Not. Never. Nix!" he called, imitating her.

"Phil, I want you," she went on.

"Nothing doing."

"If you come over—you—you—you'll have the surprise of your life."

"I don't care for your kind of surprises, Miss Endicott," he replied after a jarring pause.

"But you will, I tell you."

"Not on your life!"

"Honest. Only come," she called, now pleadingly.

No answer. Randolph stood like a statue. Janey could hardly contain herself any longer. He was making it so

perfectly wonderful for her. What a climax! She must lead
him to her discovery. In her excitement she was quite
capable of going to unheard-of limits to accomplish her
purpose. Beckyshibeta had changed the world for Janey.
She had no time to stop to analyze the transformation.

"I'll make you happy, Phil," she trilled, persuadingly.

"You've got another guess coming, Miss Endicott," he
said.

What a stubborn creature a man could be anyway! And
this one with his dream of ambition waiting for him!
Janey had a wild notion that she might include herself in
the finding of Beckyshibeta. Assuredly there was need of
her discovering herself now.

"Phillip, dear. Come," she called, despairingly.

"I *told* you not to go over there," he answered. "Now you
can get back by yourself."

"I'm terribly scared, Phillip. I—I've sort of found out—
something."

"Fly over," he replied, mockingly.

"Is that nice—when I want you?"

"Janey Endicott, every word you utter is a lie."

"No. I've stopped lying. Come and see."

"I tell you I'm as unmovable as these rocks," he shouted,
in a tone that signified considerable strain.

He just imagined he was, thought Janey, but still he
might carry his stubbornness to a point of spoiling her
little plan. Nevertheless, if she could not move him now,
she would have the pleasure of keeping it secret longer.

"Phil, dearest," she called.

"You go to the devil!" he yelled, using her very words,
but his tone was vastly different.

"My darling!" cried Janey, at the end of her rope. If that
did not fetch him!

Randolph desperately jumped into the hole he had been
digging. She could see his pick move up and down, with
speed that implied tremendous effort. Janey realized that
her plan was useless for the time being, so she decided she
had better husband her resources and attack him later.

What she could not accomplish at such long range would
be easy enough by close contact.

Whereupon she stepped out on the narrow strip. As she
did so her eye, for the first time, caught the perilous depth
and the jagged rocks far beneath. Janey stepped back with
a sudden cold sensation. Life might have grown singularly
full all at once, but death was still only a step away. But
she was not one to lose her head during excitement.

She crossed this dangerous bridge with coolness and
courage, taking no chances, and unmindful of her sore
knees. She made it successfully.

Randolph's back was turned. She approached and hiding
behind a large rock, peeped out at him. For what seemed
long moments he did not look. But at last he straightened
up and gazed around evidently to see where she had
gone. Janey took good care to keep hidden. She was tingling all over. He concluded that she had passed him and
gone on out of sight. Then he sat down on the edge of
the hole, removed his sombrero and wiped his face. He
sat there idle, lost in thought. How sad his expression! His
trouble in this unguarded moment was there to read. Janey
conquered her impulse to rush out and tell him, there
were at least a couple of reasons why he should be tickled
to death. But the moment gave her a glimpse into his heart.
And it stirred Janey so deeply, so strangely that she wished
to escape being seen by Randolph. At length, wearily and
without hope, he looked again in the direction he supposed
Janey had taken, and then resumed his work. Janey slipped
away noiselessly and rounded the corner of wall without
being seen.

Soon she yielded to a desire to sit down and think about
herself. What had happened? She went over it all. Where
had vanished the delight, the inexplicable joy she had anticipated? Randolph's sad face had checked her, changed
the direction of her thoughts. She felt so sorry for him
that she wanted to weep. Resuming her journey back to
camp she went on a little way, then stopped again. Something was wrong. Her breast seemed oppressed, her heart

too full. She felt it pound. Surely she had not exerted herself enough for that. No—the commotion was emotional. She had sustained an unaccountable transition. She was no longer the old Janey Endicott. A last time she sat down to fight it out—to face her soul. After all—how easy! Only to be honest! For the first time in her life, she was honestly, deeply, truly in love. No need of wild wonderings, of whirling repudiations! She had fallen in love with this adventure, with the glorious desert, with the lonely soul-transforming canyons, and with Phillip Randolph.

The instant the solution flashed out of her brooding mind she knew it was the truth. It seemed annihilation of self-catastrophe, yet it held a paralyzing sweetness. Janey received the blow of her consciousness, like a soldier, full in the face, while she was gazing down the canyon, now magnifying its gold and purple, its wonderful speaking cliffs.

Then she heard the thud of hoofs. A horse! Startled, she turned the corner of the wall that separated her from camp. Her alarm vanished in amazement at sight of a dudish young man dismounting from a pinto mustang as flashy as its rider. He wore a ten-gallon sombrero that appeared to make him top heavy; white moleskin riding trousers, tight at the knees, high shiny boots and enormous spurs that tripped him as he walked. Janey then recognized this young man, Bert Durland, the darling of many week-end parties, a slick, dark, dapper youth just out of college. Also she heard more thuds of hoofs and voices coming. Cursing to herself, Janey slipped in behind a section of rock that had split from the cliff, and ran along it to the far end, where she crouched down to peep through a crack.

8

JANEY WAS AMAZED, curious, resentful at this rude disruption of her rapture. Bert was a nice kid, but to meet him here! Where she was alone with Randolph!

Two riders appeared above the bulge of the bench, off to the left. One was an Indian, leading a pack horse. Presently Janey made out the second rider to be a woman. Mrs. Durland! No human creature could have looked more out of place, or uncomfortable, or ridiculous. Mrs. Durland's marked characteristic had been dressing and playing a part to improve the family fortunes. Here, if Janey had not been suddenly furious, she could have shrieked. They approached camp. The Indian dismounted and began to slip the pack. Bert went to his mother's assistance. Manifestly it was no joke to get her off a horse. She was heavy, and looked as if her bones had stiffened.

"O mercy! My muscles—my flesh!" she wailed.

"Cheer up, Mother. We're here at last," replied Bert, with satisfaction.

"*This* is the place then?" she asked, peering round in disgust.

"Beckyshibeta."

"It looks like it sounds. I don't see much of a camp. Mr. Endicott said his daughter was here with some friends."

"Perhaps this is the guides' camp. We'll look around and find them. My word! It'll be good to see Janey!"

"Bert, our Indian is riding away!" exclaimed Mrs. Durland, in alarm.

"I understood he was going to see his family."

"Suppose he doesn't come back? Suppose we don't find Miss Endicott and party! Here we are in a godforsaken

118

hole a hundred and ninety miles from a railroad. Nothing but a lot of wild Indians around. We may get scalped."

"You needn't worry, Mother," returned Bert. "You'd never get scalped. You can take off your hair and hand it over. I'm the one to worry."

"Bert Durland! How dare you talk that way? You ought at least be respectful after my being good enough to let you drag me out here."

"Pardon, Mother," said the youth, contritely. "I'm sore. This beastly trip through all that horrible desert! And no sign of comfort here. It's most annoying."

"Whose fault is it?" queried Mrs. Durland, as she carefully looked round a rock to see if there were snakes or bugs present. Then very wearily she sat down.

"Yours," returned young Durland, looking at his drooping horse. "I suppose I'll have to remove that awful saddle."

"My fault? You miserable boy!" exclaimed his mother, highly indignant. "You know I'm doing it all for you. Chasing this worthless girl! I've suffered agonies on this ride. And that horrid place where we tried to sleep last night! Will I ever forget it? And this awful sunburn!"

"Janey isn't quite worthless, Mother dear," rejoined Bert, complacently. "Her dad has several millions. And Janey is pretty well fixed. You know that's why you're here."

"There's gratitude for you," declared Mrs. Durland, witheringly. "Here I am trying to make it easy for you. You who've gone through most of your father's money. Now you make it appear I'm doing this for myself."

"All right! All right!" said Bert, impatiently. "But don't blame me for bringing you on this particular wild-goose chase. I didn't like the idea, believe me. I told you in New York that Endicott was taking Janey to a tourist hotel. That's what I believed then."

"Didn't you say Janey told you her father was taking her into one of the loneliest places in the world?"

"I sure did. Mother, Arizona looks to me to be about half of the United States. And it's lonely all right, all right.

Imagine fine-combing this desert all to hunt up a girl!
That fellow who charged a hundred dollars for a car ride
that scrambled my insides! I'd like to get hold of him.
Mother, I've an idea Endicott and that trader Bennet were
laughing at us up their sleeves."

"Humph! That dirty-looking trader laughed in my face,"
asserted Mrs. Durland. "And as for the wasting of a whole
hundred dollars—that's your fault, too. You never knew
how to bargain. You just threw money away. It drives me
mad. You have no backbone, no stamina. Otherwise you'd
have eloped with Janey before her father ran off with her
to this terrible place of rocks."

"Eloped! My dear Mother, you don't know Janey Endicott," returned her son, significantly.

"Perhaps we'd better not talk so loud or mention names,"
remarked Mrs. Durland, apprehensively.

"Didn't you try to tell that Indian guide and the car
driver our family history? . . . Hello! Here comes a white
man! Tough-looking customer!"

"Oh, dear, I hope he isn't a desperado," replied Mrs. Durland, in alarm.

This last from mother to son tickled Janey so keenly that
she was hard put to it to keep from side-splitting laughter.
She peeped round the edge of her covert. Yes, Phil was
coming. He had spied the visitors, and he was peering everywhere for Janey.

"How do you do," greeted Randolph, as he came up.
"Your Indian told me of your arrival."

"Very nice of him to find someone," returned Mrs. Durland, gratefully.

"Whom have I the pleasure of addressing?"

"Mrs. Percival Smith Durland, of New York, and her son
Bertrand. Of course you've heard of us."

"I regret to say I never have."

Janey giggled inwardly at this slight, because she had
more than once told Phil about the Durlands.

"Indeed. I see. You've never been away from this raw
crude Arizona," replied Mrs. Durland, apologizing for his

ignorance. "Do many tourists come here to this Becky—something or other?"

"Very few. We don't encourage them."

"There, Mother. I told you so," broke in Bert, who had been staring hard at Randolph.

"Is there any resort for tourists near?" asked Mrs. Durland.

"Bennet's trading post is the nearest habitation of white folks. But you'd hardly call it a resort."

"I should say not. We stopped there to get ready for this trip. . . . May I ask your name?"

"Phillip Randolph, at your service, Madam."

"Randolph? Surely that's the name we heard. You're an archaeologist, I understand."

"Yes, Madam," returned Randolph, shortly.

"Work for the government, don't you?"

"Yes."

"And you're *the* Mr. Randolph. Well, I'm sorry for you. There's a Mr. Elliot at the post now. He came the day we arrived. He's from Washington, D.C. I heard Mr. Bennet say he was furious that you had gone to this Becky—place before the time scheduled, and it would likely cost you your job."

"Mr. Elliot at the post! Well, that is a surprise," returned Randolph, quite perturbed.

"I daresay. It's too bad. I'm sorry for you. But you might find decent work somewhere. You look stronger than those bowlegged cowboys."

"Thank you. Yes, I think I am rather strong. You spoke of cowboys. Were they—did you see any round the post?"

"Cowboys! I rather think so. They nearly rode us down. Stopped our car to keep us from being killed by stampeding cattle. One of them was tow-headed, and pretty fresh, to say the least."

"Cattle stampede! Oh, Lord!" muttered Randolph, in distress.

"What did you say?" asked Mrs. Durland.

"I—I was just talking to myself," replied Randolph, hastily.

"We are looking for Miss Janey Endicott and her party," interrupted Bert, with importance. "I'll give you ten dollars to guide us to her camp."

"There you go, Bert Durland, flinging money to the four winds," declared his mother.

"Miss Janey Endicott and party!" echoed Randolph.

"That's what I said," returned the young man, testily. "Mr. Endicott informed me. I'm a very dear friend of Janey's—in fact of the family."

"Did Endicott say how many were in the—party?" inquired Randolph.

"No. I gathered there were several. People from the post. Where are they camped?"

"Not here. I have not seen any—party. Do you mean you've ridden all the way out here to see Miss Endicott?"

"Certainly. Do you know her?" replied Bert, suspiciously.

"I think I've seen the young woman," said Randolph, dryly.

"You haven't. Any man who ever saw Janey Endicott wouldn't *think* he'd seen her. He'd never forget her."

"Oh, excuse me, perhaps I'm wrong. The person I saw was about twenty, and acted fifteen, and dressed as if she were ten. Very coy and vivacious, and wild, I may say. She was not bad looking."

"Miss Endicott is strikingly beautiful, one of the loveliest girls in New York," returned young Durland, grandly.

The expression on Phil's face made Janey want to shout with glee.

Mrs. Durland had been looking at the bits of broken pottery and stone utensils which lay carefully arranged on a flat rock.

"Is this the kind of bric-a-brac you dig for?" she inquired. "You appear to be careless with it."

"It's broken when we find it, Madam. I could not be careless with such priceless relics."

"Priceless? That lot of junk!" interposed Bert, in amazement.

"We would like to see a little of your—your place here," said Mrs. Durland, graciously. "Then I will engage you to find Miss Endicott's camp for us."

"Beckyshibeta is very dangerous," returned Randolph. "You have to climb over rough rocks."

"Excuse me from climbing. But we'll take a look. Come, son."

"I don't care anything about Bechyshib—or Beckysharp," responded Bert. "I want to see Janey Endicott."

"What! After our long journey out here to see this wonderful place?"

"You called it beastly before Professor Randolph dropped in," replied Bert, scornfully.

"Oh, dear, this generation. No appreciation of art or love of the beautiful!"

"I'll have a look up the canyon to see if Miss Endicott—and party—are camped near," said Randolph, moving away with Mrs. Durland.

Bert unsaddled his horse. Janey, convinced that the Durlands would find her sooner or later, preferred to surprise Bert. So she took advantage of his occupation with horse and saddle to run back the way she had come. Then she boldly turned round the corner. Durland was sauntering here and there, inspecting the camp, plainly nonplused. Presently he heard Janey's step and wheeled.

"Oh!" cried Janey, starting back.

"Janey!" he burst out, rapturously. "What luck! By heaven, I'm glad to see you!"

"Young man, you frightened me," returned Janey. "What are you doing here?"

Suddenly his gaze took in her apparel and his eyes popped. Janey had not realized until that moment what a scarecrow she must look like.

"Janey Endicott! Good Lord! What a getup *you've* got on! You look like a ballet dancer. Mother will have a fit! . . . Why, you look . . ."

"See here, boy, you're pretty impudent."

"Why all the bluff, Janey?" he asked with a laugh. "It's great to see you again, even if you are a sight to make Park Avenue weep."

He approached her with outstretched arms and unmistakable intention.

"Don't you dare. I'll yell for my husband," cried Janey.

"Husband? Now look here. This sounds serious."

"I said my husband."

"Janey Endicott with a husband! Impossible!"

"I'm Mrs. Phillip Randolph, wife of the archaeologist in charge of the excavation here!"

"Wife? Phillip Randolph? . . . Good God! But you're Janey Endicott. Your father said you were here."

"You're crazy. Who are you and what are you doing here?"

"No, I'm not crazy, but you are."

Janey pointed imperiously down the canyon. "Take your horse and get out of here."

"Janey Endicott, you can't stall me like that," he replied, hotly. "I've come clear across the country to rescue you from your father. This is how I find you! It has a damn queer look!"

His eyes held a sharp suspecting glint of anger and jealous doubt.

"Poor boy!" said Janey, solicitously. "You must have gotten away from your keeper. There! There! Run along and find him."

Bert pointed to Janey's left hand. "If you're Mrs. Randolph, where's your wedding ring?"

"In the years I've lived here with my husband, I never saw the like of you," declared Janey. "Either you're an escaped lunatic or a college freshman—trying to impersonate Hopalong Cassidy. I'm going to call my husband."

"Go ahead. It'll be great when Mother sees you. Janey, it's your wheels that are twisted, not mine." Then he seemed to become genuinely concerned. "You know, Janey, you do look strained and queer. My God! You might have lost your memory!"

Janey backed away trying to elude him, but he moved to stand in front of her.

"No, you won't escape that way. I'm going to make you remember."

"Let me by!" cried Janey, wildly. She was really possessed with an infernal glee. What would Phil say to this? "Get out, or I'll have my Phil take care of you."

"Janey, dear, you're strange. Your eyes. Try to concentrate. I'm Bert. Bert Durland. Something terrible has been done to you or you'd remember me and how I love you. Why I couldn't hurt a hair of your lovely head."

Janey kept maneuvering for a loophole to dodge through.

"If you touch me I'll scream!"

Bert made a lunge and captured her, and before Janey could thwart his intention he had grasped her hand and looked at her ring. "There! You *are* Janey Endicott. I know that diamond as well as if it were my own. It was a present from your father."

"Stop mauling me," cried Janey, breaking free from him. "I don't know you. I never saw you in my life!"

"You do it well, Janey, if you're not truly mad. I'm afraid there's something behind all this, young lady, and I'm going to find out."

Indeed there was, Janey thought; and never in her wildest flights of imagination could she have planned anything so good. She almost wanted to hug Bert for happening along at this opportune hour. Then voices drew Bert's attention and he hurried to meet Randolph, of whom Janey caught a glimpse among the cedars. She ran up the rock slope to hide in a niche where she could not be easily discovered. When she got herself satisfactorily crouched she peeped out with eyes that fairly danced. This was better than any comedy she had ever seen. Bert and Randolph were approaching. Randolph had a baffled look. His sweeping gaze about camp explained to Janey one of the reasons

he was so concerned. She wondered what had become of
Mrs. Durland.

Bert viewed the desert camp in dismay.

"I'll be damned!" he ejaculated.

"Will you please produce the young lady?" demanded
Randolph, stiffly.

"She's gone."

"My dear young fellow, she was never here."

"I tell you she was," retorted Durland, angrily. "Janey,"
he yelled. "You come back here. This has gone far enough."

"I agree with you," said Randolph.

"She was here. I talked with her, though she denied she
was Janey. She looked awful. Her clothes were soiled and
torn—dress up to her neck. Most disgraceful! And either
her reason's gone or she's a clever actress."

At this point Mrs. Durland appeared, red and puffing.

"Bert—this Mr. Randolph—talks strange," she panted.
"He left me a few minutes ago most unceremoniously.
There's no other camp. Janey isn't here."

"Yes she is, Mother. Or she was a moment ago," asserted
Bert, positively. "But now she's gone."

"Gone! Where?"

"I haven't an idea. She just vanished."

"Why don't you find her? You've chased her long and far
—why not a little more? My son, you act queer."

"There you are," interposed Randolph, with exaggerated
conviction. "Why don't you chase this hallucination of
yours? . . . I'm sorry indeed to see a fine young fellow like
you, laboring under mental aberration."

"What?" snapped Bert.

Randolph turned to Mrs. Durland: "Have you ever had
your son under observation or er—examined, you know?"

"You—you—commoner! How dare you!" burst out Mrs.
Durland.

"Really, I don't mean offense. If he *was* all right then it's
the long ride, the heat, the loneliness of the desert. These
things act powerfully upon some persons, especially any
who are not strong mentally and physically."

Bert strode forward to confront Randolph with dark and angry mien.

"See here, Sir," he said, "cut that stuff. You're trying to string me. But you can't do it. I tell you there was a girl here not ten minutes ago. If she wasn't Janey Endicott then I *am* out of my head. But it was Janey, and it's she who is crazy. She doesn't know who she is. She forgot she's engaged to marry me."

"Engaged to you!" ejaculated Randolph, taken aback.

"Yes, to me. Ask Mother."

Randolph turned bewildered with a voiceless query.

"There was an understanding between my son and Miss Endicott," replied Mrs. Durland. "No formal announcement, but all their friends knew."

Randolph seemed stunned.

"Look here, Randolph," spoke up Bert, suddenly. "Are you a married man?"

"Certainly not," replied Randolph, surprised into the truth.

"So! That's it!" shouted Bert, triumphantly. "I've a hunch you're a damned villain. Wait until I find that girl!" He rushed to and fro, and finally disappeared round the corner.

"Mrs. Durland, don't you think I had better stop him?" queried Randolph, in real concern. "This canyon is a big place. He could get lost or fall off a cliff. He's so slim he could almost slip down into a gopher hole."

"I don't care what happens," complained Mrs. Durland. "I'm overcome at this shocking turn of affairs. I'm beginning to think Janey Endicott was here. The fools men make of themselves over that girl! . . . I wish I'd never come to your miserable old ruin. I'll crumble myself before I get away."

"Courage, Madam. All is not lost!"

"Stop calling me Madam," replied the woman, testily. "My name is Mrs. Durland."

"Pardon. . . . Shall I endeavor to locate your son before he . . ."

Bert hove in sight at that moment high up on the shelving rock. Janey had caught sight of him before the others, and she tried to melt into the niche. But she was a little too substantial. Part of her protruded and young Durland saw it.

"Aha!" he shouted, leaping down the slope. Janey wanted at least to show her face, because she was fighting a wild laugh, but as soon as Bert laid rough hands on her, she blazed with wrath.

"Here you are. Come out of it," he said exultantly. "Hey, you down there. I've found her."

"Let go of me, you—you . . ." cried Janey.

"You shameless thing! No wonder you can't face me. . . . Out you come!"

"Let go!—Phillip!" shrieked Janey, as Bert dragged her out. She wrenched free to glare at him.

"Durland, I'll knock your head off," called Randolph, loudly.

"So *he* is your party?" sneered Bert, in jealous contempt. "I'm on to you, Janey Endicott. This beats any stunt you ever pulled back East. Came out West for a real kick, eh? Well! Won't it sound sweet back home?"

"Yes, and you'll be just about the kind to blab about it," retorted Janey.

"Come on down here. You've got to face them," he said, snatching at her.

Durland did not release her even when they reached a level. In fact, he dragged her in a most undignified, if not actually brutal way, toward his mother.

"Phil!" cried Janey, in pain and mortification.

Randolph intercepted Durland and gave him a resounding slap that was certainly equivalent to a blow. Durland went down in a heap. His grand sombrero rolled in the dust.

"You blackguard!" screamed Mrs. Durland. "To strike my son! You'll suffer for this."

Bert got tangled up in his long spurs and with difficulty restored his equilibrium.

"Say, you young jackass," declared Randolph, coolly. "If you touch this young lady again, I'll take a real poke at you."

"Don't hit him, Phil," interposed Janey, trying to recover her humor. "I don't want his death on our hands."

Then ensued an awkward silence. Bert went from white to red. He brushed the dust from his immaculate riding breeches, and picked up the huge velvet sombrero. Meanwhile Mrs. Durland was staring in wide-eyed recognition at Janey.

"Well, Mother, do you know the young lady? Was I right or wrong?"

"Right, Bertrand," snapped Mrs. Durland.

Whereupon Bert turned to the others.

"Janey, I've got the goods on you," he said. "You needn't take the trouble to keep up the farce any longer. What I can't understand is that your father should tell us you were here."

"I can't understand that, either," replied Janey, soberly.

"He must have guessed it and hoped I'd rescue you," went on Bert. "Or else he saw you gone beyond redemption."

"That probably is it, Bert," said Janey, with sweet meekness.

Randolph appeared the most uncomfortable of the four, although Mrs. Durland was getting ready to explode.

"Anyway, it's too late," concluded Durland, with bitterness.

"Randolph, you told me you were not married. 'Certainly not,'" you said.

"Yes, I—did," returned Randolph, haltingly, as if his mind was not working.

"There! Janey, *you* swore you were Mrs. Phillip Randolph, didn't you?" went on the accuser, bolder as he recognized he had the whip hand.

"Yes, I—did," returned Janey, bending terrible eyes upon Phillip.

"*Miss Endicott!*" burst out Mrs. Durland, in accents of horror. "You're here with this man *alone?*"

"Yes, but not willingly, Mrs. Durland," answered Janey, with profound sorrow. "He kidnaped me."

"Kidnaped you? Good heavens! Then he isn't what he pretends to be?"

"Indeed he isn't."

"Desperado—Wild West villain sort of man?" she whispered, huskily.

"Worse than that."

Durland had turned pale at this revelation. His distended eyes, fast upon Randolph, denoted both fear and anger.

"Your name isn't Randolph?" he queried, apprehensively.

"Looks as if my name is mud," returned Randolph, coming out of his stupefaction.

"Bert, the truth is he is Black Dick, a notorious character hereabouts," explained Janey.

"Black Dick!—I heard about him from the driver," rejoined Durland, apprehensively. "But, Janey, why did you try to deceive me about yourself? Why didn't you tell me in the first place who this man was?"

"It was the shame—the ignominy of it all, Bert," she said, enjoying Randolph's discomfort. "I knew he'd drive you off and I thought I could get away with that story. I'd rather have died out here than have—anyone know."

"And he actually kidnaped you?"

"Well, I just guess he did. Ambushed me when I was in camp with friends on the way here. He caught me alone. Seems he followed all the way from the post where he'd been watching me for days. He grabbed me. I fought with all my might. But he was too much for me. Tied me on a horse. Oh, it was awful! Look at these black-and-blue marks. These are *nothing* to others I have that I—I can't very well show you. I had to ride a whole day and night in the most terrible storm. When we got here I was more dead than alive."

"By heaven, it's like a book!" ejaculated Durland. "Kidnaped you for ransom? Heard about your dad's wealth, of course?"

"No, Bert, it isn't money he's after," declared Janey. "I

imagined that at first. And I offered to give him everything from ten to a hundred thousand dollars. But the brute would only laugh and kiss me again. Swears the minute he saw me at the post he went mad over me."

Bert's consternation and fright were strong, but he laughed—hysterically—nonetheless. He rocked to and fro.

"Ha! Ha! Ha! Ha! It was coming to you—Janey Endicott! Drove him mad? Ha! Ha! He's only one of many. Prefers making love to you to a hundred thousand bucks! . . . By golly, you've finally got the kick you were always longing for!"

"Bert, I deserve all I'm getting," rejoined Janey, sadly resigned.

"Why didn't your father get word of this? What is the matter with your friends?"

"I think they must have been captured by Black Dick's outfit and are being held."

"My God! And—and where is Randolph, the archaeologist? They said he was here."

Janey managed a convincing moan. "There was a Mr. Randolph, a wonderful man, but now he's—he's gone, and there's nobody but this vicious desperado left."

Bert turned white. "You mean—"

"Hush!" Janey almost screamed. "Don't remind me!"

All this time Randolph had been standing near gazing at them and absorbing the fantastic dialogue. He had assumed a most ferocious aspect; and Janey, after a second glance, thought it was genuine. Then, the Indian guide who had brought the Durlands, appeared riding through the cedars. Randolph strode to intercept him and spoke some Indian words in very loud and authoritative tones. The rider wheeled his horse and disappeared the way he had come.

"Look!" whispered Janey. "I told you. He's driven off your guide."

"Janey, I'll beat it and fetch a horse back to save you," whispered Bert, breathless with the excitement of the idea, and he made for his horse.

"Bertrand! Don't leave me!" screamed Mrs. Durland, who had been listening, pale and mute up to this minute.

Randolph also spotted Durland, and vigorously called him to come back. But Bert only went the faster. Whereupon Randolph pulled his gun and fired in the air. Bang! Bang!

"Come hyar," roared Randolph, "or I'll make a sieve out of you!"

Mrs. Durland gave a loud squawk and promptly fainted. Bert ran back, very wobbly and livid.

"D-don't kill me—Mr. Dick," he implored. Plain it was the two shots had brought him realization.

"All right then, but no monkey business," growled Randolph, flipping up the gun and returning it to his belt. "You better look after your mother. I reckon being strongheaded doesn't run in the family."

Whereupon Randolph strode toward Janey. She saw him coming and went in the opposite direction. Randolph caught up with her at the corner of the wall.

"Something of a mess, isn't it?" he said, quietly, as he detained her.

Janey sat down upon a flat rock and fastened solemn eyes upon him. There did not seem to be need of further pretense, for she was really distressed, yet she not only welcomed the facts of the case but also meant to keep on accentuating them.

"Phillip, you have ruined me," she said, tragically.

"Oh, Janey, it can't be as bad as all that," he protested.

"Why didn't you acknowledge me as your wife?" she asked.

"My God! I guess I just didn't think about it. Durland asked me if I was married. And I said, 'Certainly not.' He suspected, of course, and I was fool enough to fall into his trap."

"Bert knows many of my friends. He will talk."

"But he said you were engaged to marry him!" ejaculated Randolph.

"Nonsense! I never was. How could you believe it?"

"I'm afraid I could believe almost anything of you," he returned, in bitter doubt.

"That has been evident all along," she replied, aloof and cold. "But it does not mitigate your offense. . . . It might be possible to keep Bert from talking. But not Mrs. Durland. She's an old gossip. This little escapade of ours will kill her ambition to see me Bert's wife. She will get it through her thick head that it always was impossible. And she'll take her vindictiveness out on me. She'll ruin my reputation."

"How can she?" asked Randolph, miserably. "I thought modern girls didn't have reputations to lose."

"That's an hallucination of yours and my father's. Granted a certain freedom and license of modern life, it's true all the same that there are still limits. In her eyes, we've transgressed the most vital one."

"Not you, Janey. I'm the one to blame."

"That'll do me a lot of good, I don't think," rejoined Janey, dismally.

"But maybe we can carry out this idea of me being Black Dick. He's well known on the reservation. Travels round with a half-breed Piute. They've been known to hold up tourists. Perhaps I can carry the bluff through."

"You can try, surely. But in my opinion it's a forlorn hope. Besides the cowboys will trail us. You heard what Mrs. Durland said. The cowboys evidently changed their plans."

"Your father—er—or something may put them off the track," said Randolph, lamely.

"Father! Why, he'll *send* the cowboys after me," exclaimed Janey. "I declare I don't know where your wits are."

"If I ever had any they vanished when you appeared on my horizon. So did my peace! And now, I may add, my character, too, is gone."

"Nonsense! What is disgrace nowadays to a man?" retorted Janey, with supreme contempt. "You ran off with a girl! . . . It'll never hurt *you*. It'd make you more attractive—after I divorce you!"

"Divorce me?" echoed Randolph, feebly.

"Certainly. You'll have to marry me, at least, to make this stunt of yours halfway decent. Then I'll get a divorce."

"But if the Black Dick bluff should go over?" he asked, hopefully.

"Fine for the Durlands," replied Janey. "But I was thinking of the cowboys and the Bennets after the Durlands go. We can't fool those sharp-eyed Westerners. However, they may hang you. And I suppose that would save my reputation, if not the notoriety."

"Hang me! I wish to God they'd come and do it," returned Randolph. "I'm surely at the end of a rope right now."

"No such luck!" sighed Janey. "You may come out of it scot free. The woman pays."

"I—I'm most deperately sorry," said Randolph, wringing his hands. "I'd like to have—somebody—here to choke. . . . But it can't be so bad. We'll fool or muzzle these Durlands. As for the Westerners—well, they're not so free at gossip and Arizona is a long way from New York. You will—"

"Phillip, don't fool yourself," interposed Janey. "You've ruined me irretrievably."

Janey wished to drive this point home. She appeared to be having fair success, for he swore under his breath, and sitting down he covered his face with his hands.

"You're a fine brave kidnaper and desperado," said Janey. "Don't let the Durlands see you look like that."

He took no heed of her banter. "I've ruined you—and—and what am I? . . . When Elliot's word reaches headquarters I'll be done for."

"Well, suppose you are fired. You can go on your own. Wouldn't it be better for you to discover Beckyshibeta *now* than when you were employed by the government?"

"You talk like a child," he replied, wearily.

"Why?" inquired Janey, in lofty surprise. "I think I'm pretty gracious, considering."

"What do I care about Beckyshibeta?" he burst out, with sullen passion. "When you step out of my life there will be nothing left."

"That is sad—if true," she returned, with proper pity and constraint. "But you have only yourself to blame."

"Bah!"

"I respected you once—liked you," went on Janey, in merciless sweetness. "Now you have made me—hate you."

"I could expect nothing else," he said, lifting his head with dignity. "I am not asking your pity—or even your forgiveness."

"Oh, as to that, of course I could never forgive. One thing you've done, an angel herself could not forgive—though I don't quite fit into that category."

"Not quite," he responded, dryly, and stood up, hard and stern. "But what's to be done? We're up against these confounded friends of your."

"It'll be best to keep them here," replied Janey. "Until something turns up. Carry on the Black Dick bluff. Let's see what an actor you can be."

"I'm no actor. I couldn't deceive a child."

"You deceived me," protested Janey. "I imagined you gentle, kind—the very opposite to what you are. Be natural now. Be a brute to me, like you were. I'll play up to it. And make these Durlands pay for butting in on our—what shall I call it?—our canyon paradise. . . . Be a monster to Mrs. Durland, and scare the everlasting daylights out of that fortune-hunting young Romeo."

"That last will be easy," replied Randolph, grimly.

9

RANDOLPH'S PREOCCUPATION with himself interfered with his acting a part. But that very grim aloofness made him the more convincing and mysterious to the Easterners.

Durland was a picture of astonishment when he saw Janey staggering into camp under a load of firewood.

"Don't you do it, Janey," he begged. "I'll get the wood." And leaving his mother, who importuned him to stay, he started off with Janey.

"Hyar, girl, don't go traipsing out of my sight with that jackass," growled Randolph, in so natural a tone that Janey knew he was not masquerading.

Then while Bert went off alone, Janey approached Mrs. Durland.

"I've money and jewelry on my person," stated that lady, nervously. "Isn't that ruffian liable to steal them?"

"Sure. He'll search you presently," affirmed Janey.

"*Search me!*" gasped Mrs. Durland.

"I should smile," replied Janey, cheerfully.

"Has he searched you?"

"Not yet. But anyone could see I couldn't hide anything. I've so little on."

"If he does I'll—I'll expire in my tracks," declared Mrs. Durland, and she looked it.

Randolph yelled for Janey to come back to the fire.

"Does he mean me, too?" asked Mrs. Durland.

"You'll know when he means you. And for heaven's sake, obey him quick. He's an awful brute. Nothing for him to give you a good sound kick!"

"The unspeakable monster! Of all acts—to kick a lady. He should be flayed alive. . . . He beats, too?"

"Oh, often. I've learned to mind him promptly, and to keep my eye on him when he isn't occupied."

"What a horrible situation!" exclaimed Mrs. Durland. "I see him eying me now."

"Girl, come hyar," yelled Phil, loudly.

Janey hurried back to Randolph, who continued, still in a loud voice: "What're you plotting with that old dame?"

"I was only sympathizing with her," replied Janey.

Bert appeared, carefully carrying a few sticks of firewood, to avoid soiling his moleskin riding breeches. Randolph noted this and glared.

"Huh! 'Fraid of dirtying your pants," he snorted, and he snatched up a blackened frying pan and wiped it brusquely on Bert's breeches.

That, for the present, however, appeared to be the limit of Randolph's duplicity. He forgot again and lapsed into silence. Janey helped him get supper. She found it no easy matter to look dejected and frightened when she felt actually the opposite. She certainly could stand this situation for a while. It would only grow more absorbingly amusing and thrilling as time wore on. The Durlands were completely taken in. They were scared out of their wits. Janey realized that for the time being her reputation had been saved. But what if the cowboys came! Or anybody who really knew Randolph! Janey groaned at the very idea. She was somewhat dubious about the reaction of the cowboys, especially Ray, to this kidnaping stunt of Randolph's. But so long as they did not resort to violence she imagined their advent would heighten the interest. Cowboys, however, were an unknown quantity to her. It was quite possible that even she could not stop them in dealing what they might believe was summary justice to an offender of desert creed.

"Come and get it," called Randolph, most inhospitably.

"Get—what?" asked Mrs. Durland, startled. The suggestion in those words and tone did not strike her happily.

"Grub—you tenderfeet!"

Randolph's mood had not hindered his capacity as a good cook, a fact to which the Durlands, once set down to the

meal, amply attested. For Janey, aside from satisfying honest hunger, the meal was otherwise a considerable success.
Conversation was lacking until toward the end of supper
Randolph told Mrs. Durland she would probably starve to
death and have her bones picked by coyotes.

"I opened your pack," he added, by way of explanation.
"You must have been going on a day's picnic."

"That Indian ate most of ours," ventured Bert.

"We can always get sheep," said Randolph to himself.

After supper he ordered the Durlands to make their beds
at the foot of the rock slope. Bert asked and obtained per-
mission to cut some cedar brush to lay under their blankets. Randolph gathered firewood, while Janey rested aside,
dreaming and watching. When the shadows of the canyon
twilight stole down, accentuating the loneliness, Randolph
stalked away.

"What a strange—desperado!" exclaimed Mrs. Durland.
"I think he must have been someone very different once.
That fellow has breeding. A woman can always tell."

"Black Dick is the most gentlemanly outlaw in these
parts," replied Janey. "Despite his habit of killing people,"
she added hastily.

"Janey, I apologize for all the nasty remarks I made,"
said Bert. "If we get out of this alive—why, everything can
be as it was before."

"Ah-huh," returned Janey, dreamily. Nothing could ever
be the same again. The future and the world had been
transfigured prodigiously. But she wanted the present to
last, even if she were compelled to stand for more love-
making from Bert Durland. The young man, however, was
still a little too perturbed over Black Dick to grow sentimental.

"Where does he sleep?" asked Mrs. Durland, anxiously.

"Black Dick? Oh, when he sleeps at all it's right here by
the fire. But he's an owl."

"Where's your bed?" asked Bert.

"Mine is high up on this ledge behind," replied Janey.

"Couldn't you let Bert fetch it down by ours?" inquired the mother.

"Black Dick might not like that."

A bright campfire dispelled the gloom under the cliff if not that in the minds of the captives. Janey, at last, stole away to be alone. Her heart was full—full of what she knew not. Yet some of it was mischief and a great overwhelming lot was a deep rich emotion that seemed strange and stingingly sweet. It threatened to take charge of her wholly; therefore, rebelliously, finding it real and true, not to be denied, she compromised by putting off resignation until later. Very difficult was it to crush down this feeling, to resist the most amazingly kindly feelings toward the Durlands, to scorn forgiving her poor old dad, who had erred only in his love for her, and to fight off generally an avalanche of softness.

What could be expected to happen?—that was the question. Randolph had settled down to a waiting game, and he would stick there if they all starved. After all, he had been tempted into this thing; there were excuses for him, though, of course, no excuse whatever for the atrocious punishment he had meted out to her. The mask of night hid Janey's blush, but she felt its heat. Contemplation of that would not stay before her consciousness.

Indians might drop in upon them, or tourists, or sheepmen, or possibly roving riders of doubtful character. The possibility of any or all of these occurrences was remote, but anything could happen. The cowboys would surely come. Janey wanted that, yet she feared it. There was no hope of Randolph keeping up his deception for any considerable length of time. So Janey was in a quandary. She wanted the Durlands to have a good scare and leave Arizona under the impression they now entertained. She wanted dire and multiple punishments to fall upon Randolph's head. If it pleased her to assuage them later, that was aside from the question. If he could be reduced to abject abasement, to want really to be hanged, as he said, to taste the very bitterest of repentance, then would be the

time for her denouement. For although he had not the
slightest inkling, even the remotest hope, of his two driving passions, Janey knew. Janey herself had done the discovering of Beckyshibeta and of the true state of her heart,
but that did not make them any the less his. What a profound thought! Janey trembled with it. There was a big-
ness about these discoveries that began to divorce her from
the old Janey Endicott. She would, she must, have her revenge; she fought this subtle changing, as it seemed, of
her very nature. She still hated, but the trouble was she
could not be sure what. Janey sighed. Oh, what a fall this
would be! Janey Endicott, on a pedestal of modern thought,
freedom, independence, equality—crash!

Nevertheless, despite everything, Janey sought her bed,
happy. For a while she sat on the ledge and gazed down into the campfire lightened circle. Mrs. Durland and her son
huddled there, keeping the blaze bright, whispering, gazing
furtively out into the black shadows, obviously afraid to
seek their beds. Presently Randolph strode out of the gloom.
Janey tingled at sight of him. She marveled at herself—
that any man could make her feel as she did.

"Madam, the hour grows late," declared Randolph, harshly, to the cowering woman. "Must I put you to bed?"

Whereupon Mrs. Durland made hasty retreat to her bed,
which was under the ledge out of Janey's sight.

"Young fellar, you sit up and keep watch," continued
Randolph, as he unrolled his camp bed near the fire. "And
remember, no shenanigans. I always sleep with one eye
open."

When Janey took a last look, Randolph appeared to be
sleeping peacefully while Bert was nailed to the martyrdom
of night watch.

The shadows flickered above Janey on the stone wall,
played and danced and limned stories there. If she could
have chosen she would rather have been here in this bed
than anywhere else in the world. But all the strangeness
and sweetness of the present at Beckyshibeta could not suf-
fice to keep her awake.

Janey's slumbers were disrupted by a loud voice. Randolph was calling his captives to breakfast. Janey sat up and made herself as presentable as possible. The face that smiled at her from the little mirror did not require make-up. It was acquiring a beautiful golden tan. Her eyes danced with delight.

She went down to breakfast. Randolph did not glance up, at least while she was close. Bert was heavy-eyed and somber, and Mrs. Durland was a wreck.

"Good heavens, you look like you've slept," was Mrs. Durland's reply to Janey's greeting.

"I sure have," returned Janey, and then ate her breakfast with a will.

"Lord preserve me from another such night," prayed Mrs. Durland, fervently. "I lay on the rocks—turned from side to side. My body is full of holes, I know. Mosquitoes devoured me. Some kind of animals crawled over me. I nearly froze to death. And I never closed an eye."

"That's too bad," replied Janey. "But you'll get used to it after a while. Won't she, Mr. Black Dick?"

"Wise men say a human being can get used to any kind of suffering, but I don't believe it myself," astonishingly replied the supposed outlaw, with somber accusing eyes piercing Janey in a quick look.

"Mr. Black Dick, you were a better man once?" ventured Mrs. Durland, almost with sympathy.

"Yes. Much better. I was ruined by a woman," he replied, somberly.

This startling revelation enjoined silence for a while, which was broken by the sound of hoofs cracking the rocks.

"Indians coming down the canyon," said Randolph, who had arisen.

"Oh, gracious! Are they hostile?" cried Mrs. Durland.

"Well, about half-friendly Navajos," returned Randolph.

Three picturesque riders rode from the cedars into camp. One of them, particularly, caught Janey's eye, as he dismounted in a sinuous action. He was tall with a ponderous

head that made him appear top heavy. He wore brown moccasins, corduroy trousers, a leather belt with large silver
buckle and shields, and a maroon-colored velveteen shirt.
His huge sombrero with ornamented band hid his features,
but Janey could discern that his face was red.

"Better eat while the eating is good," warned Randolph.

Then he spoke to the Indians in Navajo. Their actions
then signified that he had asked them to partake of the
meal. Janey was glad she had about finished hers. The
meat, the biscuits, the potatoes disappeared as if by magic.
Mrs. Durland, who had filled her plate, but had scarcely
tasted anything, appeared electrified to see her portion of
breakfast disappear with the rest. To do the Indians justice,
however, she was not holding the plate at the moment.
She had set it on a rock by the campfire.

"Ugh!" grunted the big Indian after each bite. Randolph
had made fair-sized biscuits, but one bite sufficed for
each.

"That wretch appropriated all my breakfast," declared
Mrs. Durland, astounded and angry. Evidently she took it
for granted that these Navajos could neither speak nor
understand English!

"Of all the hogs!" ejaculated young Durland. "Mother,
that Indian made away with nine biscuits. I counted them."

"Mr. Dick said they were half friendly," complained
Mrs. Durland. "I declare I don't see it."

Randolph contrived in an aside to whisper to Janey:
"That big Indian is smart. Keep your mouth shut and for
that matter stay right here."

"Don't worry, Phil," whispered Janey. "I'll stay in camp.
What's his name?"

"The cowboys call him Ham-face."

Presently Janey had opportunity to get a good look at
him. The sobriquet was felicitous. He certainly had a face
that resembled a ham. But it was also a record for desert
life. Janey could not decide whether he was young or old.
He had great black eyes, piercing and bold, yet somehow
melancholy. There were sloping lines of strength and he

had a thoughtful brow. Seating himself before Mrs. Durland he spoke to her in Navajo.

"What'd he say?" she asked, half fascinated and half frightened.

"Mrs. Durland, I regret I do not translate Navajo well," replied Randolph. "But he wanted to know something or other about why you wore men's pants."

Janey did not believe a word of that. She could tell when Phil was lying.

"The impudent savage!" ejaculated the woman, indignantly.

Ham-face addressed her again, gravely, with a face like a mask.

"He wants to know if you are any man's squaw," explained Randolph.

"Mother, you've made a conquest," laughed young Durland.

That affronted his mother who got up from beside the Navajo and left the campfire. Ham-face followed her, much fascinated, evidently, by her general appearance. It was to be admitted, Janey thought, that Mrs. Durland in tailored riding breeches, much too small for her portly figure, was nothing, if not a spectacle. When she became aware she was being followed she grew greatly perturbed, and hastened this way and that, though not far from the others. Ham-face pursued her.

"What's the fool traipsing after me for?" she cried.

Finally in sheer fright she came back to the seat beside her son, and sat there fuming, tapping the ground with her boot. Ham-face continued to walk around her and study her with grave eyes.

"Talk about the noble red men!" she exclaimed. "They're abominably rude. . . . Why don't they go away?"

The three Navajos appeared to be in no hurry. Ham-face kept devoting himself to Mrs. Durland, while the other two smoked cigarettes and talked in low tones to Randolph. Janey had taken refuge behind the packs, from which only her head protruded. Bert was interested despite his alarm.

At length Ham-face's attention to Mrs. Durland became so marked that the nervous high-strung woman burst into a tirade that might have been directed at the whole Indian race.

Ham-face imperturbably lighted a cigarette and blew a puff of smoke upward. "Pardon me, Madam, if I seem to stare," he remarked in English as fluent as her own. "But you are the most peculiar-looking old lady I've seen. I'd like to introduce you to my squaws. When I was in New York and Paris, during the war, I met some modern up-to-date women, but you've got them beaten a mile!"

Mrs. Durland's jaw dropped, her eyes popped, and with a gasp she collapsed. Janey, standing behind the packs, stuffed her handkerchief in her mouth to keep from shouting in glee. Ham-face was assuredly one of the educated Navajos whom the cowboys had mentioned.

After that he ceased annoying Mrs. Durland, but presently, after an enigmatical look at Janey, he joined Randolph and his two comrades near the horses. They conversed a little longer. Then the Indians mounted and rode away. Ham-face turned to wave a hand at Mrs. Durland.

"*Adiós,* little Eva," he called.

When they disappeared Mrs. Durland came out of her trance.

"That long-haired dirty ragged savage!" she raged. "To think he understood every word I uttered and then talked just like a white man! . . . He added insult to injury. Oh, this hideous Arizona with its lying traders, cowboys, Indians, outlaws and pitfalls! . . . Oh, my son, my son, get me out of this mess!"

"Mother, I've a feeling the worst is yet to come," replied her young hopeful.

Janey got up from where she had sprawled, and tried to catch Randolph's eye. But his face was averted and he stood motionless in a strained attitude of one listening.

"What is it?" whispered Janey.

"I thought I heard a horse," he replied. "Not the Indians'. It came from down the canyon."

"Hands up!" rasped out a hard voice from behind them. Janey stood paralyzed. She saw Randolph extend his arms high, and then slowly turn. His ruddy tan fled. "My God—it's really Black Dick himself!" he breathed, huskily.

Janey's heart skipped beating and then leaped. Turning, she saw two men in rough rider's garb. The foremost was heavy and broad, with what seemed a black blotch for a face. He held a gun which was pointed at Randolph.

"Howdy, Professor," he said. "Jest stand steady-like while Snitz gets your gun."

The second man, a little red-faced, red-headed, bow-legged person, with a greasy blue leather shirt, appropriated Randolph's weapon, and then very deftly his wallet.

"Hum! Looks flatter'n a pancake to me," said the robber, eying the latter with disdain. "Wal, mebbe these hyar tenderfeet will be better heeled."

Mrs. Durland and Bert stood rigid, with hands high and startled expressions.

"Reckon Willie Whitepants ought to have a lot of money, an' if he hain't Mrs. Hatchetface will."

A swift search of Bert brought to light a few bills of small denomination and some change.

"Wal, if he ain't a two-bit sport," exclaimed the leader, in disgust. "All them fine togs an' no yellow coin! . . . Say, lady, have you any money an' vallables?"

"Not h-h-here," stammered Mrs. Durland. It was plain that not only was she lying but very frightened.

"Scuse us, lady, fer gettin' so familiar when we ain't even been introduced. I'm Black Dick, from the border, an' this hyar pard of mine is Snitz Jones."

"Oh, my! There are two Black Dicks!" groaned Mrs. Durland.

"Wal, there's only one real Black Dick an' I'm the gent," returned the robber, with lofty humor.

"He calls himself Black Dick," burst out the woman, dropping a weak hand to point it at Randolph.

"Y-yes—so—he does," corroborated Bert, impressively.

"The hell you say! Wal, now, I call that complimentary.

But, folks, he was only joshin' you. Mebbe havin' fun with my rep!"

"You—you mean he isn't Black Dick and you are?" faltered Mrs. Durland.

"Precisely an' exactly, lady," returned Black Dick, amiably.

"Who is he, then?"

"Wal, I ain't sure, but I think he's Phil Randolph. The cowmen hyaraboot call him Profess or Bone-digger."

The guilty archaeologist dropped his hands with a laugh and sat down abruptly. Janey realized that the cat was out of the bag.

"Impostor! Liar!" burst out Mrs. Durland.

"Wal, I'll be dog-gone!" ejaculated Black Dick, with mild interest. "Snitz, somethin' up hyar, an' I've a hunch it's amoozin'. But we mustn't forget to collect all vallables fust."

"Fork over, mum," said Snitz, thus admonished, his eager hands extended.

"I—I tell you I've nothing," replied Mrs. Durland, weakly.

"Search her, Snitz," ordered Black Dick, sternly. "Hey—lady—keep them hands up."

Whereupon the little red-headed ruffian went at Mrs. Durland with an alacrity and verve that made Janey nearly choke, while at the same time she felt misgivings as to what might happen to her.

"Aha! Hyar's a lump of somethin' that feels heavy an' sounds moosical," announced Snitz, slapping at Mrs. Durland's hip pocket.

"You—thieving—lecherous—scoundrel!" Mrs. Durland screeched.

It must have hurt her to see that fat jingling bag brought to light. Snitz burst it open. Greenbacks, gold coins —jewelry!

"Whoopee!" yelled the little robber. "It's a haul, boss. This hyar lady shore didn't bulge all over fer nothin'.''

"Business is lookin' up," remarked Black Dick, with satisfaction. "Now Snitz, hand all that over to me, an' hev a look at this gurl. Looks to me she'd have a million—if you jedge by eyes. . . . Ain't she a looker?"

As Snitz approached Janey, grinning, eager, full of the devil as well as greed, she suddenly became terrified. This was not so funny.

"Phil!" she cried. "Don't let him touch me."

"Be sensible, child. They've held us up," admonished Randolph.

Janey slipped off her diamond ring and stretched it out at the length of her arm and let it drop in Snitz's palm.

"That's all I've got. Honest," she said, earnestly, in the stress of wanting to escape those rude hands.

"Little gurl, you don't look like a prevaricateer, but we jest can't trust you," returned Black Dick, soothingly.

"Peachy, if you run it'll be the wuss for you," added Snitz, reaching for her.

His touch, following the devilish little gleam in his eye, inflamed Janey. With one wrench she tore free and struck at Snitz with all her might. A quick duck of head just saved him.

"Whew!" he ejaculated, astounded and checked.

"Wow!" added Black Dick, in gleeful admiration. "She strikes like a sidewinder, Snitz. If that one had landed you've hev knowed it. . . . Wal, now what a fiery wench!"

Janey blazed at the leering astonished robber. "You damn little beast! If you touch me again I'll knock your red head off!"

Black Dick guffawed uproariously, while Snitz, though he joined in the mirth, took her seriously.

"Who'd a thunk it, boss?" he said. "Look at that tight little fist an' the way she swings it."

"Wal, I reckon I'm noticin'," added the leader, sheathing his gun and approaching. "We gotta be gennelmen, you know, Snitz. . . . See hyar, mighty little gurl, are you tellin' us true? You hain't nothin' on you but this ring?"

"That's all," returned Janey, breathing hard.

"Wal, turn round fer inspection," he ordered.

Janey did as she was bidden.

"Do it again, an' not so damn fast. This ain't no merry-go-round."

Whereupon Janey, realizing that she was to escape indignity, turned for their edification like a dress model in the Grande Maison de Blanc.

"Peachy, you ain't got a whole lot of anythin' on," remarked Snitz, fervidly.

Black Dick surveyed her with the appraising eyes of a connoisseur.

"Wal, sweetie, I reckon if you had a dime hid on you I could see it," he concluded, with finality.

10

"SAY, YOU'RE GETTIN' too big a kid fer sech short dresses," observed Black Dick disapprovingly to Janey.

"We were caught in the rain and my clothes shrunk," explained Janey.

"Reckon you're about sixteen years old, hain't you?"

"Oh, I'm a little more than that," dimpled Janey, very much pleased.

"How much?"

"Several years."

"Humph! No one would take you fer a grown girl. I'm afeared your mother hain't brought you up right—lettin' you run around with your fat knees all bare."

"Fat? They're not fat," retorted Janey, promptly insulted.

"Excuse me. Wal, they're bare. You can't deny that. An' after I give your ma a lecture I'll give you one," concluded Black Dick.

"Snitz," he said to his lieutenant, "you go diggin' round an' see if thar's anythin' more wuth takin'."

Then he confronted the dejected and crushed Mrs. Durland. "Look ahyar, lady," he began. "Your gurl says she's eighteen years old. An' I'm tellin' you she hain't been brought up decent. Wearin' sech clothes out hyar in the desert! Why, it ain't respectable. An' it ain't safe, neither. You might meet up with some hombres thet was not gennelmen like me an' Snitz."

Mrs. Durland was spurred out of her apathy into a wrathful astonishment that rendered her mute. Black Dick evidently saw that he had made a profound impression.

"I took her fer a kid, like them I see in town, wearin' white cotton socks thet leave their legs bare," he said. "An' hyar she's of age. There ought to be somethin' done about it. You ought to be ashamed of yourself to let your dotter run around like thet."

"My daughter?" burst out Mrs. Durland, furiously. "Not much! She's no kin of mine."

"Excoose me, lady. I had a hunch she was sister to this dude you've got with you," returned Black Dick, coolly. "Come to think aboot it I might have known from her looks."

Snitz approached at this moment, carrying various articles he had taken from Mrs. Durland's saddle. One of them was a light handbag, which Black Dick promptly turned inside out. It contained gloves, handkerchief, powder puff, cosmetics, and a magazine with a highly colored front page. The robber kept this and returned the other things.

"Snitz, you poke around some more," he said laconically, and turned to Janey. She, from her perch on the packs, had expected this and prepared herself with sad face and tearful eyes.

"Wot's your name?" he asked.

"Janey."

"Kind of suits you somehow. . . . Wot you cryin' aboot?"

"I'm very scared and unhappy."

"Scared? Of me?"

"Oh no. I'm not afraid of you. I think you're a *real* man.

But these people have kidnaped me—to get money out of my father."

"Ahuh. Wot'd this fellar Randolph pretend he was me fer?" asked Black Dick, growing more and more curious.

"I suppose to intimidate me. But he wasn't a bit like *you.*"

"So thet old bird is a kidnaper?" mused Black Dick, darkly. "An' Randolph's been roped in the deal. Wal, I'll be doggoned. Shore are a lot of mean people. Now, I'm only an old desert pack rat, snoopin' 'round when I get broke, but I could see you was a nice girl. Kidnapin' wimmen fer money shore ain't in my line. I was jest throwed off a little by your dress bein' so short."

"Thank you, Mr. Black Dick," said Janey, thinking that never had she received more sincere approval.

"Wal, we'll see wot can be did with this old hen," said the robber. Then he happened to notice Randolph sitting there as if he had not a friend in the world.

"Say, Randolph, my Navvy friends tipped me off about these pickin's. And what were you up to? Don't you reckon it's dangerous pretendin' to be me? There are men who'd shoot at you fer it."

"I never thought of that at the time," returned Randolph, lowering his voice. "The honest truth is I was just in fun. And I'm not so sure it was all my idea."

Then they got their heads together and conversed in such low tones that Janey could not hear any more.

"Boss, there ain't any more stuff worth hevin', onless it's the grub," announced Snitz, coming up. "Some orful fancy eats!"

"Well, I've a grand idee," said Black Dick, slapping his knee, and he winked one of his great bold black eyes at Janey. "We're goin' to have aristocracy cook for us."

Whereupon he approached Mrs. Durland with a slow rolling step, his sombrero cocked on one side of his head, his right thumb in the armhole of his vest, and his left hand holding onto the magazine.

"Lady," said Dick, grandly, "you're goin' to be honored

by cookin' a meal fer Black Dick. An' if you don't do your best I'll feel it my bounden duty to tote you off an' larn you how."

Mrs. Durland fell back with horror in her face.

"I like my wimmen with spunk," went on the desperado. "Could you larn to cuss, an' toss off a drink, an' kick me in the shins?"

"Merciful heavens—no!"

"Wal, then, you cook an' Whitepants hyar can be cookee. Rustle up some firewood. . . . An' now, sister, waddle along. An' mebbe I'll let you off."

"Beast!" screamed Mrs. Durland, and she ran toward the campfire.

"Cook dinner thar, you two," yelled Dick. "An' don't be all day aboot it."

Janey had observed that these men, despite the earlier action of robbing the party, and their later antics, took occasion now and then to gaze up and down the canyon. The younger one, Snitz, was particularly keen. These outlaws expected someone to come along or else were just habitually cautious and watchful.

Black Dick and Snitz sat down close together, with the magazine on the former's knees. They had the air of guilty gleeful schoolboys about to partake in a thrilling and forbidden act. They made a picture Janey would never forget, and reminded her of the mischievous cowboys. All these natives of Arizona had some inimitable Western quality, the keynote of which was fun.

Dick's huge dirty hands turned the pages, until suddenly they froze; then the bent heads grew absorbed.

"Jerusalem!" ejaculated Dick.

"Ain't she a looker!" exclaimed his comrade, raptly.

They turned a page and giggled. Then Black Dick looked up, swept the immediate horizon, and happening to see Janey, he waved a hand, as if to tell her to go away far back somewhere and leave them to their joy. Dick turned another page; and they whispered argumentatively. Another page brought a loud gasp from Snitz and something that sounded very much like an oath from Black Dick. Then they were as petrified.

"My Gord!" finally burst out Dick. "Snitz, do you see wot I see?"

"I'm lookin' at thet lady in the Garden of Eden," replied Snitz, breathing heavily.

"She ain't got a damn thing on," said Dick, in consternation. "Say, this must be gettin' to be an orful world."

"Wonder who tooked thet picture," returned Snitz. "It had to be tooked by a fotoggrapher."

"It says so—an' a man at thet. Shore I wouldn't been him fer a million dollars."

"I'd tooked thet picture fer nuthin'!" said Snitz.

Black Dick continued turning the pages, very slowly, as if he expected one of them to explode and blow them to bits.

"Wal, hyar's somebody with clothes on—sech as they are," he observed, presently.

"Actress. Not so bad, huh?—You'd get a hunch there ain't any men in New Yoork."

"Men don't cut much ice nowheres," said Dick, shrewdly. "When Eve got thick with thet big snake they fixed it so men did all the work, or become tramps like us, or went to jail."

"Dick, it ain't so long ago when the pictures we seen—most on them cigarette cairds—was wimmen in tights," said Snitz, reminiscently.

"Shore, but it's longer'n you think. You can bet there ain't nothin' like that these days. The world is goin' to hell."

"Hold on," interposed Snitz, halting Dick's too impetuous hand. "Heah's a nice picture."

"Nice? Snitz, you was brought up iggnorant. Thet ain't nice. Can't you see it's two girls in a room? They're half undressed an' smokin' cigarettes. Turrible fetchin' but shore not nice."

"Aw heck, I cain't see nuthin' wrong with it," said Snitz. "At least they're real purty."

"Snitz, this hyar all ain't so damn funny. Thet's the fust picture of this kind I've seen since the war. Wal, time changes everythin'. . . . But, Snitz, we ain't so bad off. Shore, we're often hungry an' oftener broke waitin' fer a chanct like this, an' we're dirty an' unshaved, with a few sheriffs lookin' fer us; but I'm damned if I'd change places with any of them people—even thet pho-toggrapher. Would you?"

"Nary time, Dick. Give me a hoss an' the open country," replied Snitz, rising to take a look up and down the canyon. Black Dick's ox eyes rolled and set under a rugged frown. Evidently in the magazine he had been confronted with a mysterious and perplexing world. Janey decided about this time that this desert rat several sheriffs were looking for was not half a bad fellow.

Presently Mrs. Durland called them to the meal she had been forced to prepare. Her face was very red and there was a black smudge on her nose, but she faced them with confidence. Snitz let out a whoop and alighted on the ground with his legs tucked under him—a marvelous performance considering the long spurs. Black Dick surveyed the white tablecloth spread upon the tarpaulin and the varied assortment of cooked and uncooked food.

"Wal, if I ain't dreamin' now I'll have a nightmare soon," he said, and squatted down. Snitz had already begun to eat. Dick, observing that he had not unfolded his napkin, took it up and handed it to him.

"Wot's—thet?" asked Snitz, with his mouth full.

"You ignorramus. Sometimes I wonder if your mother wasn't a cow. . . . Wal, I never had indigestion or colic, but I'm goin' through hyar if it kills me."

Janey had seen hungry cowboys eat, to her amazement and delight, but they could not hold a candle to these outlawed riders of the range. Their gastronomic feats were bewildering, even alarming to see. Not a shadow of doubt was there that Mrs. Durland had served concoctions cunningly devised and mixed to make these men ill, if not poison them outright. Sandwiches, cakes, sardines, cheese, olives, pickles, jam, crackers, disappeared alike with hot biscuits, ham, potatoes, and baked beans. When they had absolutely cleaned the platter Black Dick arose and quaintly doffed his sombrero to Mrs. Durland.

"Madam, you may be a disrepputable person, but you shore can hand out the grub," he said.

Snitz had arisen also, but his attention was on the far break of the canyon, where clouds of dust appeared to be rising.

"Look at that, pard," he said.

"Ahuh. Get up high somewheres, so you can see," returned Dick, and strode toward the horses that had strayed to the cedars. When he led them back Snitz had come down from the ledge.

"Bunch of cowpunchers ridin' up the canyon," he announced.

"Wal, we seen 'em fust," said his comrade, mounting. Then he surveyed the expectant group before him. "Madam, I reckon I'll never survive thet dinner you spread. Randolph, if you ain't in fer a necktie party, I don't know cowpunchers. Miss Janey, so long an' good luck to you. Bert-ie, if we ever meet again, I'm gonna shoot at them white pants."

He rode away. Snitz, swinging to the saddle, flashed his red face in a devilish grin at Janey.

"Good-by, peachy," he called, meaningly. "I'd shore love to see more of you."

Spurring his horse he soon caught up with Black Dick. Together they rode into the cedars and disappeared up the canyon.

"Thank God, they're gone!" cried Mrs. Durland, sinking in a heap. "Gone with every dollar—every diamond I possessed! . . . Bert Durland, you will rue this day."

Janey had been realizing the return of strong feeling. It did not easily gain possession of her at once. The cowboys were coming. And that recalled the bitter shame and humiliation Randolph had heaped upon her. How impossible to forgive or forget! The anger within her was like a hot knot of nerves suddenly exposed. She hated him, and the emotions that had developed since were as if they had never been.

"Mr. Randolph, the cowboys are coming," she said, significantly, turning to him.

"So I heard," he replied, curtly. He looked hard and he was slightly pale. Perhaps he appreciated more than she what he was in for. Janey was disappointed that he did not appeal to her. But she would only have mocked him and perhaps he knew that.

The dust clouds approached, rolling up out of the cedars. Crack of iron-shod hoof on rock, the crash of brush, and rolling of stones were certainly musical sounds to Janey. There was something else, too, but what she could not divine. She knew her heart beat fast. When Ray rode out of the cedars, at the head of the cowboys, it gave a spasmodic leap and then seemed to stand still. How strange a thought accompanied that! She wished they had not come. They did not appear to be a rollicking troupe of gay cowboys; they were grim men. It was very unusual for these cowboys to be silent.

Ray halted his horse some little distance off, and his companions closed in behind. His hawk eyes had taken in the Durlands. Janey noted what a start this gave him. She heard them speaking low. Then Ray dismounted, gun in hand. That gave Janey a shock. This lout of a cowboy, whom she could twist round her little finger, seemed another and a vastly different person. They all slid off their horses.

"Reckon Randolph's got a gun, but he won't throw it," said Ray. "Wait till I . . . see who these people are."

He strode over to confront Mrs. Durland and Bert.

"Who are you people?" he asked, bluntly.

"I am Mrs. Percival Durland, of New York, and this is my son Bertrand," she replied, with dignity.

"How did you get heah?"

"We employed an Indian guide."

"How long have you been heah?"

"It seems a long time, but in fact it is only a couple of days."

"What'd you come for?"

"We *used* to be friends of Miss Endicott," returned Mrs. Durland, significantly. "We heard at the post she was out here, so we came—to my bitter regret and shame."

"Who else has been here?"

"Two miserable thieving wretches," burst out Mrs. Durland. "Black Dick and his man. They robbed us."

"Reckon they saw us an' made off pronto?" went on Ray, his keen eyes on the ground.

"They just left—with all I had," wailed Mrs. Durland.

"You're lucky to get off so easy," said Ray curtly. "You found Miss Endicott an' Randolph alone?"

"Very much alone," replied the woman, scornfully. "He had kidnaped her."

"That's what *she* says," interposed Bert, with sarcasm.

"Ahuh. I savvy," replied Ray, fiercely. "You're intimatin' Miss Endicott might have come willin'?"

Bert was about to reply, when one of the cowboys, whose back was turned and whom Janey could not recognize, slapped him so hard that he fell off the rock backward.

"Wal, you better keep your mouth shet about it," said Ray, with a wide sweep of arm shoving the belligerent cowboy back.

"Thet shore won't save Randolph."

"Oh, this awful West!" screamed Mrs. Durland. "You're all alike. Cowboys—robbers—traders—Indians—scientists! You're a mob of deceiving bloody villains."

"Madam, I reckon it ain't goin' to be pleasant round heah. You an' your dandy Jim better leave pronto."

"Leave! Where and how? That man drove our guide away. We can't saddle and pack horses, and much less find our way out of this hellish hole."

"Take yourself off then, out of sight," he continued, harshly, and turned to come toward Randolph and Janey, his gun low, but unmistakably menacing. Diego, Mojave, Zoroaster, and Tay-Tay came striding after him. The musical jingling of their spurs did not harmonize with their demeanor.

Ray fixed Janey with a cold penetrating stare. She realized that for him, as a glorious entity—a girl to worship—she had ceased to exist. This escapade of Randolph's had ruined her with Ray beyond redemption. Janey was afraid to look in the faces of the others, for fear she would see the same condemnation. It was a sickening conception. It added fuel to the fire of her roused wrath at the perpetrator of this situation.

"You beat it," ordered Ray, with a slight motion of his gun, signifying that Janey was to get out.

"What for?" she asked, sharply.

"This heah ain't no place for a—a woman," he replied. He was going to say lady. Janey saw the word forming on his lips, but he changed it. She was no longer an object of respect, even to these crude cowboys. Her spirit flamed at them, at herself, at Randolph.

"After what I've gone through, I can stand anything. I'll stay," she said, heatedly.

He gave her a strange glance. What eyes he had—like hot blades! No man had ever dared to look at her with such unveiled disillusion.

"Randolph, stand up an' stick out your hands," ordered Ray. The archaeologist looked up, disclosing a dark set face and eyes that matched the cowboy's!

"You go to hell," he replied, coolly.

"Fellars, jerk him up off thet pack an' tie his hands behind him."

This order was carried out almost as soon as Ray had spoken. Randolph was a bound man.

"Thanks," returned Ray. "But I ain't aimin' to go where you belong. . . . We don't care pertickler to heah your musical voice either, but if you're any kind of a man you'll say whether you kidnaped Miss Endicott or not."

"Certainly I did, you knuckle-headed cowpuncher," retorted Randolph.

"You heah thet, boys?" called Ray, imperiously.

"We shore heered him," yelled the others as one man.

"Fetch a lasso," ordered Ray, dragging Randolph forward. "An' look fer a cedar high enough to hang this guy."

They moved off in a body toward the cedars, leaving Janey almost paralyzed. She saw them stop under one of the first trees. They were talking in low tones. Evidently Randolph spoke. The cowboys guffawed in ridicule. Then Mrs. Durland and Bert hurried up to Janey.

"What are they going to do?" panted Mrs. Durland.

"Hang him," whispered Janey, in awe.

"Serve him quite right," declared the woman, nodding in great satisfaction. "If only they had that dirty Black Dick, too!"

Janey broke from her trance and ran the short distance to the group. She heard the Durlands following. Janey would have been at her wit's end without the fright that had inhibited her. Certainly she would have to do something. If she gave way to a growing idea that the situation was beyond her—what might not happen? She gathered there had been an argument between Ray and the cowboys, for she heard sharp words on each side, and then suddenly at her approach they were silent. Randolph appeared less upset than any of them. The look of Ray gave Janey an icy chill. She had not been much frightened at Black Dick. But this lean-faced cowboy! All in a flash her hatred of Randolph and her unworthy passion for revenge were as if they had never been. She seemed as vacillating as a weather vane.

"Ray—wh-what are you going to do to him?" she asked, struggling to control her voice.

"We're going to make it the last time this fake scientist kidnaps a girl," replied Ray.

"But—that rope! You can't really hang a man for so little. Why, you'd hang too if you did such a thing. There'd be an investigation."

"Real kind of you, Miss, to worry aboot us," returned Ray, ironically. "Duty and the law are one and the same in Arizona. By hangin' this fellar we save the government expenses of keeping him in jail."

"But he didn't do anything so—so very terrible," went on Janey, still struggling.

"Look heah, young woman," said Ray, sharply. "Randolph kidnaped you, didn't he?"

"Yes," admitted Janey.

"Wal, thet's plenty. But it shore wasn't *all*—now, was it?" questioned the cowboy, his piercing suspicious eyes on hers. His jealousy probed the secret and his naturally primitive mind made deductions.

Janey blushed a burning scarlet. It was a hateful thing to feel before those keen-eyed boys who had revered her. It had as much to do with an upflashing of furious shame as the recollection of Randolph's one unforgivable indignity.

"Fellars, look at her face. Red as a beet!!" ejaculated Ray, passionately.

"Aw, Ray, cut it," burst out Mohave.

"Ain't you overdoin' it, Ray?" asked Zoroaster, darkly.

"Y-y-y-y-you—" stuttered Tay-Tay, in unmistakable protest. But he never achieved coherent speech.

"Damn you all! Shut up!" hissed Ray, in a deadly wrath. If his comrades meant to intercede on Janey's behalf, at least to save her from insult, he certainly intimidated them for the time being.

"Miss Endicott, you can't say honest that Randolph didn't mistreat you," asserted rather than asked Ray. He was a hard man to face and Janey, strangely agitated, yet still not roused, was not equal to it. Besides his words were like stinging salt in a raw wound.

"No matter what he did—you can't hang him," burst out Janey. Ray turned purple. The other cowboys subtly changed.

"Wal, for Gawd's sake!" bawled out Ray. "Ain't thet jest like a woman?"

"An' he stole my hoss, too," added Mohave, darkly.

"But, Mohave, my father would buy you a hundred horses," spoke up Janey, eagerly.

"Say, Miss, what's your father got to do with this?" demanded Ray. "He didn't steal the hoss. Randolph did. An' thet's as bad as stealin' you. Course Arizona has quit hangin' hoss thieves. But when you put the two together, why it's shore a hangin' case. . . . Miss Endicott, your friend Randolph ain't only a villain. He's a coward."

"I'm beginning to think a lot of things about you," retorted Janey, hotly. "And one of them is—you're a liar!"

Ray flinched as if he had been lashed with a whip. His eyes burned and his face became like flint.

"Wal, I ain't no kidnaper of girls—whether they're innocent—or not," he said, coarsely.

Randolph turned half round to look at the circle of cowboys behind him.

"Fellows, I'll be perfectly willing to be hanged if you'll grant me one request."

"You talk to me," ground out Ray. "I'm boss of this rodeo. What you want?"

"I'd like my hands untied so I can beat your dirty loud mouth shut," replied Randolph, ringingly.

Ray completely lost control of himself, and lunging out, he struck Randolph a sounding blow, knocking him flat.

"Oh, you dirty coward!" cried Janey. "To strike a man whose hands are tied!"

Mrs. Durland screamed: "They're all outlaws, blacklegs, murderers!"

It was Tay-Tay who assisted Randolph to rise to his feet. Blood was flowing from his mouth.

"Mebbe thet'll keep your mug shet," declared Ray.

"Say, Ray, this ain't gettin' us anywheres," interposed Mohave. "Mebbe we're far enough."

"Move along, Randolph," ordered Ray, shoving his gun into Randolph's side. He forced the archaeologist to walk on to a point under a high-branched cedar. "Somebody throw a rope over thet limb."

But nobody complied with this order. Again Janey intuitively guessed that this situation had not been what it looked on the face. The cowboys were a divided group. Ray was deadly, implacable. No doubting his real intention! Janey had sensed his jealousy and now realized his brutality. But another sharp scrutiny of the other faces convinced Janey that with them it had been a well-acted jest, which Ray was trying to drive to earnest. But he would never succeed. Janey racked her brain for some expedient to circumvent him.

Ray snatched the lasso from Mohave and threw the noose end over the branch, pulled it down, and with the skillful dexterity of a cowboy tossed the loop over Randolph's head.

"Thar's your necktie, Mr. Kidnaper," he said, with fiendish satisfaction.

Mohave seemed to pull himself together. Janey caught his quick significant glance at Diego, and she took her cue from that.

"Wal, I'm pullin' the rope," announced Mohave, stepping forward.

"Nothin' doin'. . . . I'm the little man who hangs this gent. It's my rope," replied Zoroaster.

"I weel pull the rope," said Diego, impressively.

"W-w-w-wh-where do I come in?" stammered Tay-Tay, evidently offended.

Janey was now almost certain of her ground, except for the silent Ray.

"Gentlemen, let me decide which of you shall have the honor of being the first to crack Randolph's neck," interrupted Janey, with entire change of front.

They gaped at her, nonplused. Ray's tense face relaxed to a slight sardonic grin. Janey feared him. The majority would rule here. Besides she had an idea.

"Let me decide, please," she continued.

"F-f-f-fair enough," said Tay-Tay.

"Pick me, Miss Janey. I'm the strongest," entreated Mohave, who seemed to be returning to his natural self.

The others, excepting Ray, loudly acclaimed their especial fittingness for the job.

"I can't show any favoritism among you boys," went on

Janey. "Lay down your guns. Then blindfold me. I'll pick
one of them up and whoever owns that gun shall have the
first pull."

"Fine idee," declared Mohave, and then deposited his gun
at Janey's feet. One by one the others gravely complied,
until it came to Ray. He held the lasso in one hand and his
gun in the other. Janey feared he would block her daring
scheme, which was to get possession of all the guns and
hold up the cowboys.

"Bert!" gasped Mrs. Durland. "She's a barbarian! A fit
consort for the likes of these! . . . To think I ever allowed
you to anticipate marrying such an impossible creature!"

"That'll be aboot all from you, Madam," retorted Ray,
threateningly.

"Come, Ray, your gun," called Janey, in a nervous hurry.
"Who'll lend me a scarf?"

"You're smart, but you can't fool me," rejoined Ray,
darkly. "I don't lay down my gun fer no woman. I'm onto
you, Miss. . . . Now you easy-mark cowpunchers, jest step
back. Stop! Never mind pickin' up them guns."

Slowly the cowboys edged back, and Janey with them. At
that moment Ray was more to be feared than Black Dick
had ever been. Ray had this game beaten and knew it. He
exchanged rope and gun from one hand to the other. With
a quick pull he tightened the noose hard around Randolph's neck, straining his body, lifting him a little.

"Reckon it's a doubtful honor, but I'll have it myself,"
he said, his cold eyes on Janey.

"My God!—Ray! You don't mean to go on with it?" cried
Janey, finding her voice.

"I shore do. I've got the goods on Randolph. You accused
him, an' he confessed. Everybody present heard you both.
An' there ain't a court in Arizona that'd hold me fer a day."

He was triumphant and malignant. Fierce jealousy had
brought out the evil in him. Janey had a terrible realization of her guilt—for she had flirted with this hot-headed
cowboy. She had looked upon him with caressing eyes; she
had listened to his sentimental talk and led him on. What

an idiot she had been! Vain, detestably bent on conquest—
heartless, wrong. Ray resembled a devil and he certainly
had overwhelming odds in his favor. Janey seemed to be
sinking in stupefied terror. Almost blindly she stepped out.

"Ray—for God's sake—don't—don't add murder to this—
this thing," she implored.

"So! You're intercedin' fer a man you swore treated you
out-rag-eous?" sneered Ray.

"Yes. I beg of you. Don't let your—your—whatever actu-
ates you—go any farther. Cool down. Think!"

"I've been thinkin' all right," he rejoined, with brooding
intimation.

"Randolph did not kidnap me," spoke up Janey, gathering
strength. "I came with him willingly."

"What's thet?" snarled Ray, almost crouching.

Randolph responded with his first show of perturbation.
"Ray, don't you believe a word she says. She's trying to
clear me by implicating herself."

"Wal, she's a liar all right, but mebbe this is straight,"
said Ray, somberly. "Say, gurl, if you come willin'—what
was it fer?"

"One reason was I wanted to get a kick out of it," replied
Janey, coolly. "I was sort of blasé. Tired of ordinary life.
I wanted something new, different."

"Ahuh! An' how aboot this heah out-rag-eous treatment?"
asked Ray, gruffly.

To have saved Randolph's life Janey could not have
stayed the coursing flame of red that burned from neck to
face. But her spirit flamed likewise.

"I disobeyed him," she confessed, bravely. "He—he chastised me. . . . I deserved it."

"Haw! Haw! Haw!" guffawed Ray, loudly, mirthlessly.
That laugh contained bitter doubt, scorn, hate.

"Ray, I'm afeared I hear hosses," interrupted Mohave,
sharply.

"So, you come willin', huh?" he questioned, with terrible
eyes on Janey. "Liked to be treated out-rag-eous, huh?

Wanted a new different kick, huh? . . . Wal, now watch your *lover* kick!"

Ray was a bully and a brute. But he did not know the fiber of the girl he had so grossly insulted. That was all Janey required to find herself. As Ray bent down to stretch the lasso over his hip, dragging Randolph to the tip of his toes, she sprang forward. She grasped the tightening rope above Randolph's head and pulled it loose. Then she confronted Ray.

"Stop, you madman!" she cried, imperiously. "Don't you dare— If you do I'll *kill* you!"

"Wal, fer Gawd's sake!" ejaculated Ray, surprised into his usual expression, and he momentarily slackened the lasso.

Quick as a flash Janey seized the noose and flipped it from Randolph's neck.

"Listen, cowboy!" she said. "What business is it of yours? If Randolph and I wanted to come out here to Beckyshibeta and lie about it that was *our* business. But it's gone too far for jokes now."

Janey backed up against Randolph and took his arm.

"Shore it's gone too far!" furiously returned Ray, recovering from his amazement. "An' you haven't give me one reason why he shouldn't hang."

"Very well, I'll try another," said Janey, with calm proud exterior, while inwardly she was in a state of exaltation. "I love him. Can you understand that? . . . I *love* him!"

For a long moment all her hearers seemed petrified. Ray looked shocked into credulous defeat. Then he choked out: "You white-faced slut!"

"Shet up!" yelled Mohave, sternly. "Heah comes Bennet an' some Indians . . . Mr. Endicott, too . . . all ridin' like hell! Cool down, Ray, or you'll get yours!"

11

THE INSTANT Janey had a close scrutiny of her father's face, which was when he reined his horse before the group, she knew his gay greeting and nonchalant survey of them had no depth. He had always been a capital actor, but he could not deceive his daughter.

"Hello, Janey," he had called out, before reaching them. "How are you? Little white, aren't you, for a modern amazon?"

Janey's emotion, whatever its great extent, suffered a swift transition to fury. Nevertheless she had wit enough to remember that this was no time to play against her father. Her cue was to be miserable and happy at one and the same time. At that she need only be natural.

"Howdy, Phillip," said Endicott, genially, sitting his horse at ease and gazing down upon the center of this motionless group. "Bet you're glad I arrived. Sorry we are rather late. But that darned storm turned us back."

Janey removed herself from Randolph's proximity. What had she said and done? She did not regret it, but the lofty spirit, which had prompted it, was failing. Randolph stood there, pale, with gleaming eyes and bloody lips, his hands still bound behind him. The noose that Janey had thrown off dangled not far above his head. The cowboys stood on uneasy feet. Ray still held his gun, and it was manifest that a dim realization of his part in this farce had dawned upon him. He was sweating now. The guns of the other cowboys lay where they had deposited them.

Mr. Endicott surveyed this scene with the air of a Westerner of long experience. He was too cool. Then he spotted the Durlands, and doffed his sombrero.

"Good day, Mrs. Durland. Hello, Bert. I hope you have had a nice little visit with Janey and her fiancé."

If anything could have struck fire from Mrs. Durland that speech might have done so, but she was beyond words. But Bert, now that danger had passed, showed an ugly temper.

"We've had a rotten visit, if you want to know," he howled. "We've been deceived, insulted, beaten and robbed."

"Robbed! Oh, not quite that, I'm sure," replied Endicott, laughing. "No doubt Randolph's a desperate character, but I can't believe he'd steal."

"We were held up and robbed by Black Dick and his partner," continued Bert, hotly.

"All my diamonds—and money—gone!" wailed Mrs. Durland.

"Indeed. That's too bad. It's something of a shock," returned Endicott, solicitously. "But I'll make your losses good. You see, I didn't calculate on a real desperado." Here he laughed. "It's all a little joke of mine. I wanted Janey to have a scare. So I persuaded Randolph to run off with her. My plan was to send the cowboys the very same day. But they didn't get back, and when they did the washes were flooded by the storm."

"Somebody untie my hands," called out Randolph, cutting and grim. "I'll show you what kind of a joke it was."

Mohave was the cowboy who complied with the request, and it was plain he was nervous. He whispered something to Randolph. But it did not prevent Randolph, the instant he was free, from making long strides to confront Ray.

"You're a skunk," said Randolph, deliberately. "I always had you figured as a bully and a conceited ass of a cowboy —mushy over every girl who ever came out here. But not till today did I know you to be a dirty foul-mouthed rat. You—"

"Hold on, Randolph," interrupted Endicott, aghast. "I told you I was to blame. Ray was only following my instructions."

"Randolph, we'll shore make allowance for your feelin's,"

added Bennet, conciliatingly. "But you're usin' strong language—too strong for a little joke."

"Joke, hell!" flashed Randolph. "This locoed cowboy meant to hang me!"

"Good God! Why, boy, you're quite out of your head," expostulated Endicott.

Bennet began to see something serious in the situation. And he took his hint more from Ray's face than Randolph's words. Slipping out of his saddle he strode quickly to get between the men. Randolph gave him a shove that almost upset him.

"Don't you butt in. You're a little late to save me the rottenest deal any man ever got. And you're a lot too late to save this cowpuncher of yours from the damnedest kind of a beating."

"Man! Look out for thet gun!" warned Bennet, shrilly.

"I don't care a damn for his gun," replied Randolph. "He wouldn't shoot a rabbit."

"Wal, I'd shoot a coyote damn quick—or a gurl-chasin' scientist," replied Ray, laughing coarsely.

"Drop thet gun!" ordered Bennet. "Can't you see Randolph is unarmed?"

"I'm takin' no more orders from you," said the cowboy, sullenly.

"You bet your life you're not," shouted the trader, angrily. "But you throw thet gun on Randolph an' you'll have me to deal with."

Suddenly Randolph, in a pantherish spring, leaped upon Ray, and caught his arm just as he was lifting it with the gun. Randolph threw all his weight upon that gun arm, forced it down. Ray struggled and cursing yelled: "Leggo, er I'll plug you!"

Randolph bent swiftly to fasten his teeth in the dangerous hand. The cowboy let out a howl of pain and fury. Bang! Bang! Janey screamed and hid her eyes in horror. She heard the thud of feet and wrestling of bodies, then hoarse calls from the onlookers. Her heart seemed to burst. This awful farce was going to end in a tragedy. Randolph!

Terror forced her to open her eyes. Ray had dropped the gun. The hand Randolph gripped was red with blood. On the instant Randolph gave the gun a kick. It flew to the feet of Mohave, who bent and snatched it up. Then Randolph, releasing Ray, struck him full in the face, with a blow that sounded like a mallet. Ray went down with a sodden thump.

Nobody wasted any more words. The spectators were too intense for speech, and the contestants too mad with rage. Randolph seemed a man who once in his life had let go. Ray, as he bounded up like a cat, looked a demon.

He rushed at Randolph and the fight began. Janey could not watch it, though now she had fascination added to her horror. But there was enough gentleness left in her to make her shrink instinctively. She stood there with hands pressed over her eyes. Thus blinded she could still hear. And the smash of fists, the scrape of boots, wrestling tussles of hard bodies in contact, the pants and whistles of furious breathing—these were worse to hear than to see. How must the battle go? Randolph, the gentleman, the mild-mannered archaeologist, would surely be worsted by a younger man and one inured to all the roughness of the desert. Crash! One of the fighters had been knocked into the cedar brush. He burst up again, bawling awful curses. Ray! What a hot tingling thrill Janey experienced! It seemed to change her very nature. She wanted more than anything ever before in her life for Randolph to beat down the vile-mouthed cowboy. She had known the cause of Randolph's white anger. It was because of Ray's bald insinuations. Randolph was fighting for her, to whip the cur before those onlookers who had heard. So it was impossible for Janey to keep her eyes covered any longer.

She found she stood alone. The fighters had worked away up the bench. Even the Durlands had followed the men. Janey ran. She saw Phil first, face turned toward her. He was all bloody and dirty. Then Ray's face swept round into sight. He was horribly battered, his face resembling a bloody beefsteak. He lunged wildly. He had no science.

Randolph was agile, swift, and when he struck out he landed. Ray plunged down at Randolph's legs, caught them, and dragged him down. They clinched furiously, and rolled over and over, now one on top, then the other. Ray kicked viciously. It was clear that he was trying to dig his spurs into Randolph's legs. The cowboys yelled their derision of this further evidence of Ray's cowardly tactics. He must have imagined that a rough-and-tumble fight would give him the advantage. But it soon became clear that he was as badly off as in a fair stand-up fight. Randolph was out to give the cowboy a terrific beating, and it looked as if it would end that way.

Once, when in their rolling over Ray landed on top, he snatched up a dead branch, quite weighty, and brought it down hard upon Randolph's head, where it cracked into many bits.

"You dirty dog!" yelled Mohave, who was now plainly Randolph's champion. "If you knock him out that way you'll have me on you."

But if Ray heard he paid no heed. He snatched up a rock and swung that.

"Drop it or I'll shoot your arm off," shouted Bennet, whipping out a gun.

The maddened cowboy tried to smash Randolph's head. Missed him! Bennet meant to shoot, but obviously feared he would either kill Ray or hit Randolph. Then he grasped his gun by the barrel, meaning to hit Ray with it. The cowboy struck again with the rock. Randolph dodged, but was slightly hit.

"For God's sake, Bennet, stop him! He means murder," called Endicott, frightened.

"Oh, Phil—don't let him kill you!" screamed Janey, wildly.

Mohave leaped close to do something, no one could guess what. Mrs. Durland collapsed in a faint. Randolph might not have been doing his utmost before, because his fury and strength became marvelous. With one powerful blow he knocked the stone flying out of Ray's hand. Another broke Ray's hold on his throat. Then he heaved mightily.

He tossed Ray clear of him, and was on his feet as quickly
as the cowboy. He rushed Ray. A blow stopped the cowboy.
The next staggered him. Randolph swung his left—biff!
Then his right—smash! Ray, who was falling at the first
blow, shot down with the second as if it had been from a
catapult. He fell headlong, and slid over the brink of the
bench, to crash into the brush below.

Randolph glared a moment at the puff of dust which the
cowboy had raised, then striding to his pack he picked up
his towel and went off down the slope toward the creek.

Janey was so tottering and weak that she sat down on
a rock. Bennet sheathed his gun.

"Wal, that was good," he declared, in great relief. "I
hope he broke his neck. Some of you boys go down and
see. . . . Endicott, Mrs. Durland has fainted. No wonder.
Thet came near bein' a real scrap. Young man, fetch some
water, an' we'll bring your mother to."

Janey sat dizzily conscious of the subsiding of the terrible
emotions that had swayed her. Very slowly she recovered.
Mrs. Durland was revived and lifted to a seat. Bennet appeared very kindly and solicitous. Janey's father wore a
haggard look of remorse displacing fear. Bert, who hovered
over his mother, showed the pallor of a girl, and hands that
shook. Mohave was the only cowboy left on the bench.

"What in the hell happened?" questioned Bennet, sternly.

"Boss, I swear it was as much of a surprise to us as to
you," began Mohave, most earnestly. "The boys will back
me up in that. . . . You know Mr. Endicott was awful keen
on makin' this false hangin' look like the real thing. We
had our orders to do some tall actin'—like them motion-
picture fellars. You can bet we had a lot of fun plannin'
this. Talkin' it over! We must *look* terrible mad, as if we
meant bizness. Wal, Ray acted so powerful good thet we all
was plumb jealous. Even when he began to say nasty things
we thought he was only overteppin' a little. When he
insulted Miss Janey—then I was flabbergasted. Same with
the other boys. Once I opened my trap, but Ray shet me

up pronto. Still it was all so sudden I jest couldn't see through Ray until he called Miss Janey a white-faced slut."

"Ahuh! Aboot time you seen through him, I'll say. Wal?" grumbled the trader.

"Then it all come in a flash," went on Mohave, breathing hard. "We was obeyin' orders—havin' an awful big kick out of it. But Ray wasn't actin'. He meant to hang Randolph. No doubt of thet, sir. He had it all figgered out an' knowed the facts would clear him in any court."

"But the damn locoed idget!" burst out Bennet. "To hang Randolph in earnest! What on earth for?"

"Wal, I ain't shore. But I believe Ray thought Miss Janey was his gurl," replied Mohave, manfully, though it was evident he hated to be frank. "He shore talked like it. An' when he seen—wal, that he was what you called him, boss, why he went plumb out of his haid with jealousy."

"Ahuh! Wal, I'm damned!" ejaculated Bennet.

Mr. Endicott had listened to all this conversation and now he turned to his daughter.

"Janey, you let that cowboy make love to you," he said. He did not ask; he affirmed.

"Dad, I did," replied Janey, bravely. It was confession that was accusation. "To my regret and shame—I did. I let him kiss me—talk a lot of nonsense."

"Well, that's no crime," he said, gravely. "But in this case it nearly led to murder. I hope it will be a lesson to you."

Janey dropped her face into her hands and hid it. Lesson! What lesson had she not had? She would be days accounting for them and their clarifying and transforming power. Now there was only one man in all the world whom she would allow to kiss her. And would he want to again?

Zoroaster and the other cowboys came back from below.

"Ray's not crippled, sir," reported Zoroaster. "Bad bunged up, but nothin' serious."

"Able to ride?" asked Bennet, tersely.

"Reckon so, if someone shows him where to go. Both eyes are swelled shet."

"Wal, let's see. The Indians can look after us. You boys

take him back to the post. Tell Mrs. Bennet to pay him off an' let him go. Clear out now. . . . An' say, boys, if you want to stay with me, keep mum aboot this deal. Not one little word! Savvy?"

They promised soberly, and picking up their guns, they led their horses down through the cedars out of sight.

"Reckon we might as well stay heah fer a day or two, hadn't we?" inquired Bennet of Endicott. "The Indians will look after our horses, an' pack firewood. I can cook."

"Surely. I want to see this Beckyshibeta. Besides—" replied Endicott, who, happening to glance at Janey, did not complete what had been on his mind to say. Then seeing Randolph returning he advanced to meet him. He certainly got a cold shoulder from that individual. Standing blankly a moment he threw up his hands, then stalked off tragically. Janey had noticed this little by-play. So had Bennet, who was not above chuckling. This and Randolph's reception of her father did much to spur Janey to some semblance of sanity.

"Wal, lass, it was an awful mess, wasn't it?" said the trader, sympathetically, as he seated himself beside Janey.

"Mess is the word, Mr. Bennet," replied Janey, finding her voice somewhat strained.

"Your father had good intentions," went on Bennet. "But jumpin' horn toads! What a damn fool idee! He never told me till it was all done, an' the cowboys on your trail. Shore I could have held them back, or come along. I thought somethin' was kinda queer. Sort of in the air. But, Lord, how could I guess it?"

"Don't apologize, and please don't be sorry for me," murmured Janey.

"Aw now—"

"What this—this mess has done to me I don't realize yet," interrupted Janey. "But today has been terrible. . . . When I—I get my nerve back, I'll be all right. . . . I don't blame Dad. He meant well. He wanted to give me a—a real scare. I'll say he succeeded beyond his wildest hopes. . . . Still, it was my fault, Mr. Bennet. I can't crawl out. I must have driven poor Dad crazy. And that miserable cowboy Ray! I don't know what to say. I—I wanted Phil to kill him. Think of that!"

"Wal, I'd have shot Ray myself if I hadn't been leery of hittin' Randolph," said Bennet. "Don't you waste too much pity on Ray. He's plain no good. I know a lot of things aboot Ray. He was a good man with hosses an' cattle. An' not a hard drinker. I've gotta say thet fer him. But Ray always was loony aboot girls. He wouldn't up an' marry one. No sir-ee! He always said he didn't want to be hawg-tied. . . . Wal, I reckon he had a genuine case on you."

"As far as Ray is concerned—and that terrible fight— I am solely to blame," confessed Janey, almost choking. "It makes me deathly sick. Mr. Bennet, I—I made a fool of—"

"Never mind, lass," interposed the trader, putting a rough kind hand on hers. "I heard what you said to your Dad. You're game, as we say in the West, an' takin' your medicine. You jest didn't savvy cowboys, much less a dangerous hombre like Ray. We're lucky it didn't turn out bad. . . . Randolph shore was chain-lightnin' when he rode up, wasn't he? Wal, I reckon, after all, the most dangerous men are the quiet ones. I'll never get over the surprise he gave me, though. . . . Now, you pull yourself together. Reckon I'd better look up your Dad."

With that Bennet arose, and giving the Indians some instructions, he strode off in the direction Endicott had taken. Janey felt that she had pulled herself together, in a sense, though she was far too wise to trust herself yet. Still, she had to go about facing things, and she chose the hardest first. She went up to Randolph. He had changed his stained, torn shirt for a clean one, and washed the blood from his cut and bruised face. And he did not appear such an ugly sight as she had anticipated.

"Phil, it was—fine—wonderful for you to fight that way for me. You—I—I can't find words."

"What I did is nothing compared to the way you stood up before them and lied for me," he said, with deep feeling.

Janey had forgotten about that. All in a second she felt unaccountably tender and realized she was on most treacherous ground. She had not lied, and she longed to tell him so.

"Don't look so distressed," he went on. "They all know you lied to save me and they'll think more of you for it."

"I don't care what they think," returned Janey. "I'm pretty much upset. I just wanted to tell you how I felt—about your fighting for me . . . and to ask you—please not to quarrel with Dad."

"Sorry I can't promise. It's certainly coming to that gentleman," said Randolph, grimly.

Janey was not equal to any more just then; and when she slowly ascended the little rock slope to her retreat she realized how unstrung she was. Once there she lay down on her bed and did not care what happened. She did not quite sleep, but she rested for a couple of hours. Still she did not feel up to the exigencies of this hectic situation. Curiosity, however, was an entering wedge into the chaos of her mind. She sat up and tried to make herself more presentable—thinking, with a wan smile as she saw the havoc in her face, that this was a favorable sign of returning reason.

The Indians appeared to be busy around the campfire, cleaning the mess left by Black Dick and his partner. Never would she forget them! And pretty soon she would find herself in the unique and embarrassing state of inquiring into their wholesome effect upon her. The Durlands were fixing up some kind of a shelter in the cedars, and evidently were quite interested. Janey reflected that an adjustment to their material loss might make considerable difference in their reaction. Randolph and Bennet were nowhere to be seen. But presently Janey saw her father. He had been so near, under the wall in the shade, that she had overlooked him. Hatless, coatless, vestless, collar open at the neck, dejected, he certainly presented a most unusual counterpart of himself. For an instant Janey had a wild start. What if Randolph had chastised him too! But no, that

was improbable. Nevertheless something had happened to
Mr. Endicott, and seeing him this way revived Janey's
spirit. Could she carry on? She would die in the attempt!
These two detractors had not been punished enough to
satisfy her. Especially Randolph! So after thinking it over
for a little longer Janey went down to her father.

"Well, Dad, you appear to be having a most enjoyable
time," she said.

"Ah!—Hello, Janey. Yes, I'm having a grand time. Ha!
Ha!" he replied.

It was worse than Janey had imagined. She began to
soften a little, though she never would let it show.

"How do you like Beckyshibeta?" she asked.

"Becky-hell and blazes!"

"What's happened, Dad?" she went on, quietly.

"Nothing. I've had the most uncomfortable hour of my
life," he rejoined, miserably. She saw that unburdening
himself would be well, so she encouraged him.

"I didn't know that man Randolph at all," he exploded.

"Neither did I," replied Janey, musingly.

"Janey, that confounded Westerner came up to me with
fire in his eye. And he said: 'Damn you, Endicott. I ought
to punch you good!' I thought he was going to do it, too.
So I made some feeble reply about how sorry I was to
place him in such a fix. 'Fix? Hell!' he yelled at me. 'I'm
not thinking of myself. It's the fix you've got *her* in. It's
not I who'll have ruined her reputation. It's *you!* You made
a damn fool of me. But you've *hurt* her. Those Durlands will
be nasty. Your own daughter! You made me believe she was
wild—going straight to hell!' I yelled back at him that you
were. Then he shut me up all right. I knew I was going to
get something. He was red as a lobster. He shook that big
fist under my very nose. He called me a blankety-blank
liar! . . . Then he swore at me. He cussed me. Such profanity I never heard. He must have collected it from every
cowboy in the West. He never stopped until he was out of
breath. Then he went off somewhere with Bennet."

"Is that all?" she inquired.

"All? Good God! What would you want? Have him beat me up like he did that cowboy?"

"I thought perhaps he might."

"You'd have been an orphan all right, if he had. . . . Janey, you don't mean you're dead sore at me?"

"You are an unnatural parent," returned Janey, beginning to revel.

"Why, I thought I'd been the easiest dad any girl ever had," he protested, not without pain. "Our friends always took me to task for giving you freedom—everything you wanted."

"Yes. But never the love I was so hungry for," said Janey, cruelly.

"Janey!" he exclaimed, amazed and shocked. "I always worshiped you—and spoiled you. This miserable trick I played on you—that's turned out so badly—why it was a proof of—of—"

"Not of faith, Father," she interrupted, coldly.

"Faith! Of course it was faith. I swore to myself that our rotten life in the East had not yet ruined you."

"Please do not argue with me," she returned, sweetly. "The thing's done. You have ruined me, that's certain. And I'll never, never forgive you."

This so crushed him that she had to leave before she must yield to an irresistible softness. And by way of a counter-irritant she went over to talk to the Durlands. They were cold and reserved at first, but presently her sad face, and the struggle she apparently was making to keep up, quite warmed Mrs. Durland. Her son, however, came around slowly. Finally he broke out in a tirade against Randolph and her father.

"Yes, I know, Bert, they're all you say and more. But that doesn't help me. I was perfectly innocent. You know what kind of a girl I am."

"You bet I do. But, Janey, that about coming here willingly? Then you stood up so—so wonderfully and said you loved him!"

"You ninny. I was trying to save his life," protested Janey.

"It was great of you, old girl, believe me," replied Bert, fervently. "And I believe you did."

Janey decided the Durlands would be hard to handle. Under her direct influence they would respond, but once away from it they would be likely to gossip, unless she could make them loyal to her. On the face of it that seemed an impossible task. And she was silly to hope for it, selfish to ask for it. She began to stroll around, hoping to get a peep at Randolph, conscious of a sneaking delight. She saw Bennet returning to camp, but the archaeologist had vanished. Could it be possible that the man was again digging for Beckyshibeta? If so she would have to hand him a laurel wreath. She could not, however, venture to find out, and had to content herself with waiting.

Out of sight of camp Janey found a lofty perch in the sun and there she succumbed to the glory and dream of this canyon country. There was no sense or use in trying to resist its charm. But it was a way with Janey to try to understand what got the best of her. This place had taken hold of her heart.

What was the spell of this deep fissure in the rocks? She dreamily attended to her senses. It had such a strange sweet dry fragrance, with sage predominating, but with other perfumes almost as clean and insidious. It was as colorful as a rainbow. It changed with the movements of the sun, never very long the same. It had mystic veils of light, rose and pink at dawn, amber and gold at this hour of high noon, and in the afternoon with shadows lengthening, deepening into lilac, purple, black. Then the immensity of the cliffs, the lofty rims, the far higher domes and mesas beyond, the hundreds of inaccessible and fascinating places where only squirrels and birds could rest—these added to the spell. Not a little, too, was the evidence of a wild people once having lived and fought and died here. Perhaps loved! Lastly Janey was discovering the blessedness of solitude, the something leveling in loveliness, the elevating power of the naked sheer walls with their inscrutable meaning.

All of which led to a consciousness of the thing that had

come to her. She called it "thing," when she confessed to
her soul that it was new, transforming, exalting love. And
she dared not give in to that just yet. When she must,
when she could no longer stand the old Janey Endicott,
when pride and vanity, and the host of other faults must
go by the board, then she would face the truth and its ap-
palling problems. She had a tremendous consciousness that
she would engulf all—this marvelous desert, her aging,
worrying father, her friends—and Randolph. And it was
going to hurt almost mortally.

Janey returned to camp. Sight of Randolph thrilled yet
shocked her. That hour alone in the canyon had transformed him in her mind. And the reality of him was con-
founding.

Evidently she had interrupted a conference, or at least
an argument. She caught Randolph's slight gesture to en-
join silence.

"Wal, Randolph," said Bennet. "I reckon Miss Janey
needn't be excluded."

"If I'm intruding," replied Janey, haughtily, turning to
go.

Bennet detained her. "We was jest talkin'," he said, "an'
mebbe you might put a word in. Randolph has lost his job.
Mr. Elliot, haid of the New York Museum, is now at the
post waitin' for some of his men to come over from
New Mexico. 'Pears he's been agin Randolph's explorations
out heah. Wants to find Beckyshibeta himself. After Randolph has dug up the desert! Wal, he took this unauthorized
trip of Randolph's out heah as an excuse, an' fired him.
Your father feels bad aboot bein' to blame, and he offered
Randolph substantial means to go on with his explorations
on his own hook. Randolph turned it down cold. . . . What
do you think aboot it?"

"I! Oh, I think it very unfortunate and distressing that
Phil—Mr. Randolph should be discharged—and disgraced
through Father's idiotic scheme," replied Janey. "Certainly

Father could do no less than offer to repair the material loss. And just as certainly Mr. Randolph could not accept it."

"Why not?" demanded Endicott.

"Well, Dad, if you're so dense you can't see why—I am not going to enlighten you."

"Thank you, Miss Endicott," said Randolph. "You understand, at least."

Endicott might have exploded then, if he had had energy enough left to express himself as he looked. As it was, his first exclamation was unintelligible and scarcely mild. Then he added: "If you temperamental young fools weren't logger-heads I could still save the situation."

"Yes, you could," declared Randolph, sarcastically. "Endicott, my private opinion is that you might save your face if—"

"See here, you hot-headed jackanapes!" interrupted Endicott. "You've insulted me enough."

"I could still add injury to insult," retorted Randolph.

Here Bennet stepped in and tried his Western common sense and kindliness. Janey had been thinking desperately. What astounded her now was that she simply could not stand Randolph's unhappiness. She, who had wanted to make him writhe and moan and curse himself with remorse!

"Mr. Randolph, may I have a word with you alone?" she asked, very businesslike. No one could have guessed there was a lump in her throat.

"Certainly," he said, with freezing politeness, "if you consider it necessary."

He went aside with her, manifestly with misgivings. Janey heard her father whisper to Bennet, "Now what's she up to? There's no telling about a woman."

Janey maintained an outward composure. She could rise to the moment and this one was big.

"Will you make me a promise?" she asked.

"I couldn't very well be surprised at you. And if you'll pardon my bluntness—no, I won't," he replied.

Janey was looking with a woman's penetrating intuitive eyes into his face; and what she read there made the ordeal worse, yet gave her a hint of the assurance she needed.

"Well then, *if* you make me a promise—will you keep it?" she continued, steadily.

"Yes. If!"

"Do you recall the last time I was around where you were digging?"

"I'm not likely to forget it."

"I am going to tell you the honest truth."

"Miss Endicott, are you capable of that?" he asked, acidly.

"If you were big enough to fight for my honor you can be big enough to give me the benefit of the doubt—when I particularly appeal to you. Will you?"

That struck him deep. He lost his grim cold look of doubt and became merely wretched.

"I'm not quite myself. But tell me what you want to."

"If I reveal something to you will you promise never to tell it to anyone?" she asked, hurriedly and low.

"I don't see any need of your revealing secrets to me," he replied.

"Will you promise?" she went on, appealing as well with her eyes.

"You can trust me," he said, surrendering in spite of himself.

"Thank you. The secret you have promised to keep is that *I* have found Beckyshibeta for you," she whispered. "Go at once far beyond that place where I crossed and risked my life—where I taunted you and you told me to go to the devil. . . . Go high up around the great cracked leaning rock. Find a stairway of little cut steps in the stones. Follow them. They will lead you to Beckyshibeta. Don't doubt. Don't laugh. But go!"

Janey did not wait to see his incredulity or to hear whatever he might have to say. She hurried away, up to her ledge. When she sank to her knees upon her bed, and looked back, Randolph had disappeared. Soon he would learn that her words had not been idle. The greatest ambition of his life attained! Beckyshibeta! How would he return to her?

12

JANEY HAD ANTICIPATED PEACE, satisfaction, relief from her whirling thoughts. But she was wrong. Suppose it had not been Beckyshibeta at all? What a horrible mistake! Her eloquence, her exaction of a sacred promise, her cool certainty had convinced Randolph. But she might have been wrong. How could she be sure about cliff dwellings?

So she was tortured. How to make amends to Randolph if she had blundered! Of course she could give herself. It did not seem possible that she could rival Beckyshibeta in this mad scientist's valuation; nevertheless she might be some little consolation. That would be what she must do; that was what she had intended for long endless growing hours. Only it would have to be done at once, right there where this catastrophe had happened, instead of waiting until she felt utterly and forever avenged.

An hour passed, surely an hour Janey would never want to live over. The camp was deserted. She had not heard anyone leave. And presently she felt that she could not lie there any longer, waiting in actionless suspense. She must move around, do something.

Janey wandered in the opposite direction to the one she was sure the others had taken. She went round under the cliffs farther on that side than she had ever been. But for once the speaking walls had no power of solace. She was not ready to take stock of her own spiritual needs. It was Randolph of whom she was thinking. If she had actually

discovered Beckyshibeta she would presently be the most
fortunate—the happiest of women. She did not try now to
reason out why. It was something she most devoutly believed and prayed for.

She found a clump of sage and lingered in it, reveling in
its fragrance and color. She gathered an armful of the
sprigs, meaning to treasure them in a pillow, to have near
her a memory—stirring sweetness of the desert. Then she
sat down with the sage in her lap, and tried to plan clearly
her procedure from this hour. But she could only dream,
because everything was uncertain.

Time passed, however, and upon her return to camp she
found all the others there, except Randolph. At first glance
they appeared to be friendly enough. There must be some
occasion for intimate talk. Then her father spotted her and
came running. Janey sighed with relief. Mr. Endicott was
not given to overexertion in ordinary movements or when
he was gloomy.

"I've had the very devil of good luck," he announced, as
he reached her, and quite forgetful of a former state of
mind he put his arm around her and squeezed her.

"You have? Well, that's fine," replied Janey, yielding to
him, as he pulled her to a seat on a rock.

"Randolph and I have made up," said Mr. Endicott, with
great pleasure and satisfaction.

"Made up! Indeed? I did not imagine it possible that he
would ever forgive you—either." Janey added the "either"
as an afterthought. It quite escaped Mr. Endicott.

"Janey, the lucky dog discovered the lost pueblo—Beckyshibeta!" exclaimed her father.

"Oh!—How wonderful!"

"It's true. And, well, I don't know when I've been so
glad about anything."

"Tell me about it," said Janey, composedly, although she
kept her face half averted.

"Bennet was showing us the ruins," went on Endicott,
wiping his hot face. "We ran into Randolph. I declare I
thought he was crazy. So did Bennet. At first we did not

take him at all seriously. He convinced us finally. He had discovered Beckyshibeta—the pueblo about which archaeologists have been raving for years. Quite by a strange lucky accident. He was radiant. I never saw a man so completely happy. He was so absurdly grateful to me for sending him out here. Why, the fellow embraced me. I was embarrassed, remembering how he treated me a few hours before. . . . Janey, he had actually forgotten. I declare it upset me—I was so glad. I like Randolph, and when I queered myself with him it hurt. He's one of the finest chaps I ever knew!"

"I'm glad—for his sake and yours," rejoined Janey. "This discovery must mean a great deal to him?"

"I didn't understand that until after he rushed off again," replied Endicott. "Bennet told me! It means fame and money to Randolph. In one word—success. Scientifically this is a very important discovery. Beckyshibeta is one of the greatest pueblos, says Bennet. An ancient buried city! Then the best of it is that Randolph was not working for the museum people when he found the pueblo. He was all on his own. That upstage Elliot, you know, fired him. Bennet says Elliot will practically expire. Randolph will have the credit, and everything else that comes with it. The work of excavation will be under *his* control, instead of Elliot's. I'm just tickled over it."

"Excavation," mused Janey. "He will undertake that? Won't it be expensive?"

"I'll back him. It's a big thing," replied Mr. Endicott, heartily.

"Do you think he would accept that?"

"Phillip has already accepted," went on her father, happily. "He said he could raise any amount of money. The government would want to help. Patrons of scientific research would want to donate—to have their names connected with Beckyshibeta. But I beat them to it. And Phil was delighted."

"Where is—he now?" asked Janey, with her glance downcast upon the bunch of sage. It would never have done for her to let anyone see her eyes then.

"He went back. Bennet and I tried to follow him. But he crossed a terrible place. We'd have broken our necks. So we returned to camp."

It was night with silvery radiance streaming down over the dark canyon rims. The moon was rising. Janey lay in her blankets, waiting to see the white disk slide up over the black ragged rockline above. She had not cared to trust meeting Randolph at the campfire, and pleading fatigue had retired to her ledge, where her father brought her supper.

Randolph did not return until the others had finished their meal; and then he quite forgot to eat. His ragged appearance attested to hours of contact with the rough rocks, and his radiant face to the discovery that had made him a changed man. While he talked to Bennet and Endicott his glance went so often toward Janey's perch that she feared she might be caught peeping. But she was in dark shadow there, and could revel in watching and listening. If she had ever seen three happy men it was then.

The Durlands had thawed considerably. They hovered around Randolph, fascinated, and warming to the man's enthusiasm. When at last they went off to their shack, Bennet said: "Wal, Endicott, can you dig up a drink?"

"No. I didn't bring any," replied Endicott, regretfully.

"How aboot you, Randolph?"

"I had some for possible snakebite, but it leaked out."

Bennet turned over his saddle and procured a flask. "Heah, friends, we'll drink to Beckyshibeta!"

What a long time they were in getting ready for bed! At last Randolph was left alone. He sat for what seemed an endless hour, gazing into the ruddy dying fire. What was he thinking about? Fame and fortune, the goddesses of all men's ambitions, thought Janey, jealously. Certainly he did not appear to remember her.

The moon soared across the narrow opening between the rims of rock above; the dark shadow on one side of the

canyon moved magically across to the other. An impenetrable silence enfolded the lonely place. Janey had sat up
peeping until her back ached. Several times she lay down
again, only to rise up and peep once more. Randolph was
a magnet. She laughed happily under her breath as she
watched him. If he but knew!

Endicott and Bennet lay prone in their beds, deep in slum-
ber. It touched Janey to see the silver of her father's hair,
bright in the moonlight.

Randolph glanced rather markedly and long at them.
Then stepping noiselessly he entered the zone of shadow and
vanished. But soon the outline of his head and shoulders
was silhouetted against the moonlight. Janey gave a wild
start and shrank back. He was climbing to her ledge.

The sudden burning of her face and beating of her heart
accompanied a panic she could not quell. But she covered
herself with the blankets and feigned sleep. To her own
eyes it had been almost as bright as day up there. But
Randolph, coming from the open moonlight, would find it
dark. Yet if he stayed long enough! A child could read
her heart in her face. She heard a slight rustling on the
rock, and she began to tremble. Next she felt his presence.
He was there, gazing down upon her. How could she lie
still? What was his intention? Then she realized that he
would surely awaken her, and she sought to still her nerves.
Something lightly brushed her hair. His hand or his lips?
Another instant she knew, for she caught a slight sound of
intense breathing very close to her face. He had kissed her
hair. If he dared to kiss her lips her rigid arms would fly
up round his neck. She knew it. She waited, surrendering
in her heart, ready to end the fight royally.

But instead he touched her softly and whispered: "Janey!"

That saved her. She caught at her ebbing self-control;
and her conscious swift thought balanced her emotion.

"Janey," he whispered. "Wake up. It is I—Phil."

She opened her eyes, not needing to pretend a start. She
saw him distinctly—his face pale, rapt. He knelt beside her.

"Oh!—Who?—What?" she faltered.

"Don't be frightened," he said, swiftly and low. "It's Phil. I couldn't wait till tomorrow."

"You—you startled me. What is it?—Oh, I hope my father—"

"Don't speak so loud," he interrupted. "There is nothing wrong. I simply could not wait till morning. I had to wake you."

"Why, may I ask—if all's well?"

"Janey, it was no dream," he went on with deep feeling. "You were right. You have found Beckyshibeta for me."

"Of course. Did you wake me to tell me that?"

He hesitated, and then went on explosively. "No . . . but—it—they—you all go together."

Janey did not answer.

"Janey, please don't be—be—" he added, hastily.

"What?" she asked, not encouragingly.

"Why, cold," he burst out. "At least don't freeze me to death. Let me tell you—let me unburden myself."

"It's quite unconventional, to put it mildly. But I haven't ordered you out, have I?" she replied, and put a hand out to lift her pillow.

"Thank you," he said, huskily. "I'll be relieved and happy to get this off my mind. . . . Janey, you've made my fortune. Beckyshibeta is marvelous. I have not had time to gauge its scope, but from what I've discovered already, it is vastly larger and more important than I ever dreamed it would be. In fact, Beckyshibeta is one of the great ancient buried cities. It will take years to excavate, and in a scientific way is a priceless discovery. The fact that Elliot discharged me from the museum staff is particularly fortunate for me. I am all on my own. I can dictate terms. I can raise any amount of capital, but I believe I'll accept your father's aid. It will be a fine thing for him, too."

"But, Phil," replied Janey, as he paused, "you told me all this before. When you explained what it would mean to you if you discovered the ruin."

"Yes, but I never dreamed of its magnitude. . . . Janey, I've tried more than once to make you see how my heart

was in this work. It appeals to me in so many ways. I like
delving into the musty past. But I could not advance because I had neither capital nor luck. You have made my
fortune. I'll be famous. I'll make money writing, lecturing,
and I'll have a big position offered to me. Expeditions in
foreign countries, if I want, or research work all over this
desert. I simply cannot think of all the advantages that
will come to me. But I think you should release me from
my promise not to tell you made the discovery."

"Certainly not. I am glad it means so much to you. You
know I always wanted you to succeed, even if I didn't appear interested. And I can feel that I returned some little
good for the—the evil you did me."

"Janey!"

"You have ruined my good name," she went on, gravely.
"It's Dad's fault, but that does not excuse you."

"Oh, Janey, it really all amounts to nothing—nothing," he
whispered, hoarsely. "In this age! Why, even if the kidnaping had been real, it could not have hurt you vitally."

"I can't agree with you, and we needn't discuss that."

"Listen. I loved you from the first moment I saw you. But
I had no hopes or delusions. You remember when I saw you
in New York. . . . Well, I don't think I'd ever have gotten
over it. I'd never have cared for any other girl. But my heart
would not have broken. This trip of yours out here—your
father's crazy plan—the wonderful hours in this desert—
and lastly, your finding Beckyshibeta for me—I can never
stand them. I can never get over them. I loved you before,
but I worship you now. . . . Janey, will you marry me?"

Janey tried to withdraw her hand from his warm clasp,
for fear that it might betray the true state of her heart.

"I will no longer be a nonentity," he hastened on. "Nor a
poor beggar. I can offer you a home—good enough for any
good girl. I can make you happy, Janey. Oh, you never
fooled me. That gay idle luxurious life never brought out
the best in you. There's a lot in you, Janey. What a wonderful girl to help a man make something out of himself! To
make a real American home!"

"Not long ago you thought me all that was bad," she replied, scornfully.

"I did not. I never even took you for what you appeared to be on the face of it."

"I remember what you said, Phil," she returned, sadly.

"I don't care what I said. God knows I had provocation enough for anything. I don't care *what* I thought, either. The inspiration of your discovery of Beckyshibeta has given me vision. I see clearly. I know you as you are in your heart. You are deceiving yourself, not me. . . . I beg you, listen to me. I'll never importune you again. I love you. I worship you. If you will only rise to the beauty and splendor of what I see!"

"Phil, you don't allow for a woman's feelings," she returned, earnestly. "I respected you—liked you. And I proved it by letting you alone. If you had refused Dad's miserable advances. *If* you had told me. *If* you had borne with me and been my friend—*Quién sabe?*—But now it's too late!"

"Janey, you can't be so little as that," he pleaded, in torture. "If you liked me at all, it might be lasting."

"You forget you—you beat me!" she whispered, and felt the hot blood move up to her cheeks.

"No, I don't forget," he said, stubbornly. "I'm sorry, of course. But I'd do it again under the same circumstances. Only I want you to understand I didn't beat you. I *spanked* you. There is a very great difference."

"I don't care about the difference. . . . Phil, do you honestly believe I oughtn't hate you for that?"

"Hate me? Good heavens, no! My love for you robs that terrible humiliation of any hate."

Janey knew that was true, and just then hated herself for the passion which held her to her pride and revenge. She knew also that she must end this talk abruptly or yield to him.

"Phil, any moment you may awaken the others," she said, managing a hauteur that must have been sickening to him. "But take my answer. It is all too late for the beautiful thing you vision. Too late! . . . I shall insist that you take me to

Flagerstown at once—and give me the protection of your name. I shall go to New York, and free you there."

"Oh, Janey!" he cried, in passionate disappointment, and threw her hand from him.

"You will—do that much—for me?" she asked, unsteadily.

"Yes, I'll make you Mrs. Phillip Randolph," he answered, bitterly, and went silently down the ledge, disappearing in the shadow.

Janey lay back with a long sigh. The ordeal was over. She realized that in a few moments she would be gloriously happy. Just the instant she had satisfied her insistent modern mind! As she settled back, and drew the blankets close about her shoulders, she felt the quivering of her body. She was cold and exhausted. But for the darkness she could never have carried on that intimate talk with Phillip to the climax it had attained. She had deceived him. She had tortured him with the hint of what might have been. The assurance of his love had been what she craved. Her breast swelled and her conscience flayed her as she recalled his words, his emotion, his faith. She would take exceeding great care that no word or act of hers would do anything but increase his remorse and love. Nevertheless she would go clear to the very last minute with her revenge. No longer revenge, but fun, simply love itself, something to enhance her surrender to him with the sweetest and most unforgettable turning of the tables.

A thought flashed by—was this trifling with her happiness—going too far, risking too much? No! If Phillip worshiped her—and how thrillingly she believed it—dared not yield to it!—a few more days on the desert and then that marvelous climax she must devise to follow their marriage in Flagerstown, would make him more miserable, more lovelorn, more wholly hers. How she must rack her brain to make her victory complete—something for which he could only love her more!

Janey lay long awake. Sleep would have robbed her. The night wore on. The silver gleam on the walls paled, darkened, vanished. And the canyon grew black, mysterious, silent as a tomb. But by intense concentration Janey managed to hear a very low murmur of running water and then the faintest of mournful winds. How wonderful the night, the darkness, the loneliness and wildness, the meaning of these old walls, the echo of past life there, the living powerful love in her heart, and the intimation that nothing died!

Then, as if by magic, the gray dawn came, the brightening of the canyon.

Janey lay in bed and thought and dreamed, and smiled, and pinched herself to prove she was awake. Presently she became aware of sounds of camp stirring below. They were early this morning. But she was loath to leave the warm blankets, and would rather have lingered there with her thoughts.

Then her father appeared on the ledge, carrying her riding habit and boots.

"Hello, you're awake," he said.

"Good morning, Father," she replied, demurely peeping from behind the edge of her blanket. He did not look happy and the smile he usually had for her was wanting.

"We're breaking camp. Randolph acquainted me with your wishes and intentions. We will leave for the post and Flagerstown at once."

"So soon! Leave Beckyshibeta today?" she exclaimed, in dismay.

"Assuredly. I daresay you will appreciate this place—and some other things—after you have lost them. Hurry and dress yourself. Breakfast is waiting."

Janey stared after his retreating form rather blankly. "Well!" she soliloquized. Then she laughed. What could she have expected? He was tremendously disappointed in her. All the better! Things were working out magnificently. She would certainly teach him a lesson that would last for life. Yet she was very glad indeed that he was so disappointed. She could endure a little longer that he and Randolph should continue to be sad about her and the mess she was going to make out of her life.

Janey got into her riding habit and boots with extraordinary pleasure and satisfaction. What a transformation! The scant garb she had been wearing did not harmonize with dignity, and certainly had not enhanced her good looks. All the same she would keep that shrunken skirt and torn blouse and the soiled stockings. She rolled them in the blankets. The worn shoes, too! Some distant future day she would don them to surprise and delight Phil.

Her little mirror showed a golden-tanned face, with glad eyes and a glorious smile; and shiny rippling hair, all the prettier for being wayward and free. Janey did not need to hide her feelings any longer. She would let Randolph and her father make their own deductions regarding her happiness.

As she descended the ledge she heard Mrs. Durland squeal with delight. Something had excited her. Randolph and Bennet were busy packing. Breakfast steamed on the fire. The Indians were coming up with the horses. A pang tore Janey's heart. Only an hour more, perhaps less, of these gleaming canyon walls! But she would come back. The gentlemen were not blind to her changed attire and mood, though they did not fuss over her. Indeed she could not catch Randolph's eye.

Mrs. Durland came up almost running, breathless, triumphant, and radiant. "Oh, my dear, how different—you look!" she panted. "What do you think?—That villain Black Dick forgot to take our money—and jewels. My bag was hanging —on a cedar twig. Imagine! I was simply overcome . . . and here's your diamond ring."

"Well, of all the luck!" cried Janey, surprised and pleased, as she took the ring. "I'm very glad for you, Mrs. Durland. Of course my loss would have been little. . . . So our desperado forgot to take what he stole? Well, he was a queer one."

"I can almost forgive him now," replied Mrs. Durland, fervently.

Bert came up and tipped his sombrero to Janey. But his
sour look did not fit his graceful gesture. Janey did not need
to be told that her father had passed on the important news.
The Durlands might be civil, but Bert, at least, would never
forgive her. Janey reflected that it might not matter how
they felt or what they did. She would be careful, however,
to make it plain to Randolph and her father that she feared
the Durlands and desired to placate them.

Janey had her breakfast alone. One of the Indians left
his work and stood nearby, apparently fascinated at the
sight of her. Randolph kept his back turned and worked
hard on the packs.

"Phil, please get me another cup of coffee," she called.
He hurriedly complied and fetched it to her.

"You make such lovely coffee," she said, looking up at
him. "I'll miss that, at least, when I'm home again."

"Bennet made this coffee," replied Randolph, brusquely.

"Oh!" But nothing could have hurt Janey this wonderful
morning. Nothing except leaving her canyon! She went
aside by herself so that she could feel and think, unaffected
by Randolph or her father. The gleaming walls spoke to
her. The great red corner of rock that led off toward Beckyshibeta beckoned for her to come. And she went far enough
to peep round. How wild and ragged and rocky! It was a
wilderness of broken stones. Yet for her they had a spirit
and a voice. The stream murmured from the gorge, the
canyon swifts darted by, their wings shining in the sunlight, the sweet dry sage fragrance filled her nostrils.

Janey gazed all around and upward, everywhere, with
deep reverence for this lonely chasm in the rock crust of
the earth. She would return soon, and often thereafter
while Randolph was at work on the excavation of the
ruined pueblo. She would like to plan her future, her
home, her usefulness in the world, here under the spell of
her canyon.

How soon would that be? Not yet had she planned any
farther than Flagerstown. No farther than the hour which
would make her Phil's wife! The tumultuousness of that

thought had inhibited a completion of her plan. But was not that the climax—the end? It did not satisfy Janey. It entailed confession, total surrender, both of which she would be glad to give, yet—. Suddenly she had an inspiration. It absolutely dazzled her. It swept her away. It was a perfect solution to her problem, and she could have laughed her joy to these watching jealous walls. But—was it possible? Could she accomplish it? How strange she had not thought of it before! Easy as it was wonderful! Whereupon she gave herself up to a mute reverent farewell to Beckyshibeta.

A lusty shout interrupted Janey's rapt mood: "Come on, Janey. We're off!" called her father.

Very soon then Janey was astride a horse, comfortable and confident in her riding outfit, going down the trail through the cedars. She was the last of the cavalcade. Randolph and the Indians were ahead, driving the pack animals. Bennet was looking after the Durlands. Endicott rode ahead of Janey. They crossed the boulder-strewn stream bed, climbed the dusty soft red trail, and wound away through cedars. Janey did not look back. It would not have been any use, for her eyes were blinded by tears. They did not wholly clear until she rode out of the rock walls, up on to the desert.

Janey rode alone all day. And surely it was the fullest and sweetest day of all her life. Forty miles of sage to traverse to the next camp—purple color and wondrous fragrance all around—red and gold walls beckoning from the horizons—the sweep and loneliness of vast stretches—sometimes all by herself on the trail, far behind the others —these were the splendid accompaniments of her happy dreams and thoughts, of long serious realizations, of the permanent settling of convictions and ideals, of consciousness of a softened and exalted heart.

Sunset fell while they were yet upon the trail—one of the incomparable Arizona sunsets that Janey had come to love. A black horizon-wide wall blocked the West. The red

and golden rays of sunlight swept down over it, spreading
light over the desert. Above masses of purple cloud with
silver edges hid the sky. And it all gloriously faded into
dusk.

A flock of black and white sheep crossed the trail in front
of Janey. The shepherds were a little Indian boy and girl
both mounted on the same pony. How wild and shy! The
dogs barked at Janey. The sheep trooped over the ridge
top. And lastly the little shepherds and their pony stood
silhouetted against the afterglow. Janey waved and waved.
The little girl answered—a fleeting shy flip of hand. Then
they were gone.

Soon after that a bright campfire greeted Janey from a
bend in the trail. She rode into camp and dismounted, to
discover she felt no fatigue, no aches, no pains—and that
the exhilaration of the morning had not worn away in that
long ride. Mrs. Durland was bemoaning her state; Bert
limped to his tasks; and Endicott showed the effect of long
sitting in a saddle. The Westerners were active.

The camp was in the open desert, in the lee of some
low rocks. Coyotes were wailing and yelping out in the
darkness. A cold wind swept round the rocks and pierced
through Janey. How good the blazing bits of sage. She
was ravishingly hungry.

Janey ate her supper sitting on an uncomfortable pack,
and she had to eat it quickly while it stayed warm. Firewood appeared to be scarce, and the desert wind grew
colder. There was little or no gayety in the company. Bennet tried to make a few facetious remarks to Mrs. Durland,
but they fell flat. Janey edged so close to the fire that she
almost burned her boots. Randolph kept in the shadow. She
felt him watching her, and needed no more to keep her
spirits high. Endicott huddled on the ground on the other
side of the fire, and his head drooped. Bert was silent and
dejected. Mrs. Durland complained of the awful effects of
the ride, the food, the cold, the wind and everything.

"Are those terrible wild creatures going to keep that din
up all night?" she asked.

"Wal, I reckon so," replied Bennet. "Coyotes are noisy an' they'll come right up an' pull at your hat, when you're in bed."

"Heavens! And we must sleep on the flat ground!"

"You might bunk up on the rock. It'll be tolerable windy. . . . Miss Janey, aren't you scared and frozen stiff?"

"Both," laughed Janey. "But I think this is great. I love to hear those wild coyotes."

"No more desert for me," sighed Mrs. Durland.

"Bert, surely you will come back to Arizona someday?" asked Janey, curiously.

"What for?" he asked, fixing her with gloomy eyes.

"Of course, Janey, you'll be coming back often to see your husband digging in that heap of stones?" added Mrs. Durland.

"Y-yes, but not very soon," replied Janey. "Father is coming back shortly to start the excavating of Beckyshibeta. Aren't you, Dad?"

"Sure. I'm going to dig a grave for myself out here," growled her father.

"Haw! Haw! Haw!" bawled the trader. "Did you heah that, Randolph? . . . Wal, folks, you'll all come back to Arizona. I've yet to see the man or woman who'd slept out on this desert an' didn't want to come back."

"You all better turn in," said Randolph. "Firewood is scarce, and you'll be called at dawn."

"I forgot about bed," exclaimed Janey, giving her palms a last toast over the red coals. "Phil, where's my couch?"

"Here," he replied, and led her a few steps.

"Ugh, it's windy. I hate to think of bed on the cold rocks," returned Janey, trying to see in the dark.

"Yours won't be windy or cold or hard," he replied, briefly. "Here. There's a foot of sage under your blankets, and a thick windbreak. You'll be comfortable."

"Oh! . . . You found time to do this for me?" she asked, looking up at him. The starlight showed his face dark and troubled, his eyes sad.

"Certainly. It was little enough."

"Thank you, Phil. You are good to me," she said, softly, and held out her hand.

Randolph gave a start, clasped her hand convulsively, and strode away without even saying good night.

Janey gazed a moment at his vanishing form. Then she plumped down on her bed. "Gee," she whispered, "I want to be careful. He might grab me—and then it would be the end!"

Removing only her boots Janey slipped down into the bed. How soft and fragrant of sage! Her pillow was a fleecy sheepskin, one she had seen in Randolph's pack. Then her feet, bravely stretching down, suddenly came in contact with something hot. It startled her. Presently she ascertained it was a hot stone wrapped in canvas. Randolph had heated this and put it in her bed. Let the desert wind blow! The white stars blinked down at her from the deep blue dome above. Had she ever thought them pitiless, indifferent, mocking? The wind swept with low moans through the sage; the coyotes kept up their wild staccato barks; the campfire died out and low voices of men ceased. Tranquil, cold, beautiful night enfolded the scene. And Janey lay there wide-eyed, watching the heavens, wondering at the beauty and mystery of nature, at the glory of love, marveling at the happiness that had been bestowed upon her unworthy self.

Next day about mid-afternoon they rode across the wide barren stretch of desert to the post, the pack train far ahead with Randolph in the lead, and Bennet trying to hold Mrs. Durland in the saddle to the last. Janey brought up the rear, so late that when she reached the last level all the others had disappeared in the green grove that surrounded the post.

Mohave met Janey at the gate, bareheaded, respectful, but with a face of woe.

"Why, Mohave, have you lost your grandmother—or something?" exclaimed Janey.

"I reckon it's worse, Miss Janey," he replied, meaningly.

"Oh—goodness! For a moment I felt sorry for you. Mohave boy, you keep shy of Eastern girls after this. They're no good."

"Most of them ain't, I reckon. But I know one who's an angel. An' she's gonna be married to a—"

"Mohave, who told you?" interrupted Janey, as she slipped out of the saddle.

"Thet big-mouthed, lop-eared, hard-headed Bennet. He came aroarin' it to everybody, an' no winter cyclone could have knocked us flatter."

"Mohave, honest now, aren't you glad—for my sake?" asked Janey, sweetly. She liked this frank clean-cut cowboy.

"Wal, Miss Janey, since you tax me—yes, I am, seein' I cain't have you myself," he replied, with reddening face. "I never liked thet kidnapin' stunt an' didn't understand. Shore, if we'd known you was engaged all the time there'd never been such a mix-up. Poor old Ray, he was the hardest hit, I reckon."

"How about him, Mohave?" asked Janey, anxiously.

"Gone. An' mighty shamed of himself. Asked me to tell you he'd plumb lost his haid. An' wanted you to know it wasn't the first time."

"Well! ! What did he mean?"

"I reckon Ray figgered thet if you knowed he'd made a fool of hisself over a gurl before, you wouldn't feel so bad aboot what you did to him."

"He was man enough to confess his weakness. I call that square of him, don't you, Mohave?"

"It shore is. Wal, Ray was a good sort, when he wasn't loco over a gurl, or full of licker."

"How are the other boys?"

"They wasn't so bad, till this news came. Reckon now they're down at the bunkhouse drownin' their grief. They shore left the work to me an' the boss."

"How funny! What did they say?"

"Wal, I can't recollect all, but one crack I'll never fergit. Tay-Tay busted out like this. 'W-w-w-what the h-h-hell you

think of thet grave robber? He's s-s-s-stole our gurl an' he's
got a face like a sick c-c-cow!' "

"Well, I never," laughed Janey. "Mr. Randolph ought to
look well and happy, oughtn't he?"

"He shore ought. I reckon, though, he feels turrible bad
aboot your goin' East an' him havin' to stay on account of
Beckyshibeta. Bennet told us. You can jest bet, Miss Janey,
no cowboy would let you go off alone."

For once Janey was startled, but she maintained her outward air of coolness. Somehow she had forgotten that the
cowboys would wonder why she did not stay here with Randolph until his plans were complete. To let Mohave or any
of the others guess her secret would upset all her plans.

"I fancy not," she said, quickly. "But you mustn't think
ill of Mr. Randolph. The discovering of the pueblo has upset all our plans. It's very important. I'm hoping to per-
suade him to go East with us for a few weeks, but I have
some very urgent business reasons for going back im-
mediately with Father. Please regard that as confidential,
Mohave. And tell the boys we'll be leaving early in the
morning. I wouldn't want to miss saying good-by."

When Mohave had left Janey breathed a sigh of relief.
Her excuse had been a lame one, but the honest cowboy
had apparently swallowed it without a second thought.

Janey then went on into the house, first encountering
Mrs. Bennet, to whose warm greeting she responded. The
Indian maid showed shy gladness at Janey's safe return.
Bennet came bustling in with Endicott, both of them blushing and coughing. Janey thought her father looked much
better and she guessed why. The Durlands were evidently
in their rooms, and Randolph was not in sight.

"Mr. Bennet, we shall want to leave early in the morning," said Janey.

"Aw, Miss Janey! One more day," he entreated.

"I'm sorry, but we must go. Some other time we shall
come and stay longer. . . . Dad, I'll change and pack now.
Will you please tell Phil I want to talk to him presently.
Say in an hour. Tell him to knock at my door."

"All right, star-eyed enigma," returned her father, with a puzzled glance upon her.

Janey rushed to her room, and lost no time in bathing. She put on her most fetching gown, one of those scant creations that Randolph had hated, yet could not resist. How swiftly her blood ran! What a glow on her face! Indeed her eyes were like stars. Would Randolph see—would he be proud and wretched at once—would he betray himself? While she packed her mind whirled, keeping pace with her racing pulse. If she had not conceived a grand finale to this desert romance she was a poor judge of wit and humor. Her father would be completely floored, and best of all, won forever. Randolph? But no stretch of imagination could picture Randolph as she hoped to see him.

A tap sounded on the door. It startled Janey. She caught her breath and her hand went to her breast. She glanced at her mirror and the image she saw there quickened her agitation. But as quickly she recovered her composure.

"Come in," she said.

But the door did not move, nor was the rap repeated. Janey went swiftly and opened it. Randolph stood there. She had not seen him like this.

"Oh, it's you, Phil. I'd forgotten. Come in. I want to talk to you."

He did not make any move to enter and apparently he was dumb.

"Well, you're very reserved—and considerate, all of a sudden," she said sarcastically. "Pray don't be shy about entering my bedroom *now*. . . . Please come in."

Randolph entered reluctantly. There was no bully about him now.

"What do you want?—Was it necessary to ask me here?"

"Yes, I think so. The living room is not private. And I want to ask a particular favor of you. Will you grant it?"

He went to the window and looked out. Then presently he turned with an almost grim look.

"Yes—anything."

"Thank you, Phil," she went on, going close to him, quite closer than was necessary. Every moment made Janey more sure of herself. There was a strange and magical sweetness in this sincerity of deceit. Yet was it deceit? She risked a great deal, trusting to his mood, his humility. It was a woman's perverse thrilling desire to tempt him. But if he should seize her in his arms! Even so, she would carry out her plan.

"Before I ask the favor, I want to tell you that I would rather have had this otherwise."

"Ha! Maybe I wouldn't!" he exclaimed. "But what do *you* mean?"

"It's hard to say. Partly, I'd like to have spared you this."

"Never mind about me. What's the favor you'd ask?"

"Phil, you are going to marry me—aren't you?"

"Certainly. Unless you change your mind."

"Everybody knows it. Everybody thinks we've been engaged."

"That appears to be the way Bennet and your father have spread it on," he replied, in bitterness.

"What is the object of this marriage?" she asked, proudly lifting her head.

"Your father says—and *you* say—to save your reputation."

"Yes. My honor! . . . And I fear your sacrifice will fail if you continue to look and act as you do. You are no happy bridegroom-to-be. Tay-Tay said you had a face like a sick cow. You certainly look wretched. If you don't cheer up and change—act and look like a lover—the Durlands will guess the truth. So will the cowboys. Not to mention those in Flagerstown with whom we come in contact. It is a tremendous bluff we are playing. I can do my part. You see that I look happy, don't you?"

"Yes, I do," he answered, miserably. "And so help me God, I can't understand you. Always you seem a lie."

"All women are actresses, Phil. I shall not fail here. And I ask this last favor of you. Look and play the part of an accepted lover. For my sake!"

"My God!—Janey Endicott, you can ask that of a man whose only crime has been to love you so well? . . . And who must lose you!"

"Phil, if you loved me *that* well you could die for me."

"I could, far more easily than do what you ask. It is almost an insupportable ordeal you set me. I was never much at hiding my feelings."

"Phil, the Durlands and the cowboys must not guess this marriage is a—a fake."

"I grant that. And I know I look like a poor lost devil. But I thought that'd seem natural to everybody. They all heard I was not going East."

"You don't know women, my desert friend. Mrs. Durland is keen as a whip. If you can deceive her—make this engagement seem real and of long standing, you will stop her wagging tongue. Then after I get to New York I can find ways socially to please her. Right here is the danger."

"Perhaps you see it more clearly than I," Randolph said, mournfully. "Anyway, I'll accept your judgment."

"Then you will grant my favor?" asked Janey, beginning to succumb to repressed emotion.

"Favor! I call it the hardest job ever given me. Marrying you will be nothing, compared to this damned hypocrisy you ask."

"I do ask, Phil. I beg of you. Now at the last I confess I'm not so brazen. I'm afraid of scandal. Nothing bad ever has touched my name yet. All this modern stuff about freedom, independence, license is rot. Face to face with the truth, I beg of you—do this thing for me. At any cost."

"Yes—Janey," he gulped, and leaned against the window.

Janey's reserve strength had oozed out in expression. She waited in suspense. She saw his lean jaw quiver and the cords set in his neck. He turned to transfix her with accusing eyes.

"On one condition," he said.

"Condition!—What?" she whispered.

"This, then, is the last time you and I will ever be alone together?" he asked, huskily.

She was past falsehood and could only stare mutely at him.

"Of course it must be. Well, my price for your favor is that you let me . . . No! I will not bargain. . . . You lovely heartless thing—you'd only refuse. I'll *take* what will give me strength to do your bidding!"

Janey backed against the wall, her hands against her breast, as if to ward him off. But when like a whirlwind he seized her in his arms he never knew those trembling hands locked round his neck. Mad with grief and unrequited love, he crushed her to his breast and pressed wild unsatisfied kisses upon her closed eyes, her parted lips, her neck. And releasing her as suddenly, he staggered to the door, like a blinded man, and leaned his face against it, sobbing: "Janey! Janey! . . . Janey!"

He did not turn to see her outstretched arms, her convulsed face. And as Janey could not speak he bolted out in ignorance. Janey closed her eyes, slowly recovering.

"I thought—that was—my finish," she whispered, pantingly. "Poor boy—he never looked at me! . . . Well, it'll only be—all the sweeter!"

13

THE SUN HAD SET when the car entered the heavy forest of pine that skirted the mountains. Snow was blowing. The wind was bitter cold, and moaned in the trees. How the car hummed on! Night fell, and the forest was black. The headlights cast broad gleams into the forest at the curves of the road, making specters of the dark pines.

Soon, then, the street lamps of Flagerstown terminated that wonderful ride.

In the hotel lobby, Janey, indifferent to loungers there,

held frozen ungloved hands to the open fire. She had
learned the real good of fire, its dire necessity, as she had
begun the learning of many other things.

As Janey turned, she saw a tall stoop-shouldered man,
rather lean and scholarly, rise from a chair to accost Randolph.

"How do you do, Mr. Elliot," replied Randolph, constrainedly. "How are you? This is my friend—and patron, I
may add—Mr. Endicott, of New York."

"Ah! How do you do, Mr. Endicott," returned Elliot,
rather slowly, extending his hand to meet Endicott's. "Patron? Of what, may I ask?"

"Hardly patron, just yet," replied Endicott. "Randolph is
a little previous, naturally."

"Yes, he is, indeed," returned the doctor, not without sarcasm. "Overzealous, I may say, in estimating things. Dreamy
when he should be scientific. Witness the ridiculous rumor
just phoned in from Cameron."

"Rumor? What was it?" asked Randolph, tersely. Janey
liked the lift of his head, and grew interested. No doubt this
was the museum director who had discharged Phillip.

"Some nonsense about your having discovered Beckyshibeta," replied Elliot, with a dry laugh. "It was telephoned in
to the newspaper by a chauffeur. Annoying to me, to say the
least."

Randolph glanced at Endicott and said, "We stopped at
Cameron for gas."

"Must have been Driver Bill," replied Endicott, sprightly,
with a shrewd eye upon Elliot.

"Yes, Dr. Elliot, it was—rather previous," said Randolph
in as dry a tone as the director's. But there was fire in his
eye.

"Ahem!—I'm waiting here for two of our men due from
New Mexico. Expect to put them on the job from which I
removed you. I trust Mr. Bennet, the trader, informed you
of this move."

"Yes, Bennet told me you had fired me. Mr. Endicott here
will corroborate it."

Endicott nodded in reply to the doctor's questioning look, but he did not speak. Janey knew the gleam in her father's eye. He would say something presently.

"Randolph, I was very sorry indeed to remove you," went on Elliot blandly. "There's no need to repeat my reasons. You've been advised often enough."

"Dr. Elliot, you need not distress yourself over doing what you considered your duty," rejoined Randolph. "It certainly doesn't distress me. In fact it was the only lucky thing that ever happened to me since my connection with the museum."

"Indeed. Excuse me if I fail to see any good fortune in that for you," replied Elliot, stiffly.

"You never could see much about me. Perhaps you will when I tell you that *after* you removed me I discovered Beckyshibeta."

"What!" exclaimed Elliot, incredulously.

"I discovered Beckyshibeta," repeated Randolph, forcefully, truth clear in his paling face and piercing eye. "Probably the greatest of all pueblo ruins. I have my proof. Mr. Endicott and his daughter can substantiate my claim. Bennet, the cowboys, and a Mrs. Durland with her son were all there."

Speechlessly Dr. Elliot turned to Endicott for corroboration of this astounding assertion.

"Fact," said Endicott, shortly. "I'm about to wire Dr. Bushnell, head of the museum. Also Jackson, a good friend of mine. Want them to know that I stand behind Randolph. It remains to be decided whether we shall let the museum in on the excavation work."

"Dr. Bushnell! Jackson!" ejaculated Elliot, weakly. "May I ask—are you Mr. Elijah Endicott?"

"The same, sir," returned Endicott, bowing, and abruptly left the astounded director to join Janey beside the fire.

"Janey, old girl, did you get that?" he whispered. "I'm simply tickled pink, as you say. . . . Now listen to Phil lay him out cold."

Dr. Elliot seemed to be in the throes of amazement and consternation.

"Ah! Indeed!—So it's true," he began, floundering to retrieve himself. "Most remarkable. Incredible, I may say. But of course, I understand—a fact. You are most fortunate, Randolph, in your discovery and to have gained the interest of Elijah Endicott. I congratulate you. . . . And I—er—ahem—perhaps it is I who is somewhat previous. Pray forget your hasty dismissal. It really was not authentic—going through a third party. Somewhat irregular. We can adjust the matter amicably. In fact I—I'd consider it a favor if you will not mention the matter to our New York office."

"I've accepted my release, Dr. Elliot, thank you, and shall wire the museum to that effect," replied Randolph, with cold dignity, and bowed himself away.

The director looked a dazed, beaten and frightened man.

"Say, Janey, didn't Phil look great?" crowed Endicott, with gleeful pride. "What a coup for him! That will cost Elliot his job. And by gad, I'll see that it's offered to Randolph."

"Daddy, you like Phillip, don't you?" asked Janey, softly.

"Love him, you icicle. And you bet I'll push him for keeps."

"You're kind and good. I'm glad you—you care for him," responded Janey, and turned to gaze into the fire. "It's too bad you—Phillip—I— Oh, words are idle and useless."

"Janey, darling, just then you reminded me of your mother," said her father, with feeling. "It's a long time since you've done that."

"Mother? . . . I'm glad, Daddy. Perhaps—after this—this lesson of yours I will grow more like her."

"Janey," whispered Endicott, bending over her, "you mean to go on with this cruel marriage and—"

"Yes," she returned, dropping her eyes.

"It will kill Phillip."

"Nonsense. Men don't die of unrequited love."

"If your mother had led me to the altar—and left me—I'm sure I'd never have lived to face it."

"Phil Randolph is made of sterner stuff. Besides he has a brilliant future. . . . I'm tired now, Dad, and very hungry."

The sunshine poured in at Janey's window, telling her that she had slept late, though this was to be the day of days. She lay watching the gold shadows on the curtain, aware of the fresh cool dry air on her face. Her active mind took up the development of plans where the night before she had left off. Her father had secured a Pullman drawing room on the Limited. The securing of this, or at least a compartment on the train, was of paramount importance. Only one more detail to arrange—the strongest link in the chain to her climax!

Janey arose, conscious of inward excitement and suspense. After all, she could not be sure of anything until she was Phillip's wife. That would be the consummation of hopes, the allaying of fears. The rest would be like the denouement of a good play.

She looked out of her window. How blue the sky! The mountain peaks stood up like dark spears. Patches of snow shone in the sunlight, running down to the edge of the vast green belt of forest land. She could see into the fields adjacent to town. Horses were romping with manes flying in the wind; red and white cattle were grazing on a grassy hill; the scattered pine trees seemed to call to her to come and ride. Cutover timberlands led her gaze to distant foothills and these to far-off black bluffs and hazy desert. Arizona! There was no place in the world so full of romance and beauty, and the natural things that stirred the soul.

Janey went into the little open parlor of the hotel, where her father sat before a cozy fire, reading a newspaper.

"What a lazy bride-to-be!" he said good-humoredly. "We had breakfast long ago."

"Mawnin', Dad," drawled Janey. "Reckon I'll have a cup of coffee and some toast up heah."

"You look very sweet and lovely for a prospective murderess," he said. "Janey, old dear, I give up forever trying to figure women."

"Fine! Now you will be the best of fathers. Where's Phil?"

"He was here a moment ago with the marriage license. Lord, but he's funny. Like a sleepwalker! I have made a ten o'clock appointment with a minister—Dr. Cardwell. Nice old chap. He's from Connecticut. Came here years ago with lung trouble. His life had been despaired of in the East. But he's hale and hearty now. I tell you, Janey, this Arizonie, as Bennet calls it, is a wonderful country."

"Arizona. Mellow, golden, sustaining, beautiful, clean with desert wind," murmured Janey, gazing down into the fire. "Presently I shall tell you what it has done for me."

"I'll fetch your coffee and toast," returned Endicott, with alacrity.

The moments passed with Janey musing. Presently her father entered, carrying a small tray. Randolph also came in. He wore a dark suit that showed his stalwart form to advantage. Janey admired again the clean-shaven tanned face, lean and strong.

"Good morning, Miss Endicott," he said, with courtesy, but his steady gaze made Janey almost feel a little uneasy in spite of herself. She gazed at him over her cup of coffee.

"Howdy, Phil. Are the horses ready?"

"No," he flashed. "But the taxi is."

Janey laughed, her composure restored. How eager Randolph was to get this awful business settled!

"Dad, you said our train left at seven something, didn't you?"

"Seven-ten. It's the Limited and always on time," he replied.

"So long to wait. I wish for Mr. Randolph's sake it left hours earlier."

"Don't worry about Phillip, my dear," returned Endicott. "We've got a lot to talk over and won't bother you."

"Thank you. . . . I'll get my things on and be back pronto," said Janey, and hurried away to her room.

Randolph showed that the strain was wearing upon him. Janey thought it would be wise for her to see as little as possible of him after the wedding up until nearly train time. She felt nervous and tense herself. It wanted but a few minutes to ten o'clock. She put on her coat and hat, and a veil, which she carefully arranged. How white her face and big her eyes! Then she hurried back to join the gentlemen, who rose at her entrance.

"I'm ready," she said, rather tremulously. "Is—everything arranged?"

"Why, I'm sure it is, Janey," returned her father, turning to Randolph. "There's not so much. Minister, license, taxi. What else?"

"Mr. Randolph, did you purchase a wedding ring?"

"No," he replied, with the strangest of glances at her.

"Then you must do so at once. I'll go with you. Surely there's a jeweler here."

"I have a wedding ring. It was my mother's. It hardly matters whether it fits or not."

"Doesn't it?—That's all you know," said Janey. Her hands were trembling while she tried it on. "Oh, it's a perfect fit. . . . What a pretty ring! I like old-fashioned wedding rings best."

"Old-fashioned weddings, too," added her father. "Lord, Janey, I always dreaded one of those swell weddings for you. Might have saved myself a lot of worry. Come on. We'll have this over in a jiffy."

He led her downstairs, through the lobby, and out to a waiting taxi. Randolph had evidently stopped behind for something. Presently he came out, and squeezing into the taxi he laid something on Janey's knee without a word. She tucked aside a corner of her veil and opened the loose paper package on her lap. Flowers of some kind! Then she thrilled. The tiny bouquet was composed of bits of cedar and juniper foliage, with their green and lavender berries, several wild roses, and a sprig of sage with the exquisite rare purple blossoms. Janey was so deeply touched that she could not speak, and she quickly dropped the corner of veil, lest Phil should see the havoc wrought by these sweet symbols from the desert.

The short ride, the simple brief ceremony, and the return to the hotel were like changing moments of a trance to Janey. She would not have exchanged the simplicity of her marriage for all the pomp of royalty.

Once more safe in her room she laid aside the bouquet, flung her gloves, tore off the veil, and threw aside hat and coat. And she did not recognize the face in the mirror. Janey had never raved about her looks, but she gloried in them now.

"It's over. I'm his wife," she whispered, kissing the slim band of gold on her finger. "Now! Now I'm safe—and oh, so unutterably happy! . . . How can I wait to tell him? Suppose he ran off to his desert before I could! . . . Oh, my bursting heart!"

Janey wept in the exaltation of that hour. It was long before composure returned, and then it was such composure as she had never known. No one would have guessed that she had cried like an overjoyous girl.

Her father knocked at her door and called: "Janey, we've arranged a lunch over here at a restaurant. Will you come?"

"Indeed I will. Just a minute, Dad, and I'll join you." She dispensed with the veil this time. Let them be mystified at the glow on her face and the light in her eyes! They were only men who knew nothing of the wondrous strength and generosity of a woman's heart. Then she went out.

"My word, Janey, but you look great!" exclaimed Endicott, with conscious pride.

Randolph stared at her as if she were an impenetrable stone image hiding the truth of woman. Nevertheless, once seated at table, the constraint eased, and they enjoyed a capital luncheon.

"Well, that was fine," said Endicott, with satisfaction. "Now, Janey, we'll take you back to the hotel, where Phil and I must go into an important conference over plans for work at Beckyshibeta."

"I shall not be lonely. I'll visit the stores—and look out for cowboys," replied Janey, gaily.

"You'll find cowboys on every corner," warned Endicott. "Be careful, Janey," he grimaced.

"Wait, Dad, please," replied Janey, catching his sleeve. "I've something to tell you and—my husband."

Randolph winced at the first use of that word between them. Endicott dropped back in his chair, sure of catastrophe.

Janey transfixed them with a glance in which long-past resentment and pain blended now with some emotion they could not name.

"Gentlemen, do you recall one late afternoon at Bennet's trading post when you planned to kidnap me?"

Randolph looked stricken and Endicott gulped: "No. Can't say I do."

"Tax your memory, Dad," went on Janey, dryly. "It never was good. But this was a special occasion."

Randolph coughed uneasily. "I remember, Miss Endicott."

"I am no longer Miss Endicott," corrected Janey.

"Pardon, Mrs. Randolph," he corrected himself mockingly.

"Dad, I was lying out in the hammock beside the open window when you made your infamous offer to Phil Randolph," said Janey.

"My God, no!" cried her father, thunderstruck. "I don't believe you."

"Listen. You'll believe your very own words," replied Janey, and went on to repeat many things that had been burned indelibly on her memory.

"That's enough," suddenly interrupted her father, very red in the face. "I can see you were there."

"All the time you knew!" exclaimed Randolph, wide-eyed and ashamed.

"All the time," replied Janey, smiling at them.

"Lord save me from another daughter," burst out Endicott, helplessly.

"I'll run along now," added Janey, rising. "Thanks for the luncheon. I'll remember it. . . . Dad, we will wait for dinner on the train. . . . Mr. Randolph, you will go to the train with us to say good-by? Please. It will look better. Must I remind you—"

"No, you needn't remind me of anything," interrupted Randolph, almost violently, dark and passionate pain and reproach in his eyes. "I'll be at the train to bid—good-by—to my wife—forever."

"Ah— Thank you. Then all is well," replied Janey, averting her eyes. "*Adiós*—till then."

As she glided away from them, out into the main restaurant, she heard her father say: "Phil, my God—I need a drink."

Randolph's reply followed with a sudden scrape of a chair on the floor.

"Eli, you old villain, I'll need two," he said, weakly. "And we'll drink to all that's left to me—Beckyshibeta."

Janey went out tingling, blushing, glowing. It was even more fun, more satisfaction than she had anticipated. How flabbergasted her father had been! And she had dared only one fleeting look at the stricken Randolph. "All the time you knew!" he had cried. Janey reflected that when he had returned to sanity he would recall many things that might embarrass her. But she would take good care he never recovered his sanity. Then she went about the last few tasks needed to insure this blissful future for Randolph.

First she engaged the hotel porter to fetch Randolph's bag to the train with hers and her father's. She made it clear to the bright-eyed colored lad—as well as remunerative—that Randolph was not to see this removal of baggage. Next she set out to look for some cowboys.

But not until actually embarked on this quest did she realize its absurdity and risk, not to consider embarrassment. It was an early afternoon hour on Saturday. Flagerstown appeared full of cowboys and those she passed on the street were certainly not unaware of her presence. Finally, near the post office, Janey located three typical cowboys standing beside a motion-picture advertisement that graced the corner of the block. It happened to be a vacant lot, which accounted, perhaps, for the cowboys being comparatively alone.

Janey walked slowly by, calmly appraising them. How like Mohave, Zoroaster, Ray! Cowboys all resembled one another. Janey expected to be noticed and commented upon. She was not disappointed.

"Andy, did you see what I seen?" broke out one.

"Wal, I reckon. An' I'm shore dizzy," was the reply.

"Some looker, pards," added the third.

The encounter ordinarily would have ended there, but these cowboys, or some cowboys, at least, were indispensable to her plan. She had to have them. She was prepared to go to the limit of making eyes at them to carry her point. Thinking hard Janey decided to walk by them again, down the street, then return, and ask them to come into the post office. To that end she turned back. As she neared them she was afraid she was smiling. What a warm feeling she had for these lean, hard-faced cowboys!

She passed, with ears acute to catch any whispers.

"My Gawd—Andy, look at them legs!" hoarsely whispered one. "Wimmin ought to be arrested fer wearin' them short skirts."

"Only seen her eyes, but thet was aplenty," came the reply. "My pore little Susie! I'll never love her any more."

Janey did not hear the third man's remark, and was glad she had not. Her face burned. What keen devils these cowboys! Right then and there Janey's plan, so far as they were concerned, went into eclipse. Still she would not give up. Crossing the street she went into the department store, made a few purchases, and going out, crossed the street again, at the other end of the block, and came down to enter the post office. She was cudgeling her brain. If those cowboys saw her and followed her into the post office she would risk speaking to them. Most cowboys were chivalrous gentlemen at heart, for all their coarseness and deviltry.

There appeared to be only two men in the post office. One was huge and dark, the other small and fair. Suddenly Janey stood transfixed. She recognized bold black eyes in the giant and sly twinkling ones in the other. She knew these men.

"Black Dick! Snitz!" she exclaimed, in astonishment. "Oh, I'm glad to meet you."

"Same hyar, Miss Endicott," replied Dick, smiling broadly, as he removed his ragged sombrero. "How about you, Snitz?"

"Me? I never was so tickled in my life," said Snitz, gallant and bareheaded. "It shore is fine of you to speak to us—after the deal we gave you."

"Never mind that. But aren't you afraid to be in town? Aren't you in danger of being arrested?"

"Wal, Miss, not that we know of. You see I'm not exactly the fellar you took me fer."

"Oh, then you're not Black Dick, the outlaw?" asked Janey, in disappointment.

"I'm awful sorry, Miss, but I ain't. Honest. Didn't your father tell you aboot us?"

"My father! No," replied Janey, ponderingly.

"Wal, he shore ought to have. Fer he hired me an' Snitz to give you a scare."

"Ah, I see. . . . And it was no accident that you left Mrs. Durland's jewel bag behind?"

"Accident? I should smile not. I jest hung it on a tree where she'd bump her haid on it."

"Well! Well! My Dad's the limit, isn't he?"

"If you want my idee, Miss, I think he's a prince," replied Dick, heartily.

"You'll always be Black Dick and Snitz to me. But I'm

indeed glad you're not real desperadoes. What a trick you played on us!"

Suddenly a thought like a bright flash struck Janey into radiance.

"Come here, both of you," she whispered, and drew the grinning men away from the door into a corner. Here they were out of sight of the post-office employees. No others had yet entered. What luck! Janey felt a gush of riotous blood heat her veins. "Will you do me a favor? Do you want to make fifty dollars apiece?"

"Well, Miss Endicott, your voice is sweet music," whispered Dick.

"Lady, I'll lay down my life fer you fer nothin'," declared Snitz.

"Listen," began Janey, hurriedly. "I am no longer Miss Endicott. I was married to Mr. Randolph today. . . . Never mind congratulating me. Listen. Father and I leave tonight on the Limited. Mr. Randolph—my husband—I'm afraid he doesn't want to go East with me very bad. But I want him to go. I want him terribly. Will you help me kidnap him?"

"Wal, we'll hawg-tie the cold-hearted scoundrel an' throw him on thet train," declared Dick, his eyes rolling.

"I never heard of the like," added Snitz, most forcefully. "The lucky son-of-a-gun! But them archaeologists are plumb queer ducks. Lady, we'll shore do anythin' fer you."

"Splendid. Can you get another trusty man—a friend— one who is big and strong? Randolph will fight."

"Shore. I know a fellar who's bigger'n a hill. He can throw a barrel of flour right up into a wagon. Reckon the three of us can put Randolph on thet train in less'n a couple of winks."

"Very well. Then it's settled," went on Janey, now calm and serene. "Here are your instructions. The three of you be at the station when the Limited comes in. Keep sharp lookout for me. I'll be with father and Mr. Randolph. Follow us a little behind—not too close—and when we reach our Pullman you wait a little aside. I'll stop at the car entrance nearest the drawing room. I'll wait until the con ductor calls all aboard. When I step up that will be your signal to seize Randolph and carry him after me. Be quick. And don't be gentle. Remember, he is powerful and will fight. I want this to go off just like that."

And Janey snapped her fingers.

"Lady, say them instructions over," replied Dick, earnestly.

She repeated them word for word.

Black Dick lifted his shaggy black head.

"Jest like thet," he said, snapping huge fingers. "Lady, it's as good as done."

"Then here's your money in advance," said Janey, producing some bills. "You won't fail me?"

"I wish my chanst fer heaven was as good," rejoined Dick, fervently.

"Lady, you shore picked the gentlemen fer thet job," added Snitz, warmly.

"You are my very good friends," concluded Janey, all smiles. "You are helping me more than you can guess. I'll never forget you. Good-by."

She left them there, rooted to the spot, and swept out of the post office in a state of supreme bliss. The gods had favored her. Suddenly she saw the three cowboys not far ahead, standing expectantly. They had seen her come out. Janey checked a wild impulse to break across the street in the middle of the block, so she would not have to pass them. Then, very erect, with chin tilted, she went on and by, as if she had never seen them.

"Say, Andy, did you feel a cold wind round heah?" asked one, in disgust.

"Huh! I been stabbed with a pitchfork of ice," came the reply.

"Pard, she's a goddess, an' I like 'em hard to win," said the third.

If they could have seen Janey's convulsed and happy face, when she reached the corner, they would have had more cause to wonder about the female species.

The afternoon passed like a happy dream. Janey spent

most of it trying to think of things to say to Phillip when
the revelation came. She changed it a hundred times. How
could she tell what to say? But every moment that brought
the climax closer found Janey's state more intense. She
must hold out. She must stay to the finish. When the porter
knocked she leaped up with a start.

"Mr. Endicott is waiting," he announced. "The Limited is
in the block."

"Where is—Mr. Randolph?" asked Janey, with lips that
trembled.

"He's waiting, too. I'll fetch your baggage—*all* of it, right
after," he replied, and he winked at her.

Janey hurriedly got into hat and coat, and omitted the
veil. How white she was! Her eyes looked like great dark
gulfs. She went downstairs. Her father looked exceedingly
uncomfortable. Randolph had not a vestige of color in his
face. She joined them, and they went out in silence. Dark
had fallen. The street lamps were lit. The air had mountain coolness in it. On the moment the Limited pulled into
the station, and slowed down to a stop, steam blowing,
bell clanging.

It was only a brief walk from the hotel to the broad platform where the Pullmans stood. Janey had the glance of
a hawk and saw every group of persons there. Not until
she spied Black Dick and his comrades did the tension in
her break. What a stupendous man the third one was! He
made Dick look small. Janey knew Dick had seen her,
though he seemed not to notice. He and his allies kept
outside the platform, where Randolph was oblivious of
them. Indeed he seemed oblivious of everything.

"Here's our car," spoke up Endicott, with an effort.

"See if our drawing room is at this end," replied Janey,
and she stepped to face round. That made her confront
Randolph. Over his shoulder she saw her three accomplices
scarcely a rod away, and Black Dick was watching. It was
going to be a success. Janey felt a blaze within her—an
outburst that had been smothered.

Her father touched her arm. He looked miserable, shaken.

"Drawing room at this end. I'll go in. So long, Phil."

And he fled. Janey edged nearer to Randolph, close, and peered up at him, knowing that a blind man could have read her eyes. But he was more than blind. She pulled at a button on his coat, looking down, and then she flashed her eyes into his again.

"Phillip, I'm sorry. Promise me you'll never—*never* kidnap another girl."

"God! I'd do it tomorrow if I thought it'd hurt you," he returned, hoarsely.

The engine bell rang, to echo in Janey's heart.

"*All aboard!*" yelled the conductor somewhere forward.

Janey wheeled and ran up the car steps, and turning, was in time to see three dark burly forms rush Randolph, and literally throw him up the steps, onto the platform. Janey ran into the hallway, shaking in her agitation. She heard loud exclamations, the tussling of bodies, the thud of boots. Then the men appeared half dragging, half carrying the fiercely struggling Randolph.

Janey fled to the door of the drawing room. They were coming.

"Soak him, Bill. He's a bull," said Dick, low and hard.

Janey heard a sodden blow. The struggle ceased. The men came faster. They were almost carrying Randolph. Janey's heart leaped to her throat.

"In—here," she choked, standing aside.

They thrust Randolph into the drawing room, and rushed back toward the exit. Black Dick turned, his big black eyes rolling merrily. Then he was gone. The train started—gathered momentum. Outside the porter was yelling. He slammed the vestibule doors and came running.

"Lady—what's wrong?" he asked, in alarm. "Three men upset me. I couldn't do—nothin'.'"

"It's all right, porter," replied Janey. "My—my husband had to be assisted on the train."

"Aw now, I was scared."

Janey's father appeared from down the aisle.

"What was that row?" he asked, nervously.

Janey barred the door into the drawing room.

"Dad—I've kidnaped Phillip," she said, very low and clear. Endicott threw up his hands.

"Holy Mackali!" he gasped.

Janey closed and locked the door. The drawing room was dark. She turned on the light. Randolph was breathing hard. He had been dazed, if not stunned. There was grime on his face and a little blood. The bruise Ray had left over his eye, and which had not wholly disappeared, had been raised again. Janey darted to wet her handkerchief. She wiped his face—bathed his forehead. She had told that ruffian Dick not to be gentle. Remorse smote her. Suddenly she touched Phillip's face.

He was staring with eyes that appeared about to start from his head. He grasped her with shaking hands. He gaped at the car window and the lights flashing by. Then he seemed to realize what had happened.

"They threw me on the train," he burst out, incredulously.

Janey rose to stand before him.

"You—you—"

"Yes, I've kidnaped you," she interrupted.

"My God!—Janey, could you carry revenge so far? Oh, how cruel! You pitiless woman!"

He fell face down against the cushion.

"Phillip," she called, trying to stay the trembling hands that leaped toward him.

When he did not look or speak, she went on softly: "Phil."

No response. Her head fluttered to his shoulder.

"Husband!"

At that, his haggard face lifted and his terrible eyes stared as those of a man who knew not what he saw.

"I have kidnaped you—yes—*forever!*"

He fell on his knees to clasp her blouse with plucking hands.

"Janey, if I am not drunk or mad—make me understand," he implored.

She locked her hands behind his head. "Indeed you are

hard to convince. Have we not been married? Are you not my captive on this train? Is this not the eve of our honeymoon?"

"It's too good—to be true," he replied, huskily. "I can't believe it."

She bent to kiss the bruise on his forehead.

"Will that do?"

"No!"

She kissed his eyes, his cheeks, and lastly, as he seemed rapt and blind, his lips.

"Phillip, I love you," she said.

"Oh, my darling, say that again!"

"I love you. I love you. I love you. . . . It was what you did to me. Oh! I confess. I deserved it. I *was* no good—and if not actually bad I was headed for bad. . . . Oh, Phillip, you *spanked* some sense into me in time, and your desert changed and won me. I bless you for making me a woman. I will give up what was that idle, useless, wasteful life— and work with you—for you—to make a home for you. . . . Forgive this last little deceit. Oh, you should have seen Dad's face. . . . Kiss me! . . . Come, let us go tell him I'm your Beckyshibeta."